The Hierophant

The Hierophant

By

James Tripp

Sir Nice Fellow Press
New York • Los Angeles

https://www.facebook.com/TheHierophantNovel
http://jamestripp.blogspot.com/
http://thejamestripp.wordpress.com/
https://www.facebook.com/thejamestripp
https://twitter.com/thejamestripp
jamestrippblog@aim.com

Library of Congress Control Number: 2012915134
ISBN-13: 978-0615674087
ISBN-10: 0615674089

𝕾𝖎𝖗 𝕹𝖎𝖈𝖊 𝕱𝖊𝖑𝖑𝖔𝖜 𝕻𝖗𝖊𝖘𝖘
New York • Los Angeles

Author's note: Portions of this work are based on sayings from *the Old and New Testament, the Bhagavad Gita* and *the Upanishads.*

Empire

It is another time.
There are wars and revolutions.
Ancient dynasties fear their end.
Simple creatures walk the land,
Led by an empire of mock power,
Or another political ideology,
Or some dichotomous morality.
They give control of their lives away too easily to
*   an outside force*
By re-forging manacles which were self-imposed,
Giving rise to an unnatural order.
It is another place.

The Hierophant

The Hierophant

The Prison

The Self listens to the song of *the Self.* The song of *the* Self is *the Self.* In the stillness of its song, *the Self* hears the song of *Being.* The song of *the Self* is the song of all *Being.* It is the thing that is the same in all things that *the Self* hears. It is the song of *Being* that makes *the Self* sing.

And while *the Self* sings the song of *Being,* there is no *Self,* only *Being.*

In a prison rising from the scorched hills above the Still Sea, deliberate steps without rhythm creep stealthily towards a cell. *Being* is not interested in the prison or its cold stone floors or its dark fortress halls and the fox steals up on its prey.

The song of *Being* is the song of all things, it is known to all *Being.* *The Self* marvels and wonders in introspective revelation. Is it a mad delusion brought on by the isolation? Is it brought on by hunger? Is it truth?

Below the hills, next to the Sea, a shepherd runs his flock of sheep. The shepherd is a lazy man and does not pay attention to his flock and one wanders away, in search of something that the shepherd or the flock cannot give him. The lamb does not look back at the man with the whipping cane.

At first no one knows the sheep is gone. The shepherd does not know. The other sheep do not know. The Sea does not know. No one knows.

The man who approaches the cage of *Being* is a varmint, a mercenary, a creature unkind and unloved. He wants no more *Light* than the dark provides, a fool who would walk away from a fire on a cold night. He is a man without compassion or reason. He is a soldier, a spy, a murderous scum. He fancies himself to be a man of God. He is a man of ambition. His name is Loki, the lowest name in this story.

Eyes close and *Being* is one with all things. *Being* is one with friends. *Being* is one with the jailers. *Being* is one with the sheep. *Being* is one with the earth. *Being* is one with the sky. *Being* is one with the mother. *Being* is one with the murderer. *Being* is all the songs of *the Self.* It is the *Being* that is the same in all *Being* that *Being* is.

Loki has trained for this dark day. Still a boy in his early twenties, not yet a man, a malleable mind, capable of following orders, a soldier and terrorist, he is proud to do his duty for his God and Tribe. The taste of another man's blood is on his tongue. He actually tastes it.

Never is a noise on a quiet dawn as unheard as are the footsteps of the encroacher at the fortress. *The Self* is powerless to flee. *The Self* does not know why the footsteps come. *The Self* does not know that it is not safe in prison.

Below the fortress, the shepherd notices the one lamb wandering off. Clutching his whipping cane, he moves to corral the renegade. He runs after it and dives for the lamb to try and take it in his hands. The lamb escapes and starts to run.

Inside the prison, the cell door opens and though it is dark in the hall, it is lighter than inside the cell. *Being* comes back to *the Self* and squints. "Who are you?"

Loki does not say anything. He moves closer.

"What do you want?" *The Self* does not sense the danger. *The Self* does not see the dagger strapped to the intruder's belt.

"Get up," says Loki. "It is time to go."

"Go? Where?"

"You are free," says the spy.

"Free?" *the Self* laughs. "Free?"

"Get up."

Trusting, seeing no reason not to comply, *the Self* stands.

"Come," says Loki, standing just inside the door.

"Who are you?"

The spy is impatient and steps into the cell and grabs the prisoner's arm. He swings around the back of his captive and with one arm held across the prisoner's chest, he holds the prisoner's arms still. In one swift motion, he grabs the knife from his belt and cuts the prisoner's neck from ear to ear. The murder is done before the prisoner knows it has begun.

Loki has never tasted human blood and he relishes the thought. While his victim is dying, the spy flips the dagger back and forth in his hand and considers wiping it off on his target's cloak. He brings the blade up and licks the blood in an almost sensual way. He likes the taste and wants more. It is the taste he had tasted before he had a taste. Licking the wet knife, he cuts his tongue and tastes his own blood and he laughs.

Loki leaves the door to the cell open when he goes. It takes only about two minutes for the body to lose enough blood to die. A prison guard finds the corpse.

All have a path they choose. Loki has chosen a path of blood to his God. It is for his God he has committed his first murder. The infidel is dead. Loki's offering of blood will secure him a spot in his afterlife. 'I am an instrument of God,' he thinks.

In the world below, the lamb runs and runs. When the other sheep see him, at first they resent him, and then they start to run after him. The lamb is their new leader. He leads them away from the shepherd.

John is dead.

Skull Hill

The bones of the Tribes are scattered on Skull Hill. It is the place of an Empire's warning, where an execution is a cause for the regulars to bring picnics and wine, as if it is a celebration. They are used to Skull Hill, the landmark outside the wall of the Holy City. They even have their own spots.

The bleached skulls from previous executions are perched on long spiked sticks scattered across the hill, with a concentration towards the gate of the Holy City. The birds are picking at those with meat still on them. Some have dragged heads to the ground. Others perch themselves on the head itself.

Tommy Trigger plays his syrinx while he waits for Timothy and Bobby and the show to begin. The stray dogs that followed him from the Holy City have settled and are resting comfortably around him. Tommy has three dogs with him this day. They are large hunting dogs. They are dogs that would eat the severed heads if Tommy did not stop them. The sun is approaching midday. It is a day like any other.

Tommy Trigger is agitated and he stops playing. His face is worn for thirty-two. His nose is short and broken from a life of fighting.

Tommy Trigger has two lists of players in his life. He has a list of friends and a list of enemies. It is easy for a friend to become an enemy, but once an enemy, always an enemy, never a friend. Once you lose his trust, you never get it again. He has a list of people who have made love to him and a list of people who have fucked him. He has a long memory and a taste for revenge.

Tommy Trigger thinks he is the only one who cares about freedom. He thinks that makes him better than other people. A lot of people don't like Tommy Trigger. He doesn't care. He is disgusted with the timidity of the Tribes. If they do not follow him and the call of *the Sons of Light,* the Nations will perish. Tommy does not hold out much hope for the picnickers of Skull Hill. He waits for genocide to be impressed on his people by an evil Empire as the people passively stand by. What is needed is a leader; someone the people will follow. What is needed is someone like Tommy Trigger.

There is a raised altar around which everyone is gathered. A path is cleared through the revelers and the soldiers and priests of the Emperor escort the prisoners through the Holy City gate to the place where they will die. Their hands are tied behind their backs and they are tied to each other. Tommy Trigger looks at each man as they settle in a line behind the altar, where all can see.

Bobby Tarmac mourns those who are not yet dead. He knows the men who will be executed today. They are his kinsmen. The blood of the Tribes will flow like rivers to drench the sun-cracked ground.

Bobby was a warrior before he had ever heard of the word. For him, it is just a matter of time before the Tribes rise up against the Empire and thrash it with justice. Like Tommy, he waits for a voice to lead the fight. He does not feel that he is that voice. Bobby is a follower.

Bobby is young, twenty-three. He is a good man. The things he believes in are good things. He is righteous and honorable. These are not righteous times. He feels the only honor is in revolution.

Bobby is drawn to Tommy by his syrinx, a familiar sound. Tommy looks like a mischievous pan and he stops playing when he sees Bobby approach. The dogs stand up at attention. Bobby watches them with caution.

"There must be justice for this," Tommy says.

"They're from our Tribe, one and all," says Bobby with anger, tears in his eyes. "I know them all. I used to see them walking in the market."

Tommy blows into his syrinx again and a dirge sounds. The dogs start to settle and lie down again, one by one. It is a dark, rebel dirge, both sad and soothing. The Imperial High Priest is now on the altar saying an opening blessing. A soldier hands him the sharpest of swords and he blesses it.

"It is a great dishonor for our warriors to be killed in this way," says Tommy, "as a tribute to a pagan God."

"I know these guys," Bobby says, exclaiming to the lineup. "They're guys like you and me. That one there's not even a warrior. Soon he will be dead."

Tommy stops. "Soon we will all be dead," he says. "He should have been a warrior. Then his death would have meaning." He looks at the picnickers. "Look at them. They brought picnics! The picnickers of Skull Hill!"

He puts the syrinx to his lips and writes *the Song of the Picnickers of Skull Hill* as they bring the first prisoner to the altar to be sacrificed.

Timothy comes upon Bobby and Tommy, stops and listens. He looks at the line of men. "When we succeed," he says, joining the conversation, "they will not have died in vain."

The dogs look up. They know Timothy and are not moved. They rest their heads again.

Tommy stops his playing. "If we succeed," he says. "Where's your picnic?"

Timothy looks at the people around him and smiles at the people of the Tribes. He has a vision of the picnicker's heads at the top of their own long poles.

Tommy Trigger wets his lips and balances the mouthpiece of the syrinx on his tongue. His cheeks swell as he fills the pipe with air. He looks straight ahead at nothing in particular. He plays a funeral song.

"You only die once," says Timothy. "It does not matter where or when. What matters is how you live. It is better to die young by the sword than to live a slow, passive life."

Timothy is the oldest of the three, in his forties. His cunning mask is crowned with horns of red hair, which rest like curls of blood on his shoulders. His beard is more gray than red. The lines in his face run deep. He doesn't care what he looks like, where he sleeps, or who he sleeps with. He has a scar stretching from the corner of his right eye, through his beard, to his ear, from a knife fight long ago. He is the leader of the three and both Tommy and Bobby seek his approval.

The prisoner is made to kneel and stick his neck over the chopping block/altar. He does not struggle, but there is defiance. He does it with honor. There is dignity in his composure. He is from a proud Tribe. The prisoner stills. The picnickers still. The High Priest raises the blessed sword over his head and brings it down on the warrior's neck. It does not go all the way through. The High Priest brings the sword up again and brings it down. This time the head rolls off of the altar. The crowd is silent.

The desert wind blows through Bobby's hair and he pushes it back from his eyes. He does not like what he sees. He has never felt such anger. He wants to make this his battlefield, but it would be futile. The Emperor has too many soldiers. Bobby's warriors would be slaughtered.

"Let us meet force with force and violence with violence," growls Tommy. "Give me an eye for an eye. Give me a tooth for a tooth."

"Let us not talk about that here," says Timothy, looking around at the soldiers and priests from the Temple of the Tribes who are there.

"Let's get out of here," says Bobby.

"You think this is fucked up," says Timothy, "what about the Games?"

"Let's just get out of here." Tears are swelling up in his eyes. "These guys are my friends. Let's just get out of here. I don't want to see them die and not do anything."

"If you did anything now, you would die," says Timothy. "The time will come when God's vengeance will reign down on this Empire."

Tommy tucks his pipe into his belt. "The descendants of our fathers hide while their brothers are slaughtered by an evil Empire," he says, "and so they are accomplices in their own genocide."

"I hope they like their picnics," says Timothy. He looks to the line of men who are about to die. "These are the first martyrs who will usher in the new age."

"They must be avenged," says Tommy.

"They will be," says Timothy. "Let us go meet Tracy. Let us go to the Games."

"What kind of game is it when two slaves are made to fight to the death?" Bobby asks with derision.

"The Emperor's game," says Timothy. "The game of Empire. At least they are not from the Tribes."

"Not yet," says Tommy.

"Not yet."

"They spill our blood outside the city walls," says Bobby. "Let's get out of this place. Let's go to the Games. Let's see why we fight."

"Let us go," says Timothy.

"Let us go," says Tommy.

They walk away from the hill, the soldiers, the Temple Guards, the priests, the picnickers, the dying and the dead. The stray dogs spring to attention and follow.

One of the Emperor's soldiers rushes over to the edge of the altar where the rebel's head has rolled off and spears it securely on the end of a long spiked stick. He finds a place in the crowd in need of a new decoration and plants it firmly in the ground. Some in the crowd cheer. The vultures flock to the fresh meat as the Imperial High Priest raises his sword.

No Man's Land

On a cliff in *No Man's Land, the Self* sings the song of *Being* like a God in creation. The colors that emanate from the earth and sky are like an explosion from the mind.

Each thing that *the Self* looks on in the desert *Being* is. When it is day, *Being* is the sun. When it is night, *Being* is the moon. When it is still, *Being* is the earth. When it is in motion, *Being* is the wind. When *the Self* drinks, *Being* is the river. When it is dry, *Being* is the desert. When *Being* crawls, it is the lizard. When *Being* flies, it is the bird. *Being* is all the songs of the desert.

Being is the grass. *Being* is the sheep grazing on the grass. *Being* is the wolf feeding on the sheep.

Being is the beach. *Being* is the ocean. *Being* is the hunter. *Being* is the hunted. *Being* is timeless. *Being* is without beginning or end.

The vultures start flocking on the first day. When *the Self* looks up, that which is the same in all things becomes the first bird it sees. *The Self* soars. The thing that is the same about all flesh is that it is hungry. Flesh can feed on flesh, but only one survives. For one to live, one must die.

The Self looks down on the man and that which is the same in all things becomes a man sitting on the pinnacle of a cliff in *No Man's Land.* There are no others. There is no civilization. There is no river. There is only the desert and a skin of water. There is loneliness. There is hunger. There is the body. There is *the Self.* There is *Being.*

The history of man emboldens *the Self:* the rule of Sumer, the empire of Sargon, the fall of Babylon, the Pharaohs of Egypt, the Caesars of Rome, the champions of the Empire, and the history of the Tribes. These are the grains that blow like sand across the desert.

The Self meditates on the empires of man that have come and gone and all the empires that will come and go. *The Self* meditates on the terror men inflict on other men to maintain power. *The Self* meditates on all the revolutions and all the men who have died fighting in them. *The Self* wonders at the varieties that have sprung up from the same seed.

All of history blows across the desert, spitting headlines of sand against the white cloak that covers the face. *The Self* smiles at the dunes in the desert. *The Self* smiles as they swirl and change. One day one dune is bigger than another. The next day another dune is bigger. The number of grains of sand is constant. Everything is in motion.

The Self turns away from the world and meditates on that which is the same in all things. And it is *Being* that is the same in all *Being. The Self* emanates from the center of *Being.* The center of *the Self* is that which is the center of all *Being.* The unity of all *Being* is *Being.* It supports everything that lives. It is the connecting force. When *the Self* knows the *Being* in its own *Self,* it knows the *Being* in all *Selves,* the oneness of all things, the all pervading truth that exists everywhere. It is the *Being* in everyone, directing the musings of all living things. And when *the Self* sees its own *Being* in everything that lives, it sees the true equality of all life. *The Self* is the sum of what it has done and what it will do and it can change what it will become by what it does next.

Being is incorporeal. *Being* exists without *the Self,* but *the Self* cannot exist without *Being. The Self* is created by *Being.* It is *Being* that assumes different forms when incarnated. *Being* is not born. It does not die. It does not germinate from anything but itself. It is *the Self* that is temporal. It is not the flesh in the *Being,* but the *Being* in the flesh.

Being beholds all *Being* in its *Being,* and its *Being* in all *Being. Being* inhabits all *Being,* is immortal, and controls *the Self* from within, whose body is manifested by *Being.*

The Self comes into awareness in *No Man's Land.* The illusions of *the Self* and of this transitory life wash away from it like moist rain, and it becomes wet in the desert.

Being sheds the desires of *the Self* and knows it is immortal. Steady in spirit, free from all material wants, *the Self* becomes one with all *Being.* It becomes impressed with the individual nothingness of *the Self* and renounces ego. It embraces all things, without which it has no *Being.*

The Self remembers the words of John, "You must accept your destiny or live without peace."

The Self lurches from darkness into awareness and becomes a creature without judgment, a senseless animal, without a body, pure *Being.* It is the *Being* that is hidden in all creatures, the all pervading, the inmost *Being* of all life, which abides in all things. *The Self* feels a searing *Light,* familiar yet strange, knowledge the living rarely have. Is this death? Is this an illusion brought on by fasting?

The Self hears the sound of marching soldiers. They are coming closer. The soldiers are approaching from beyond the horizon. They are the occupying soldiers of an unrighteous Empire. *Being* snaps from awareness and is once more in the world.

Men are the only creatures to fashion the resources of the Earth into weapons of destruction. They have arrows of metal and swords of steel. They have tall spears. The Empire uses the stretch of desert below the cliff where *the Self* sits to conduct war games. Every year at Festival, as a show of strength to the religious pilgrims in the Holy City, they regularly fight mock battles. Every year they clash. It is the reason this part of the desert is known as *No Man's Land.*

There is no truth in the Empire's order the soldiers represent. There is no truth in the Gods of the Empire. There is no truth in the God of the Tribes or the order of the priests who rule the Temple of the Tribes of the Holy City. The Great Chief has his truth. The Priests have their truth. The Emperor has his truth. There is no truth in man-made order. There is only division.

The Self looks at the birds flying over the soldiers. The thing that is the same in all things becomes one of the flying scavengers. When *the Self* looks down on the soldiers below, that which is the same in all things becomes a soldier. It becomes a man with a citizen's name and upbringing. It becomes a stranger in an occupied territory. It becomes a body marching mindlessly into the desert, surrounded on all sides by other men. They are all marching. Soon, they will break up into two opposing divisions to play their games. What is one will become two. What is truth will become a lie.

The Self looks up to the cliff and sees the man and that which is the same in all things becomes that man. 'If they only knew,' *the Self* marvels, 'if they could only see with their eyes. Someday they will build a tower around themselves and what they wall out will also keep them in.'

The Self closes the eyes. *The Self* does not say anything. *The Self* does not hear anything. Its only sense is silence. *The Self* falls into a deep sleep.

The body has a different kind of sleep when it fasts in the desert. It has less energy and it sleeps more often. *The Self* has more and different kinds of dreams it cannot remember.

The Self relinquishes the religion of the Tribes in the desert. *The Self* smiles to think of the priests. *The Self* smiles at their God and the Gods of the Empire and all the Gods that have come before.

The Self closes the eyes and when they open again *the Self* is a soldier helping other soldiers set up camp. This is where they will stay for the night. Soon the mock battle will begin. *The Self* does not know how long it will be in the desert. It does not know when or where it will fight its battle. Only the Centurion knows. A soldier waits for orders.

That which is the same in all things is a Centurion with bills to pay. It has an expensive wife and daughter. It is estranged from his only son. *The Self* is far from home. It is far from its center. It is not happy. It has taken on burdens that heap on more burdens that cannot be controlled. This life has gone awry. *The Self* is not free. *Being* is covered.

The Centurion looks up at the sky and sees the bird. That

which is the same in all things becomes the bird.

The scavengers continue their watch over the man on the cliff and keep vigil over the soldiers because they know that when men gather in uniforms against one another there is always death. It is a matter of time. They are patient birds.

The thing that is the same in all things is a man on a cliff in *No Man's Land. The Self* comes back into the body to sleep and dream. And when it dreams, it dreams of this world. When it wakes, it feels like a man on a cliff in the desert. It becomes that body. *The Self* is aware again and it watches the soldiers. *The Self* does not know how long the body was asleep. It does not matter.

The Self rubs the face to check if it is awake. The eyes blink like a lizard's. Is *the Self* a lizard? *The Self* looks at the skin of water the body has brought. There isn't much left. The throat is dry from the desert sun, but *the Self* leaves the water undisturbed. The body sleeps again.

While the body sleeps, a spring appears in the desert like a door opening. *Being* leans back and falls into the water. As it descends into the spring, it vanishes from the surface, seemingly dried up in the desert sun. *Being* penetrates the water.

When *Being* comes back to *the Self,* it is out of the desert, at the river. *The Self* is a man again, the son of a farmer. And *the Self* says, "I am not a farmer. I am a farmer's son."

He is also a man who is the brother of all because he sees the thing that is the same in all things. He knows that he will not return to *the Settlement,* where he once considered the priesthood. He knows that he will live in the world. He knows that he will proselytize. He knows that he will stay hungry. He knows that he will die.

And he says, "I will not be ruled. I will rule my own life. This is the new seed I will plant."

Douglas Trigger feels no glory, though he is about to enter the world stage.

And though he is awake, he asks himself, 'Is this not all a dream?'

Empire Games

Tommy Trigger plays his syrinx as he walks through the streets of the Holy City with his friends and a pack of stray dogs in tow. It is a dirty, crowded city. Its sewage seeps along the same paths as its people. Thankfully, it is a short trip to the stadium.

The song is over and Tommy has not thought of another tune.

"You ever been to the Games?" Timothy asks Bobby.

"First time."

"It is always the same," says Timothy. "Criminals and slaves fight all day long. There is lots of blood."

Tommy starts playing the syrinx again. It is a rebel song called *Proud Warrior*.

"The first game happened this morning," says Timothy, "during the executions. They keep them going all day long, just like in the capital. By the time we get there, those who have had their fill of blood will be leaving. There will be plenty of seats."

"What's the main attraction this afternoon?" asks Tommy between blows.

"Two slaves are going to fight today. The prize is freedom. The younger one is favored to live."

"What if they don't want to fight?" asks Bobby.

Timothy laughs. "They both will die," he says.

Proud Warrior is a somber tune. It is the lay of a man who dies in the arms of his lover fighting for her freedom. Tommy stops playing when they come to the stadium and tucks his syrinx in his belt. He turns to the dogs and says, "Stay." They can't go in. They don't.

Timothy, Tommy, and Bobby pass through the gates of the stadium. The entrance is festooned with statues of the Emperor. *The Sons of Light* regard them with contempt.

There isn't a game on when they enter, and there are just as many people leaving as coming. Those who have stayed are just milling about. They start looking for somebody.

"*The Medicine Man* could've played to this crowd," says Tommy, "He could have made them listen."

"You saw *the Medicine Man?*" asks Timothy.

"We both saw him," says Tommy.

"What was he like?"

"He was good with the crowd," says Tommy. "He had a lot of fans."

"*The Ghosts?*"

"Yea," says Tommy. "It's too bad he's dead."

"Why would a guy like that kill himself?" asks Timothy.

"I don't know."

"He didn't," says Bobby. "Somebody murdered *the Medicine Man.*"

Timothy thinks about it. "Cowards," he agrees. "This government has no honor. Who do you think murdered him?"

"He was in the Great Chief's prison," says Tommy.

"The Great Chief is a puppet of the Emperor," Timothy says what all know. "*The Medicine Man* was not the leader we were waiting for, that is for certain. The leader we are waiting for does not die before the battle."

"We can always use a martyr," says Tommy.

"The heads of martyrs are scattered outside the walls of the Holy City. We do not need another."

"Maybe we need this martyr," says Tommy.

"He was not our martyr."

"People don't know that," says Tommy.

Timothy smiles. "Where is Tracy?"

They look for their friend with more earnestness.

"What was the *Medicine Man's* act?" asks Timothy.

"He talked about *the Voice* of nature," says Tommy.

"Did he say he was that *Voice?*" asks Timothy.

"No," says Bobby, "but *the Ghosts* said he was."

"Yea," says Tommy. *"The Medicine Man* said there would always be a *Voice."*

"What *Voice?*" asks Timothy.

"He said his wouldn't be the last one," says Bobby. "He said there would always be another."

"He prophesied the coming of a *Voice?*"

"I suppose," says Tommy. "He said one would come like a *Voice* from nature. It would be *the Voice* of the Earth. He said *the Voice* would act like a hoe in a weeded field and plant new seed. He talked about a change in the world order. He called *the Voice the Hierophant."*

"The Ghosts thought *the Medicine Man* was *the Voice?"*

"A lot of 'em still do," says Tommy.

"What do you think?"

Tommy laughs. "He wasn't a military voice. He wasn't our *voice.* He said *the Voice* would come. He said *the Voice* would be like a door that opens when it speaks and closes when it is silenced. He said *the Voice* would invite others to go through the door."

"A poet, huh?" says Timothy. "What the hell does that mean? That does not sound like *the Voice* to me."

"He said *the Voice* is perfectly centered," says Bobby.

"I do not think *he* was," Timothy says facetiously. "Did he talk about fighting?"

"No," says Tommy.

"Another peace freak," says Timothy. "What else did he say?"

"A lot of stuff about *Light* and dark," says Tommy. *"Settlement* bullshit. The crowd loved it. Too bad it didn't make any sense. John, *the Medicine Man*---spokesman for a generation." Tommy laughs. "Not any more. He talked about freedom. Who was he to talk about freedom? You have to fight before you can talk about freedom. Freedom is something you fight for."

"He spoke about truth," says Bobby.

"Truth and freedom," says Tommy. "His truth. His freedom."

"I find truth in my dagger," says Timothy, "You fuck with me and you fuck with my dagger. That is my truth. That is my freedom."

"He said you don't have to fight for freedom," says Bobby.

"Of course you have to fight for freedom," says Timothy. "Nobody is going to give it to you. What else do you fight for?"

"He said you don't have to fight for anything," says Bobby.

"That is bullshit," says Timothy. "Even the slaves here fight for freedom."

"It's the only thing worth fighting for," says Tommy.

"He said prisoners of the Empire can be free," says Bobby. "Slaves can be free."

"*The Medicine Man* is free alright," says Timothy. "This afternoon, one slave will be free."

"That's not what he meant," says Bobby.

"What did he mean?" asks Timothy. "The only way a slave can be free is if he fights. No master is just going to free him."

"No free man has a master," says Bobby.

"Whatever the fuck that means," says Tommy.

"What if none of them fought?" says Bobby. "What if all of the slaves just said, 'No?'"

"They all would die," says Timothy, "every one of them."

"But they'd be free," says Bobby.

"If death is freedom," says Timothy. "Why did people follow *the Medicine Man?*"

"*The Ghosts?*" asks Tommy. "I don't know."

"How can a man be free behind prison walls?" asks Timothy.

"I don't know," says Tommy. "I can't figure it out."

"How can he be free following another man?" asks Timothy.

"I don't know," says Tommy.

"It is good he is dead," says Timothy. "Let us just hope this *Voice* he was talking about does not show up and lull our people into complete genocide. No wonder they call his followers *Ghosts*. How can we be free if we do not fight?"

"I don't know," says Bobby.

"If we could find this *Voice* before it starts speaking," says Tommy, "this *Hierophant,* maybe we could get him on our side."

"Where would we look for such a man?" asks Timothy.

"It's probably someone who's already in his movement," says Tommy. "He was probably at the river that day." Tommy wonders about his twin brother, Douglas. He was at the river. He stood with *the Medicine Man.*

"There's Sean Tracy," says Bobby.

Tommy and Timothy look over. "In the good seats," says Tommy.

The three men walk up the hill towards the center bleacher seats where Tracy is sitting.

"He said freedom doesn't come from without," says Bobby, "it comes from within."

"You sound like you are beginning to believe it," says Timothy.

"Medicine Man bullshit," says Tommy.

"Freedom comes to those who see it," says Bobby. "That's what he said."

"I see freedom, Bobby," says Timothy. "But we have to fight for it."

"Even a slave can see freedom and say, 'I am free.' That's what he said."

"But he must still fight, Bobby," says Timothy, "or he will die."

"A free man won't fight," says Bobby.

"Then the slave would die," says Timothy. "Just because a slave says, 'I am free,' it does not make him free. A man with shackles on his feet cannot run free."

"But isn't a human being more than just this body? Can't the soul run free? How can you shackle the best part of a man?"

"That is a lot of philosophical shit," says Timothy.

"That's bullshit," says Tommy.

"You have to defend freedom."

"Then you are not free," says Bobby. "What you defend

controls you."

"Are you sure you are in this fight?" asks Timothy. "Even if *the Medicine Man* was right, even if you cannot shackle the best part of a man, you can put chains on the rest of the man. You can hang him in his cell. This is not a time for philosophy. This is a time for kicking ass. Right now an evil Empire occupies our land and if we do not do something right now, we are going to be seriously wiped out. It will be genocide."

The crowd is getting restless. The sun is starting to cast shadows. The mob drools to watch another man's blood. The ritual swells up from them. They smell the scent of death. They feel a lust for killing.

"Sean, you know Bobby, do you not?" says Timothy as they sit down with Tracy.

"Yes, I know Bobby. Good to see you, son."

Sean Tracy is a very rich priest. He has money and is willing to spend it on the cause. He is the oldest of the four, in his early fifties. He has white hair and a young face with a hard expression. He is a priest who has made a small fortune as a merchant and owner of a number of sailing vessels. He is in a position where it would hurt his business if it were known that he is a rebel, but he is not afraid to help finance their operations.

"Empire culture," Tommy snorts. "Empire cu---lture."

The crowd roars. Imperial soldiers throw a naked man into the ring. He seems weak and almost falls to the ground with the force of his entry. As he steadies himself to regain his balance, he looks up at all of the people in the stands. He covers his nudity with his hands. He seems terrified. His eyes search for an escape route, but there is none. He is alone and he is about to die. The crowd cheers.

The four rebels are at their seats but they don't sit down. They stand to watch the spectacle below. "I wonder what he did?" asks Tommy.

"He fucked up," says Timothy. "He got caught."

"Whatever it was," says Tommy, "he won't do it again."

"He doesn't look like he's ready to face death," says Tracy.

The man in the ring sees something. The crowd turns to what he sees. They cheer again. It is the lion. Bobby can see him in his cage. He is pacing and he looks hungry.

"You ever see a lion before?" Timothy asks Bobby.

"No."

"You are going to see one in action today."

"This is fucked up," says Bobby.

"This is the world," Tracy sighs.

"This is the world an Empire has built," says Tommy. "This is not something the Tribes would ever do."

"Well, maybe your Tribe," jokes Timothy. The others laugh. "Look around you. Look in the stands. It is not just citizens filling all these seats."

The crowd can hear the sound of a chain wrapping around a pulley, the sound of the cage door being raised. The man falls to his knees and prostrates himself, a supplicant to his God.

"I wonder which God he's praying to?" asks Bobby.

"I will bet it is not ours," muses Timothy.

"Good bet," says Tommy.

"Would he be any safer if it was our God?" asks Bobby.

"Maybe," says Tommy. He laughs his silent laugh.

"Do not mock that which is without name," scolds Tracy. "It is through our obedience that we will regain *God's Promise.*"

The condemned man looks up at the lion's cage. Soon the door will be fully raised.

"Do you think this is moral?" Bobby asks Timothy.

"This reminds me of a time when I was a kid," says Timothy. "Me and some of my friends caught a snake and a mouse, and we put them in a pit together. We were expecting the snake to win, you know, to swallow the mouse whole, but pretty soon, the mouse started to win. He was biting the shit out of the snake. When that started to happen, we tried to put in the fix for the snake, and we stunned the mouse and he was knocked out. The snake bit him. It tried to swallow him, but he was already done. He died before the mouse died. The mouse regained consciousness briefly, and then it also died in the snake's mouth.

"Looking back on it now, I can say we were cruel. But were we immoral? When you are a child, there is no right or wrong.

Seeing the world as a dichotomy of right and wrong is something adults do. It is a judgment. That is why I do not want to grow up, boys. I do not want to judge."

"But don't we know better?" asks Bobby. "Even if this man feels no remorse for whatever crime he may have committed, should we, who have a moral sense, a knowledge of right and wrong, condone these acts by our presence here? Is this justice? Shouldn't we say something?"

"Hey," says Timothy, "It is not our Empire. Do not worry about the small things. We are not trying to save the world. We are just trying to save ourselves. We cannot be responsible for the life of one criminal. As a matter of fact, we are here for a reason." He nods to Tracy.

"What if he's an innocent man?" says Bobby. "What if it's a frame-up? Who made what he did a crime?"

Timothy looks at Bobby eye to eye. "We are all innocent, kid. Look at you."

Slowly, the cage is being raised. The crowd roars. The lion roars. The man grows weaker still. Slow, the cage. Slow, the lion. Down, the man.

"What's he praying to?" asks Tommy. "What's he thinking?"

"He is thinking he is about to die," says Timothy.

In life, the victim had probably been a murderer. In the ring, he is a coward. Many men are cowards in the ring.

The lion approaches his next meal cautiously, with his eyes on the man at all times. His back is arched, his walk deliberate and slow. The man trembles at his impending defeat. He wears no protective covering of any kind. Naked, he is another animal. He lives in the same jungle as the beast that stalks him. His entire body is exposed. The weeping man raises himself up; covering his groin with his hands as if that is the first thing the lion will go after. The throng roars.

"That lion looks like *the Medicine Man*," Bobby says to Tommy with a smiling laugh. "He's got the same mane of hair."

"That criminal kind of looks like you," jokes Timothy, pointing.

"Very funny," says Tommy. "I have a bigger shlong."

The others laugh.

When the man stands up, the lion steps back, but quickly leaps on his victim. The crowd cheers. The man trembles with his hands covering his groin. He offers no other resistance. The crowd boos at the man and starts throwing stones at him. This mob wants him to die.

The lion takes his first chunk out of the man's right side, just next to his stomach, and below the rib cage. The crowd cheers. The priest and the rebels are unmoved.

The man in the ring arches his back and his hands go to his side. The man goes down. Soon he will die.

"Look at that shit," Bobby says in a tone mixed with wonder and disgust.

The man slithers around on what is left of his belly. The crowd boos. The lion licks his lips, soaked with the blood of the man.

"They ought to just kill this guy," says Tommy. "There's no reason for this."

"There's no reason for Skull Hill," says Bobby.

"The Empire is the reason." says Timothy. "These people are examples. These people are here to warn us not to mess with the Empire."

"I don't think we're going to listen," says Tracy.

"I am not a very good listener," says Timothy.

"I know," says Tommy, playing the straight man.

The criminal in the ring starts to heave. The lion springs on him again, biting into his head, his teeth crushing the man's eyes. The man's face is covered in his own blood. He is dead.

"That's it for him," reports Tommy.

"No shit," says Bobby.

The lion bites into the man to eat him.

"I wonder what that guy did," says Bobby.

"Whatever it was," says Tommy, "he'll never do it again."

"The Medicine Man," says Timothy casually, "You think he was the real thing?"

"He had the bullshit down," says Tommy.

"What do you think?" Timothy asks Bobby.

"Maybe," says Bobby. "He could've been the genuine article."

"Would he have joined us?"

"I don't know," says Tommy. Bobby looks at Tommy. Tommy senses that Bobby is about to bring up seeing his twin at the river and he puts his finger over his lips to tell Bobby to shut-up.

The lion continues to eat his prey, and the crowd continues to boo. They continue to throw rocks at what remains of the dead man in the ring. The match had been a disappointment. It had been too easy a kill. There was no play. The man did not challenge the lion. There was only resignation.

"This criminal will break no more laws," says Timothy.

"Watching this spectacle makes *us* criminals," says Tommy. "We're co-conspirators."

"It all depends on which side of the law you are on," says Timothy.

"Which side are you on?"

"That all depends on which side wins."

"There's nothing wrong with a good conspiracy," says Tracy. "I rather like it."

On Skull Hill they are still dying.

The Baptism

The Self is at the edge of the river when it comes back to the body. John is gone. *The Ghosts* are gone. Something has happened to scatter the sheep.

'John?' *the Self* wonders. 'Where's John? Where're *the Ghosts?* Where's Peter?'

Douglas is weak from his desert fast. His throat is dry and it hurts when he tries to swallow. He feels alone at the edge of the river. He feels more alone than he felt in the desert. The campground is deserted.

'No John,' he thinks. 'John's gone.' He feels hungry. 'Hungry. So hungry.'

Douglas goes to where *the Ghosts* stored their food at the river. He finds only some old bread. It is hard. He breaks off a piece. He goes back down to the river's edge.

'John? John? Where is John?' He takes the piece of the hard bread and puts the morsel in his mouth. He chews, but he cannot swallow.

'Sick. I feel sick,' he thinks. 'Sick. I feel sick.'

He remembers the river.

'The river. I feel sick. The bread. The bread.'

He stands up. He bends over into the river. He vomits.

'Sick in the river. I am sick in the river. Polluting the water. Losing balance. Falling into the river. Into my own sickness.

Wet. Wet in the river. Drinking my own sickness. Wet. Baptized.'

Douglas sinks deeper into the water. He opens his mouth and lets it flow into him. He floats in the river.

His hunger goes away from him. His eyes close. He goes away from this world. It is dark. His *Self* is absorbed into a greater consciousness of *Being* and for the first time, he feels whole. He is one. For Douglas Trigger, all is *Being*. *Being* is all. There is no time in the water. While he floats in his own sickness, he comes to incarnate all things, for the *Being* within him is the *Being* within all creatures. The darkness becomes *Light*. His body wrenches. His eyes open. He is back at the river. He is getting sick again. He raises himself up.

'Sick,' he thinks, 'I'm getting sick again. There is no bread for me. I need no other man's bread. I am filled with the river. Drinking my own sickness, I am the water.'

Douglas's fast is over. He will not be hungry again. He is ready to enter the world once more. He is reborn.

Freedom

It is between games. People are coming and going. Soon the main event will begin. Two slaves will fight for freedom. A bag of money rests on the ground between Timothy and Tracy.

"It will happen in one year," says Tracy, "at Festival. I can already relish the victory."

"We will have our forces in position," says Timothy, "and once the fighting starts, the pilgrims will have to be on our side. They will have to join the fight."

"Aye," says Tracy. "How can a whole people stand idly by while it is extinguished by an evil Empire?"

"They cannot. And if they do, then they deserve to die."

"All of the pilgrims will join in our fight," says Tommy. "While the Emperor's Imperial Army practices war games in *No Man's Land,* we will regain *God's Promise.* This is the land of the Tribes. It has always been thus. It must always be."

Two slaves enter the arena from different gates. The main event is about to begin.

"And so the fight boils," says Tracy. "The taste of victory makes me feel young."

The bigger of the two slaves comes closer to the other, who does not move. Each man has a dagger and a net.

"See how quiet the crowd becomes," says Tracy.

"The one guy's just standing there. He isn't taking any evasive action," says Bobby.

The larger slave is quickly approaching the other with his blade raised.

"He's just gonna kill him," says Tommy. "There's not even gonna be a fight."

"He's gotta do something," says Bobby. "He's got to defend..."

The large slave plunges his dagger into the weaker one. He feels no remorse and looks with disdain on the life he is taking.

"We stayed for this?" says Timothy. "Bring back the lion."

The victor rips open the defeated man's chest and pushes him onto the ground. The crowd boos.

"There are no good kills today," says Tracy. "You always expect life to put up a fight."

"Maybe the life was not worth fighting for," says Timothy.

"Life is always worth fighting for," says Tracy.

The crowd continues to boo. They start to throw things. The slave in the ring looks around. There is no escape. None of the exits have opened. Suddenly, there is the sound of a pulley, the sound of a gate being raised. The slave turns to the noise just as the gate is raised and a bear is released. The crowd cheers.

"The slave is betrayed," says Tracy.

"He was supposed to win his freedom," says Bobby.

"Not yet," says Tommy.

The slave does not look like he understands. He did what he was told to do, and yet he is not free. He raises his dagger and net. The Bear charges. The crowd cheers. It will be the first good match of the day.

The Ghosts

Peter had come to the Campground with Douglas to try to find his younger brother, Andy. Peter had come to bring his brother home. He didn't want Andy to become one of *the Ghosts.*

Now that John is dead, there is no reason for Andy to stay. They remain because they cannot find Douglas. He is missing. The last time anybody had seen him was the last day anybody saw John. He had said he was going into the desert. That was many days ago. The desert is large. Peter is worried about him. He doesn't want to leave without him.

Two of Andy's friends, Philip and Barty, have come back to the river to help look for Douglas.

"If he isn't here," says Peter, "we'll go back to *the Settlement.* If he isn't at *the Settlement,* we'll go into the desert."

"He'll be alright," says Andy. "He's a grown man."

"I worry about him," says Peter.

"You worry about me," says Andy. "You worry about him. You worry too much."

"Look," says Barty, pointing to a man in the river.

At first Peter thinks it is just another one of *the Ghosts.* "It's probably just one of your friends," he says. "Does anybody recognize him?"

"I can't see that far," says Philip.

"I can't really see him either," says Barty. "He's not facing us."

They move closer.

Douglas feels the light refract in the droplets of water on his face. He is warm in the sun.

"Who is it?" asks Philip as they come nearer.

"I can't see from here," says Peter as he picks up the pace. The others follow his lead.

"Do you think it's John?" asks Andy. "Has he risen?"

Peter scowls at his brother. "John is dead," he says.

Douglas senses the coming of the men. He stands up. He is weak. He turns and lifts his head to meet them.

Peter stops in his tracks. "It's Douglas," he says.

Andy doesn't stop. He walks into his brother with a *thump.*

"We've found him?" asks Philip.

"Do you think he knows?" asks Andy.

Peter looks at his friend in the distance. He shakes his head. "No," he says. "No."

Douglas recognizes three of the men in the distance. "Hey," he calls out, though his voice is weak.

They wave. Peter quickens his pace and the others match his step.

Douglas rises out of the river and walks towards the beach. Peter grabs him by the shoulders when he reaches the shore. Douglas needs the support to stand. "Doug!" he says with amazement and joy. "Where have you been? We waited for you. Where have you been?"

"Hey, Doug," says Andy.

"Hey, Andy." His throat is sore and dry. His speech sounds like a whisper. He looks at Peter. "I have been where I said I would be," he says. "I have been in the desert. I have been in *No Man's Land.*"

"I don't know if you remember me," says Philip, from behind Peter. "My name is Philip. We met here once when John spoke."

"I remember," says Douglas.

"I'm Barty," says the remaining one. Now everyone is friends.

"Pleased to meet you. I'm Douglas."

"I know."

"You look weak," says Peter. "Have you eaten anything?"

"Where's John?" asks Douglas, ignoring the question. "Where are all the campers?"

The smile leaves Peter's face. He looks at the others.

"Something's wrong," says Douglas.

"They arrested John," says Peter.

"Who arrested him?" asks Douglas. "Great Chief or Emperor?"

"They were the Great Chief's soldiers," says Peter.

"And Temple Guards," says Philip.

"He was in the Great Chief's jail," says Andy.

"What do they say he did?"

"They arrested him the day after you went into the desert," says Peter. "It could have been any one of a number of things he said that day we all heard him."

Douglas nods. Nobody says anything. "You guys are spooked," says Douglas. "What's wrong?"

"Trig, he's dead," says Peter, his voice strained. "John is dead."

"Wha...?" Douglas's legs go out from under him, he is still weak and Peter struggles to hold him up. Gradually, Douglas regains his balance and speaks again. "Dead?" he says, standing on his own, his voice strained. "Dead?" He is disbelieving.

"There was nothing we could do," says Peter. "We looked for you. We didn't know where you went."

"I told you where I went."

"The desert is large," says Peter. "Anyway, there nothing you could have done. There was nothing any of us could do. It all happened so quickly."

"What was the charge?"

"Charge?" says Peter. "Sedition."

"Against the Great Chief?"

"You heard him," says Andy.

"He said a lot of stuff about the Great Chief," says Douglas.

"And the Emperor," says Peter.

"And the priests," says Andy.

"Did they bring him before the Great Chief's Council?" asks

Douglas.

Peter hesitates.

"Let's hear it," Douglas weakly whispers. "I won't find his head on Skull Hill?"

"They said he hung himself in his cell," says Peter. "They said it was a suicide."

Douglas opens his mouth in disbelief. He looks at the water. "John knew this would happen. He knew he'd be killed. He warned me about this."

"What should we do?" asks Peter.

Douglas looks at him. "Do?" he says. "Do? What should we do?" He is silent for a moment to think about it. "It's over. Take Andy home." Douglas is staring into his mind's eye. It is not over. It has begun.

"Just like that?" says Peter.

"That's why you came here."

"That was before this happened. Now, everything is different."

Douglas nods.

"What are you gonna do, Trig?" asks Andy.

"What did they do with John's body?" he says, ignoring Andy's question.

"We tried to collect his body," says Peter. "They wouldn't release it. They said we weren't kin."

"Do they know at *the Settlement?*"

"Yes," says Andy. He is not their first martyr. "What're you gonna do?"

Douglas looks at him. "There's nothing more we can do here," he says. "We might as well go home." Douglas is not going home.

"You don't think he killed himself, do you?" asks Andy.

"No. They probably beat him to death."

"Was it an accident," asks Peter, "or was it deliberate?"

"Who's responsible for John's death?" says Douglas.

"The Great Chief," says Andy. "It was his prison."

"What about the priests?" says Douglas. "Why were there Temple Guards? Have those same priests been at the river before?"

"Yes," says Barty. "It was the younger one, I think."

"Yes," says Philip.

"He asked John which God is the true God, the God of the Tribes or the Gods of the Empire," says Andy.

"What did he say?" asks Douglas.

"The question was designed to trap him," says Andy. "Either way he answered, he would have been in trouble."

"They were going to arrest him no matter what he said," says Barty.

"What did he say?"

"He said, 'Do not worship outside *the Self,* worship inside. Know *the Self,'*" says Philip.

"Well, of course they didn't know what he was talking about," says Andy.

"Maybe they did," says Douglas. "Maybe it scared them. They must be from the Holy City."

"Probably," says Andy. "They were definitely interested in John."

"They have the ear of the Great Chief," says Douglas. "They did this."

"The Priests of the Temple," says Peter. "What, are you crazy?"

"The people who listened to John didn't need a Temple," says Douglas. "They are a Temple. They are born knowing. The lie is that we must be taught what we already know. It's the knowledge which lies beneath this incarnation. It is the center of all *Being.* We're born knowing, but the world man has built is full of lies and we are educated to think the way some power elite wants us to think until we forget the truth and we don't believe in that which is the same in all things. We believe in division."

"You want to get yourself killed?" says Peter. "Keep talking like that. You were right. Let's get out of here. Let's go home."

"You're right," Andy says to Douglas.

"Are you coming with us?" says Peter.

"No. I still have to pick up the seed."

"We'll go with you," says Peter.

"I have something to do in the Holy City."

"What are you gonna do?" asks Peter.

"I'm gonna visit the Temple. I'm gonna visit *the Holy Place.*"

"Don't," says Peter. *"The Holy Place* is for priests only."

"Everyone knows there's nothing in that *Holy Place.* That's why they guard it. To hide the truth."

"It isn't worth it."

"John is dead."

"I know."

"He didn't hang himself. They can't shut him up, because his was *the Voice* of truth. I'm not gonna let them do that, Peter."

"I know. Be careful. Truth can be dangerous in a world governed by lies. We will go with you."

"No. I'll go alone."

"What're you gonna do?" asks Andy. "Are you gonna take up where John left off?"

"I don't know," says Douglas.

"How long will you stay in the city?" asks Peter.

"I don't know."

"We'll wait for you," says Peter.

"Thanks."

Douglas's weakened body collapses onto the ground. The others rush to his aid. Peter lifts him up again and supports him. "When was the last time you ate anything?" Peter asks.

"Probably a Tuesday," Douglas jokes.

"Man, there are easier ways to get high," says Peter. "We have to get you something to eat. I'm not gonna leave you alone just yet."

Douglas leans on Peter's shoulder. "Thanks," he says.

The Ghosts are not alone. Loki listens from a place undetected. He has been watching *the Ghosts* since before they left the river and now they are back. Loki is a thorough assassin. It is his purpose to make sure that John's fire has been extinguished. He will leave no sparks or embers burning. It is Loki's purpose to assure that *the Ghosts* have been disbanded. Loki watches them from a distance, though he cannot hear. As the group heads away from the river, the spy follows them.

The Settlement

Douglas met John when they were at *the Settlement,* a farming commune of priests at the northwest edge of the Still Sea. It is a sect apart from the priests of the Temple of the Tribes of the Holy City, who fight amongst themselves for power. One sect is conservative. Another sect is liberal. The sect of *the Settlement* doesn't care about that argument. They know the truth. What one side or the other says it is does not change it. They are farmers.

It was the beginning of a new millennium. People were waiting for something to happen. They were waiting for a *Voice.* John was young. He wanted to save the world. He wanted to be that *Voice.* They talked about it all the time. It was just one of those nights under the stars.

"It's got to give," says John. "It's got to give. People are just waiting for it. We've got the message and they want it."

John and Douglas are both in their mid-twenties. John wears a cloth headdress to keep his long hair out of his eyes. He has no facial hair. He still has the skin of youth.

"They can have it," says Douglas. "I don't want to be a prophet."

"I'll do it," says John. "I don't mind."

Douglas is silent for a moment. He lets out a sigh. "I don't like it," he says.

"I don't mind."

"I won't have anything to do with it," says Douglas. "You know what they do to prophets."

"I don't care," says John. "That'd be a relief for me. It's my ticket out, on to the next level."

"I don't like it."

"Everybody has to die sometime."

"I think you *want* to be a martyr."

"I don't want to be a martyr," says John.

"What if you speak and they don't listen? What if you die for nothing?"

"I want everybody to see what we see."

"I don't see anything," Douglas jokes.

John laughs.

"Everybody's got different eyes. What if they're all blind? You're never gonna reach everybody. There are always people who just don't get it. There's always gonna be people trapped in the old order, whose conditioning is impossible to overcome. What if you just create more division? What if they build a Temple to you? There's nothing you can say that hasn't been said before. It's the same old message. We aren't saying anything new. The messengers are just different."

"Exactly," says John. "It's always been there. It's the same old *Voice*. There's only one truth. We're just taking it to the next level."

"Do yourself a favor and keep it to yourself. Nobody ever listens."

"I can't," says John. "You can't either."

"What happens when they kill you? What happens when your followers, who don't have your vision, start teaching what they say is your vision? It's the story of the farmer, who sowed good seed in the field. He went away and left the field in the hands of his workers. When he returned, tares grew amongst the good wheat. When the farmer saw this he said, 'The seed I planted was good seed. How did this happen?'

"One of the workers said, 'We're sorry, but we planted the tares. We thought it was good seed.'"

"But there was still some good seed that grew, wasn't there?" asks John.

"Sure."

"As long as some of the good seed grows."

"I'm gonna leave *the Settlement* and go back to the farm," says Douglas. "I don't want to be a priest and I don't want to be a prophet."

"Do you believe in destiny?" asks John.

"Do you mean, do I think I have a destiny?"

"No. Just...do you believe in destiny? Not just for you, but for everybody."

"Yea," he says. "I guess I believe in destiny. Everybody came into this world at this time and place for some purpose."

"What is your purpose?"

Douglas thinks about it for a minute. He lets out a sigh. "I just want to be a farmer. I want to have a wife and a family and grow old."

"I don't believe you."

"Most people don't believe enough in themselves to realize their destiny. I see my fate and I see the choices I can make to affect my destiny. I am called, but I don't have to answer."

"If it is your destiny, you must answer."

"Most people have their life imposed on them and then it just kinda stays out of their control. Everyone has a destiny. A destiny is built on fate, but a man who does not control his fate forfeits his destiny. They allow their fate to rule their sacred lives. A great man sees his destiny. A great man makes great choices. He rules his fate to meet his destiny or to walk away."

"You must accept your destiny or live without peace."

"That's your choice, but it isn't mine," says Douglas. "My destiny is to be a husband, father and a farmer."

"On every journey, there is a point of no return, a mark beyond which you have exhausted the necessary supplies to return home and you must keep going, though your destination may be unknown and beyond your reach. But you must keep going. I have passed that point. If you wish to return home, I will continue the journey alone."

"You have not reached the point of no return. Continue your inner journey alone. Save yourself. Once you go public, it's too late."

"It is already too late," says John. "I have passed the point of no return. I think you have too. You can't forget what you know. Even if you do not speak, people will listen."

Sarah's Inn

Sarah's Inn is a rebel bar in a rundown section of the Holy City. Tommy's dogs lie outside as if in guard of the entrance with their menacing presence. They are large, muscular dogs, all strays like their human counterpart. Tommy and his dogs are creatures from the same streets.

Citizens of the Empire are not welcome at this inn. Collaborators are not welcome. Tourists and traveling businessmen are not welcome at this inn. And though the Empire is despised, at *Sarah's Inn* they take the Empire's money.

It is a regular watering hole for Tommy and Bobby. They sit at a dark table in the corner. There are only five other customers at the inn and they all sit at the same table across the room. It is Douglas, Peter, Andy, Phillip and Barty. Tommy and Bobby watch them. 'What are they doing here?'

"Are you gonna say something?" asks Bobby.

Tommy doesn't say anything.

"First at the river. Now here. Maybe he's looking for you."

"I don't think so. He hasn't seen me. If he was looking, he would have seen me."

"I also know some of those guys he's with," says Bobby. "If you're not gonna say something, I am. They were also at the river."

Tommy looks at the men at the other table more intently. "They were all at the river," he says.

"There's only one guy at that table I don't know," says Bobby, pondering the other.

Tommy is filled with all kinds of repressed feelings. He misses his brother but he never wants to see him again. The longer he has been away from him, the more he resents him.

"Where do you know the other ones from? Are they *Sons of Light?*"

"I don't know. I grew up with them."

"Are they *Ghosts?*"

"I don't know. I haven't seen them in a long time."

"Are they warriors?"

"They're from Swifton." All men from Swifton are warriors.

Tommy sighs. He is also from Swifton. He only knows his twin.

"Are you gonna go talk to your brother?"

"I don't know."

"How long has it been?"

"Longer than we were together."

"Why didn't you want to talk to him at the river?" Tommy doesn't answer. For the same reason he doesn't want to talk to him now. Bobby doesn't get it. "He doesn't look so good. He looks like you when you're sick. I'm going over there to talk to them. I'm gonna find out what they were doing with *the Medicine Man.* They might know something." Bobby stands up. "Well, you gonna come?"

"Yea." Tommy stands up.

Douglas is trying not to pass out. He needs something to eat. Tommy watches him and thinks he is drunk.

They walk to the other table.

"Andy," says Bobby as he approaches.

Andy looks up. "Bobby," he says. Andy stands up and hugs his old friend. "You remember my brother, Peter."

"Yea," says Bobby, "Nice to see you again."

They shake hands.

"This is Barty."

They shake hands.

"Nice to meet you," says Bobby.

"Nice to meet you."

"And you know Douglas and Phil."

"Yea," says Bobby and he hugs Phil.

Douglas looks up and smiles feebly at Bobby. He shakes his hand. Douglas sees the tattoo of a dagger on the fleshy part of Bobby's hand that connects his thumb to his index finger. It's the mark of *the Sons of Light.* He did not have it the last time they met. He looks up from the dagger and sees Tommy.

Is he hallucinating? Is this all a dream? Is he still in the desert? He can barely whisper, "Tommy?"

Tommy nods his head.

"I never knew if I'd see you again."

"Yea, well, here we are."

Douglas stands up to hug him. Tommy is not the huggable type. He stiffens up when Douglas holds him. Douglas is weak and begins to fall. Tommy has to catch him.

"Hey, what's wrong with you?" asks Tommy. "You drunk? That would explain the hugging."

"I'm just weak."

"You sick?"

"I have been fasting."

"Well, eat."

Tommy sets him back down in his seat.

"I'll be alright."

"Sit down and join us," Andy says to Bobby. "Tell us how you've been."

Tommy sits down silently.

"I've been pretty good," Bobby says as he sits.

"So you're Trigger's brother," says Peter.

"Tommy." He has an instant dislike for Peter.

"Is this where you live now?" Andy asks Bobby.

"Yea, I've been living in the Holy City." Bobby looks at Douglas. He looks at Tommy. "When's the last time you two saw each other?"

"Twenty years," says Tommy.

"We were kids. I didn't know if I'd ever see you again. I didn't know if you were alive or dead."

"Alive."

"Did you ever find our father?'

"It turns out he wasn't our father."

"Yea. Mom told me the same thing."

"She told you? When did she tell you?"

"Right after you left. I guess she didn't want me to run away too. She did the best she could."

"Yea. Did she tell you who our real father is?"

"She said he was dead."

"Did you believe her?"

Douglas smiles. Maybe not. "How long did it take you to find him?"

"It took forever. He wasn't a *Son of Light.* I stopped looking for him. I woke up every day hating him. I hated him all day long. I went to bed every night hating him. The next day I'd wake up hating him more. And then I found him."

"You really want to talk about this now?" says Douglas.

"I have nothing to hide."

"So what's there to do for a fisherman in the Holy City?" Peter asks Bobby to lighten the conversation.

"I've been fishing for other things," says Bobby.

"What things?" asks Peter.

Tommy looks at Bobby. This guy is asking too many questions. He doesn't like questions unless they're his.

"What do you guys do?" asks Tommy.

"We're fishermen," says Peter, "just like Bobby."

Tommy looks at Bobby. He didn't know he was a fisherman. "I saw you at the river," Tommy says to his twin. "I saw you standing with *the Medicine Man.* Are you *Ghosts?"*

"No," Peter says with a laugh.

Tommy stares at Peter for a moment. He is annoyed that Peter answered his question. He looks at Bobby. He believes Peter's answer. They are not *Ghosts.* And if they are not *Ghosts,* who are they?

Douglas's head is bowed. He is weak and listless.

"You'll have to excuse your brother here," Peter says.

Tommy winces to think that someone would excuse his brother to him. He regards Peter as if he were a fly who just landed on his arm. "You drunk?" Tommy asks his brother.

Douglas has no energy to speak.

"Is he drunk?" Tommy asks Peter.

"It's like he said," Peter says, "He's just hungry."

"You shouldn't drink on an empty stomach," says Tommy.

"I wasn't drinking," whispers Douglas.

"You ought to eat something."

"We ordered something," says Peter. He doesn't like Tommy.

Tommy turns around to look for the innkeeper. He is heading their way with arms full. He stops when he sees Tommy has joined the group.

"What is this," the innkeeper jokes, "a conspiracy?" He laughs. Tommy and Bobby also laugh.

"This is Michael," says Tommy as the innkeeper puts some hot stew in front of the men from Swifton. "Look who's here after twenty years…my brother." Tommy points to Douglas.

Michael looks at Douglas. "Well, I'll be. It's your own image. I thought he was you. What's your brother's name?"

"It's Douglas," says Tommy.

"Douglas Trigger. That's a good name." He gives him a big gregarious handshake which almost overpowers Douglas, who sees that Michael has the same tattoo on his hand--- another *Son of Light.* "Well, Douglas, don't ask me about your brother because I have no eyes, ears or tongue."

"He's got no balls either," says Tommy, and he laughs his silent laugh. The others also laugh. Douglas stares at the stew.

"Well, I'll be," says Michael, shaking his head, not believing it, looking at Douglas. "Anything else I can get you boys?"

"A new waiter," says Tommy.

"I'll get you a new line."

"As soon as you get one."

"We're all set," says Peter. "You guys want anything?"

Tommy and Bobby shake their heads. "This'll put some life in ya," Tommy says to Douglas, pointing to the stew. "That's rebel stew."

"Are you a rebel?" Douglas says weakly.

"This is a rebel bar. My friends are rebels. We are *Sons of*

Light."

"I never shook your hand." Tommy gives Douglas his hand. Douglas sees that Tommy has the tattoo too, a dagger in the fleshy part of the skin between the thumb and forefinger. He is a *Son of Light.* Tommy watches his brother discover his tattoo and smiles. Douglas's eyes turn from the dagger design into his brother's stare. It is the first time they have looked into each other's eyes since Tommy left. "So our stepfather wasn't a rebel."

"I never met a man of honor who ever heard of him. He was a liar, a drunk and an abuser of women and children."

"That was a long time ago."

"Not so long."

"What were a couple of *Sons of Light* doing at the river?" Peter asks Bobby.

Tommy looks at Bobby as if to say, 'This guy again. I'll handle it.' "We try to see all points of view," says Tommy. "We heard about your boy there."

"What is your point of view?" asks Peter.

"It's very complicated," says Tommy. "But let's talk about you. This is a rebel bar. Are you *Sons of Light?"*

"I didn't know this was a rebel bar." says Peter.

"You didn't know?" says Tommy. He is openly disgusted.

Douglas stares at his food. He hasn't eaten anything yet. He tightens his grip on his cup of water.

"Oh, but it is," says Tommy. "I saw you guys at the river. You were standing with *the Medicine Man.* You must be *Ghosts."*

"No," says Peter. "Just watching. What about you? Are you a *Ghost?"*

Tommy's laugh is his answer. When his laugh dies down, he doesn't say anything. He turns away from Peter. He looks at Douglas. "You don't look so good," he says.

Douglas takes a sip of water. His head drops. He is weak.

"Eat some of this," says Peter. He lifts the plate up to Douglas's nose. The smell of the food revives him and his head jerks up and he looks at his dinner. Peter puts it back down on the table.

Tommy looks at Douglas. "You alright?" he asks.

"Yea," he says.

"You don't look so good. Eat your stew. It'll make you feel better."

The door to the inn opens. It is Loki blocking the light. Tommy feels him in the room and watches him cross to the bar. He nudges Bobby. "Look who it is," he says.

Douglas does not notice the spy. He looks at the food on the table. Now that it is there, it is repugnant to him. He feels nauseous. His throat is sore and dry. He takes a sip of water. It makes him cough.

Tommy and Bobby know Loki. Loki ran with *the Sons of Light* until he did not. Without warning, he walked away from the Struggle. This is something you do not do. This is something you do when you are gathering information. Tommy does not say anything to the others. He comes back to the group, still watching the spy. "You musta got pretty drunk for Festival," he says to his twin. "You look like you just crawled out from under a rock."

"I am not drunk," whispers Douglas. "I was fasting."

"That's commendable," says Tommy, not really getting it and not really caring. "For how long did you fast?"

"I don't know."

"You don't know?"

"I was in the desert."

"The desert?" Tommy looks at the spy. He lowers his voice. "The Imperial Army is in the desert during Festival. What were you doing in *No Man's Land?*"

"I was meditating."

"Meditating. The Emperor's army surrounded you and you were meditating? About what?"

"That which is the same in all things."

"That which is the same in all things? My brother's fucked up. I got a fucked up brother." He looks at Bobby. He looks at Douglas's burned, dry, cracked skin. "Definitely fucked," says Tommy. "Are you a *Son of Light?*"

Douglas doesn't say anything.

"I guess you heard about *the Medicine Man,*" says Tommy. Douglas nods.

"That was no suicide," says Tommy. "He didn't hang himself."

Douglas makes no comment.

"The Great Chief killed *the Medicine Man,"* continues Tommy. "Everybody knows the Great Chief is a puppet of the Emperor."

"He also takes counsel from the priests."

"You think the real reason they arrested him was for blasphemy?"

"In addition to the I.A., Temple Guards arrested John," says Douglas. "If the Great Chief had John killed, he was not alone."

Nobody knows what to say to that. Douglas tries to take in some of the food. He puts a small piece of meat into his mouth and chews slowly. He stops. Douglas sees Loki. He looks out of place.

Tommy looks at the spy. He is facing the bar. "Keep your voice down," says Tommy, though Douglas's voice is already weak. "I know that guy." He looks at Loki again. "He's no good. I think he's some kind of spy. I just don't know whose. Why would the priests want him dead?"

"Perhaps you did not listen to him that day at the river," says Douglas. He chews between words. "Perhaps you did not see the priests from the Temple of the Tribes of the Holy City. He was challenging their authority."

Loki takes a sip of his drink. He strains to hear.

"The priests?" Tommy laughs.

Douglas tries to swallow the piece of meat he has been chewing on. It goes down slowly and sorely. He takes a swig of water. Douglas looks at the rest of the food. He cannot eat it. He feels sick.

"Don't like the stew?" asks Tommy.

Douglas does not answer. He drinks some more of the water. He feels a little better.

"Will you avenge his death?" asks Tommy.

"I'm not that kind of warrior," Douglas whispers and shakes his head. He drinks some more of the water. "It was not a beheading," says Douglas. "His death did not come from an

Emperor or even the Great Chief. His death was at the hands of his own people."

"It was the Great Chief's prison," says Tommy. "The Great Chief is an illegitimate ruler. He's the Emperor's stooge. They got warriors back home?" asks Tommy.

"Some are warriors," says Douglas.

"You're not a warrior?"

"No."

"But you'd fight if you had to fight," says Tommy. "You must be a warrior. You're my twin. This is our generation. This is our fight. This is our future. You must join the Struggle, you and the rest of *the Ghosts.* It's us against them. It's survival. So maybe it wasn't the Emperor, but it all boils down to the Empire in the end anyway. If they weren't here, our leaders wouldn't be so paranoid. As it stands, they're puppets."

"If they were alone in the world, our leaders would be paranoid," says Douglas. He feels woozy. "They are paranoid because they do not keep the truth. They do not do what they preach. They do not know what they preach."

"Don't you want revenge?" asks Tommy.

Douglas finishes off the rest of his water. He puts his cup on the table. "No," he says. "I only want truth."

Tommy looks at him with disbelief. "What truth?"

Douglas doesn't answer him. Tommy looks at the others. "What about you guys?" he asks. "Don't you want retribution?"

They look at each other, none with a voice to speak.

"Wasn't he your friend?"

Nothing.

"Tell me about this *Voice* your friend spoke about," says Tommy.

"It is *the Voice* of nature crying out in the wilderness."

"Will it be a *Voice* of peace or a *Voice* of war?"

"Peace," says Douglas.

Tommy looks at his brother. "This *Voice* sounds dangerous. We wait for a *Son of Light* to lead us. A philosopher will get us killed."

Douglas closes his eyes. His head falls forward. Peter catches him. He says, "Trig, you alright? You don't look so good. How long were you out in the desert anyway? Were you there all this time?"

Douglas opens his eyes and looks at his friend. "I'll be alright," he says.

"I'm worried about you," says Peter.

"Don't worry about me," says Douglas. He looks at Tommy. "I mourn for John. He was a friend of mine. Do not use him to champion your cause."

"Drink some water," says Tommy. "Don't mourn for *the Medicine Man*. You leave that to me. The Day of Judgment is at hand. It's the end time. Soon, the wrath of God will swoop down and crush every citizen of the Empire in his or her own land. The Tribes will regain *God's Promise. The Kingdom of God* is upon us." He looks at Douglas. "You don't know what I'm talking about, do you?"

"My brother's crazy," Douglas whispers. "I got a crazy brother." Douglas feels weary. "I know what you're talking about. I know. You're talking about a revolution."

"You're no different than me, brother," says Tommy. "Here you are in this rebel bar. The same blood surges through our veins."

"Sure," Douglas says. His eyes close again. He takes a stab at eating another piece of meat. He chews slowly.

"So is everyone still alive?" asks Tommy. "The mother? The brothers?"

"Mom's dead."

Tommy is unmoved. "Still got the farm?"

"Jimmy's got it."

"That figures. Anyone married?"

"Jimmy. He married a girl named Kay."

"Kay."

Tommy looks over at Loki at the bar. He looks away from him when they make eye contact. Loki turns away and smiles. He doesn't care if he gets made. It's a game. "He's an infiltrator," says Tommy. "He's a traitor. Someone ought to tell him to leave this inn."

"Don't get in a fight," says Bobby.

Tommy ignores him. He asks Douglas, "Where are you staying while you're in the Holy City?"

"We're not," says Peter. "We're leaving."

"I'm staying," says Douglas.

"Where are you staying?" asks Tommy. He's looking for a place himself.

"I don't know." Douglas swallows some more stew.

"I know a place you can go," says Tommy. "When you're ready to leave, I'll take you there."

"I'm ready to leave right now," says Douglas. "I can't eat anymore."

"Alright," says Tommy. He looks at the spy and lowers his voice to a whisper. "I don't trust that scum. You go first. Act like you're going to take a leak. I'll leave second. I'll meet you four blocks north from here. Make sure you're not being followed."

"Okay," says Douglas.

"We'll wait for you at the boat," says Peter.

"Thanks."

Douglas gets up and heads for the door. Tommy watches the spy watching Douglas. He stays at the bar. After a couple of minutes Tommy grabs Douglas's uneaten stew for the dogs and leaves. The spy remains with *the Ghosts.*

Safe House

Douglas waits at the appointed place. It is the middle of the day. He is tired. People are passing without stopping. Nobody cares. It is a busy, smelly city.

"The coast is clear," Tommy says as he joins up with his brother. "This way."

Tommy checks behind his shoulder. These are paranoid times. The stray dogs finish Douglas's stew outside *Sarah's Inn.* They follow when they are done. They know the way.

Tommy isn't taking Douglas to his home. He has no home. Tommy usually stays wherever his dick can take him. Tonight there is a girl at the safe house. He will take Douglas there.

"We're gonna go to the safe house," says Tommy. "It's an alright place, and if I'm lucky, there might be a girl there waiting to blow me. Mandolin likes the helpless type. You'll get along great. Maybe she'll blow you too. Twins. It's her fantasy. Two of me." He laughs his silent laugh.

"I'm not looking for a blow job."

"I'm always looking for a blow job," says Tommy. "See, brother, already you know a lot about me."

The streets of the Holy City reek. They walk along at a steady clip, trying to keep one step ahead of the smell. Nobody stops to look at them. This is the Holy City.

"I was sorry to hear about *the Medicine Man,*" Tommy

says. "I only heard him that one time. He had the fire to get people to listen to him. People would have followed him. Our cause needs such a man. How well did you know him?"

"I don't think your revolution was his cause," says Douglas.

"What about you? What do you do?"

"I work the farm."

"You're a farmer?"

"I'm in town picking up seed."

"What kind of seed?"

"Good seed."

Tommy laughs. He's not going to ask him again. They come to the safe house door and Tommy knocks a coded knock. It is on a busy street and there is a great deal of people noise, people walking and talking, people sneezing, people breathing, the sounds of the Holy City.

Tommy opens the door on a big, open room with a table and chairs at one end where the fireplace is, and a couple of mattresses at the other. The house is empty. The dogs fill the room before the people can. This is one of their places.

"C'mon in," says Tommy. He shows Douglas the way in. "It looks like no one's here. We got the place to ourselves. You can't tell anyone you were here. This is a secret place."

He brings Douglas in.

"No one will ever know I was here," says Douglas. "I won't even know."

"You look tired. There's a bed over there. Go ahead and crash on it."

"I appreciate it."

"No problem, brother. Next time stay out of the desert. You should go drink from the well before you crash."

"I'm alright."

"Okay. Hey, what was *the Medicine Man* before he was a preacher?"

"A listener." Douglas lays down on one of the beds.

"That figures," says Tommy.

Douglas is already asleep.

Tommy sighs with nothing to do. He isn't tired. It's the middle of the day, but he doesn't want to leave his newly found brother alone in the safe house. He gathers some wood to build a fire. Once ignited, he lays down on one of the other beds and falls asleep.

He wakes up in the morning and his twin and the dogs are gone.

A New Recruit

Douglas and the dogs are gone when Tommy wakes up. The house is empty. The smell of food is in the air. Mandolin was there. Tommy springs from his bed. They cannot have gone far.

As he reaches the front door, it opens without a knock. The dogs run in and get comfortable on the floor. Douglas and Mandolin follow them in. Mandolin is startled. Tommy faces his brother. He looks at them to see if they have had sex. He doesn't trust Mandolin. He doesn't know his brother. They have not. Douglas is lucky to be able to walk.

Mandolin is a *Son of Light* groupie. She is a pretty, peasant girl with big, dark lips that make you want to kiss them. She wears a desert flower in her long, kinky, black hair. She looks like an Ætheopian slave girl.

Mandolin is a child of the streets of the Holy City, who struck out on her own at an early age. She left her home in Shacktown long ago. She misses the place of her unhappy childhood. She wants to return in glory.

Mandolin has taught Tommy more about sex than any other woman has. It's why he likes her around.

"Good-morning," says Douglas, as they walk into the room. "Thanks for putting me up."

"I see you've met Mandolin," says Tommy, eyeing him

suspiciously.

"Yea. She made me some breakfast."

"She's a pretty good cook."

"Thanks," says Mandolin.

Tommy gives her the eye.

"I couldn't eat all of it. I gave most of it to the dogs."

"They stick around you, they'll never go hungry. You were in pretty bad shape yesterday. What were you drinking?"

Douglas is still weak, and he loses his balance and falls into a chair.

"You alright?" Tommy says. Mandolin runs to him. "You still drunk?"

"I wasn't drunk," Douglas says as he readjusts himself in the chair. "I was in the desert."

"The desert?" says Tommy. "That's right, you said that. What were you doing in the desert, brother?" Douglas doesn't respond. "Doing some reconnaissance on the Imperial Army?"

"No."

"How long were you there?"

"I don't know."

Mandolin goes to get Douglas some water.

"Are you a *Ghost?*"

"No."

"I saw you and your friends at the river." Tommy sits down in another chair. "You were standing with him. You were talking with him."

"You saw me at the river and you didn't say anything?"

"Why the desert?"

"It's just where I went to be."

"You and the Imperial Army," Tommy laughs. "What made you go there during Festival?"

"I just went to be alone."

"Alone with the Imperial Army. Why?"

"I thought I might learn something about myself."

"What did you learn?"

"I learned something about myself that is the same in all things."

"What do you mean? What did you do in the desert?"

"I meditated."

"On what?"

"On that which is the same in all things."

"For how long?"

"I don't know. After a while, you don't notice. Time doesn't matter. It isn't real."

"Did you eat?"

"I brought only water."

"When was the last time you ate?"

"You ask a lot of questions." Tommy waits for an answer. "I ate something this morning."

"I mean before that. When was the last time you ate?"

"I had a couple of bites of that stew."

"Before that."

"I found some stale bread at the river when I came out of the desert."

"Before that."

"Before I went into the desert."

It makes Douglas sick to think about food. He can feel his breakfast coming up the way it went down, only faster. "Excuse me," he says and quickly walks outside to an alley where he proceeds to vomit.

Tommy and Mandolin follow him out. They come to him after he is bent over.

Mandolin brings Douglas the water. He takes it from her and drinks slowly.

"I was not ready to eat so much," he says. "I ate more than I needed."

He drinks again.

"Don't make it a moral dilemma," says Tommy. "Come back inside. We shouldn't be out here. Come lie down again. Sleep. When you wake up, you will be ready to eat again. Next time, don't eat so much."

Tommy takes hold of Douglas under his arm. "Lean on me," he says. "I'll help you back into the house."

Douglas turns himself over to Tommy and is led back into the safe house.

"When you wake up, we will talk again," says Tommy.

Douglas lies back down on the same mattress. He is

instantly asleep.

"Sleep," Tommy whispers, "but do not dream. When you awake, I will give you your dreams, brother."

Mandolin listens to his boast with trepidation.

When Douglas wakes, he does not stay. He thanks his brother and invites him to the farm for planting season.

"Come home."

"That is not my home. I have no home."

The dogs run to the door as Douglas goes.

The Temple

The Temple is ornamented with gold, a tribute to its wealth. It is the largest manmade structure in the Holy City. Its north tower is a fortress, with the best strategic view. It is more fortified than the Great Chief's palace. It would be a good headquarters for anyone invading the Holy City.

'They worship the Temple,' Douglas thinks as he passes through its gates of an Empire design, 'not the God.'

He is still hungry. He is still tired. He is still dehydrated.

Inside the gates, the Court of the Infidels is a ring of activity. It is an outdoor marketplace, filled with beggars, whores and spies. As soon as Douglas enters, a beggar accosts him.

"Alms?" the man says.

"Not today."

"How about tomorrow?" the beggar sells as Douglas passes and smiles.

The beggar mutters something to himself. Someone else enters the Court. "Alms?" The man gives him something. "Oh, bless you, sir," he says as the man walks away. He looks at his take. "He coulda given more."

Douglas passes the booths of moneychangers who exchange the Empire's money with money of the Tribes, the only currency acceptable to the Temple. He passes the goat and bird merchants who sell life to the rich, who will sacrifice it on an altar to their God to atone for their sins. It would make more sense if the animals had sinned.

Zacharus and Aron are also in the Court of the Infidels this morning. Zacharus is the High Priest and a Counselor to the Great Chief. He is the older of the two and ruler of a secret cabal. Aron is waiting in the wings for a time when Zacharus will yield power.

Zacharus is not a powerful looking man. He is bald except for some thin, white hair around the sides of his head. He has a beard too, but it is stubbly. He has lines sprouting from the corners of his eyes from years of squinting in the desert sun.

The peace Zacharus had in him when he was young is vanquished. It is a peace gone awry in the real world. As a younger man, the world was more black and white. He is asking himself questions now he should have asked then. He is looking for answers but asking the wrong questions. He is worshiping the wrong God.

Aron is a puppet on Zacharus's strings, a fall guy. The only reason that Aron is in line for the top spot is because he's married to Zacharus's daughter. It is the only reason. Zacharus does not like the younger priest. Nobody likes Aron. Zacharus uses Aron to do things he doesn't want people to think that he's done.

Aron has blood-shot bulging eyes. He has the stature of a bony, withering old man, but he is in his early fifties. He has high cheekbones, a fragile jaw and crooked, rotting teeth. He has a tiny thin-lipped mouth and a pimply, slimy pallor. His frame is wiry. His hair is white. His beard is splotchy. He is a squat man with protruding ears and a square head. He has a fawning manner.

Douglas does not see the priests. He has a destination. He looks ahead, up the stairs at the Temple proper and the gate through which non-believers are forbidden to enter. It is known as the Court of the Tribes. Douglas must pass through there.

Zacharus is the first to notice Trigger. He watches him for a while without telling his son-in-law. Zacharus recognizes him from somewhere other than the Temple. He thinks it is

Tommy. He wonders what the rebel is doing there.

Loki is also in the Court of the Infidels. He is the next to recognize Douglas. He already knows where Zacharus is in the crowd, so when he spots Douglas, he steps up behind the priest and whispers in his ear, so that Aron cannot hear him, "One of *the Ghosts* I told you about is here." The spy points out his target with a nod of the head. It is the man Zacharus is already watching.

"Tommy?"

"It looks like him, but I think it is somebody else. Tommy Trigger's nose has been in more fights. I think he has a brother. It may be his twin."

"Twin?" Zacharus remembers seeing him at the river.

"I saw them together at *Sarah's Inn,*" says the spy.

"What's the twin's name?"

"I don't know."

"Did you hear what they were saying?"

"They spoke in whispers. I followed this man to *Sarah's Inn* from the river days after *the Medicine Man* hanged himself. He was with several *Ghosts.* Tommy met them there."

"I thought he was Tommy."

"Perhaps they were both at the river that day."

They were. Zacharus does not tell his spy. The High Priest is unsettled. Rebels. *Ghosts.* Twins. "Go wait by the gate," he says. "Prepare to follow him when he leaves. Find out his name. Find out if he is a *Son of Light.*"

Loki bows his head and retreats to his new position. Zacharus decides to follow Trigger.

"Hey, where're you going?" says Aron, running after him. Aron looks to where Zacharus is looking. "Who's that?" he says.

"Shhh," says Zacharus. "That's Tommy Trigger's brother."

"Who's Tommy Trigger?"

Zacharus's answer is silence. He watches Douglas walk up the stairs to the gate of the Temple. He goes inside, where he is alone. He enters the Court of the Tribes. There are no worshipers there. If it were not for the market outside in the Court of the Infidels, the Temple would be deserted.

Zacharus hurries after him and Aron after him.

Douglas passes through another gate covered with silver and gold and enters into the Court of the Priests. There are no priests. He continues at a fast pace.

Zacharus races through the Court of the Tribes and heads for the Court of the Priests as quickly as possible. Aron finally makes it through the gate into the Court of the Tribes.

Douglas looks around the Temple. He looks from one wall to another. He looks up at the ceiling. He steps past the altar, upon which sinners sacrifice burnt offerings to their God.

Zacharus stops when he marches through the gate, into the Priests' Court and looks in disbelief on Tommy's brother. He steps onto the porch. Aron catches up.

"What's he doing?" asks Aron.

"Let's not find out!" Zacharus rushes into the Court. Douglas passes through huge bronze doors, overhung with a golden grapevine, and enters into *the Holy Place.* It is built of white marble. Its facade is plated with gold.

"He goes where only you must go!" Aron shouts. He rushes after Zacharus.

There is a scarlet veil separating Douglas from the final chamber. He pushes it aside and enters into *the Holy Place.* The chamber was built to store an amulet, *the Holy of Holies,* a gift of their God, but it was stolen while the Temple was being built. Now it only houses the emptiness of their beliefs. Without the amulet, the shrine is vacant and meaningless. It is like sex with a nameless, faceless partner. His people worship an empty shrine.

Zacharus races in after Douglas, followed by Aron, who is using the incident to gain entry to *the Holy Place* for the first time.

"Son," says Zacharus, who is catching his breath, "you should not be in here."

Douglas does not say anything. He has lost his innocence. He stares at the empty chamber.

"What are you doing here?" asks Aron. Zacharus wonders the same thing about Aron. Aron looks around at his unfamiliar surroundings. He looks for the amulet.

"It's true," says Douglas, nodding his head.

"This chamber is for the High Priest only!" says Aron.

"This chamber is empty."

"What are you doing here?" asks Zacharus.

"I wanted to see for myself."

"It is blasphemy to enter *the Holy Place.*"

"And why is that? Is it because now I know the truth?"

"You don't look well," says Zacharus, trying to befriend him. "Are you feeling alright?"

Douglas pauses before answering. "I know who you are."

Zacharus is unsettled. "You look thirsty," he says with diplomacy. "Do you want something to drink?"

"No," says Douglas.

There is a long, awkward silence.

"What weighs on you?" asks Zacharus.

Douglas isn't sharing.

"You were at the river," says Zacharus. "You're a *Ghost.* You must still follow the Law of the Tribes."

"Shall the Law become the master of the men who made it? There is only one natural law."

"The Law is not our master," says Zacharus. "God is our master. These are God's Laws. We must follow God's commandments."

"Bah!" says Douglas. "Your Laws are manmade. They are not natural law."

"You may talk about the Law," says Zacharus, "but do not question it."

"I do question it," says Douglas. "I have no allegiance to manmade Laws. There is only one natural law."

Aron is flabbergasted.

"How do you know this?" asks Zacharus. He almost believes him.

"I have been in the desert," says Douglas.

"Why did you go into the desert?" asks Zacharus.

"I had to decide whether or not I was going to follow your Law. I had to know whether or not I would become a part of your order."

Zacharus's voice is shaking when he asks, "What did you decide?"

"I will not."

"You must leave this sacred chamber," says Zacharus.

"You may stay in the Court of the Tribes, or you may go, but you must learn to show some respect."

"I will go," says Douglas.

"Do not go," says Zacharus. "Stay."

"Someday this Temple will crumble from the weight of its gold plating and no one will be able to rebuild it."

"Are you an anarchist?" asks Zacharus. "Are you a *Ghost?* Are you a *Son of Light?* Are you a disciple of *the Settlement?* Who are you?"

"I am your enemy," says Douglas. "I am truth."

Douglas turns to go without another word. He walks by the two men without looking at them. He makes his way back to the Court of the Infidels. Zacharus goes to the gate of the Court of the Tribes and watches him go. Zacharus sees his spy positioned outside in the crowd. He motions for him to follow Douglas.

Douglas is gone and the two priests are still filled with him.

"What sort of man is this?" says Zacharus. "He talks without respect. He does not keep the Law."

"These kids today," says Aron. "Who does he think he is? Who is he to challenge us? If he's not a *Ghost,* he's from *the Settlement.* I know it. Half *the Ghosts* are from *the Settlement.* We ought to do something about that."

"He has rejected the Law," says Zacharus. "He has rejected our authority over him. He follows *the Medicine Man.* He came here to challenge us. He could be one of many, one of thousands of seeds. Perhaps *the Medicine Man* was only the first one. Perhaps he is their first martyr. He entered into *the Holy Place.* He knows the chamber is empty. This man may be more dangerous than *the Medicine Man* ever was."

As Zacharus looks after Douglas, he thinks about John and his own complicity. Was it for naught? Was it starting to happen all over again?

The Good Seed

The Settlement is a good place to go to get seed. The priests of *the Settlement* are farmers and have cultivated some of the best seed over the years. Ælfric, who was his teacher, helps Douglas load a mule with the sacks of seed he will use for this year's planting.

"Some men cannot live in isolation," says Ælfric. "Some men are compelled to the world of action. John was such a man. Now you say you are such a man."

"I cannot know what I know and keep it to myself," says Douglas. "I thought I could, but I can't."

"You are young. You have suffered a great loss. Do not take yourself too seriously. What you know has always been known and will always be known. You just can't show everyone."

"You can try."

"It is a noble cause," says Ælfric. "It is the cause of youth."

"The martyrdom of John is the first spark of the revelation."

"Be careful what you do and why you do it. Be careful what you say. Every step must be deliberate. You can be a prophet or a martyr. You can be a martyred prophet. Know what you are doing. You hold the secret. You can keep it and live. Know what you're getting into."

"I know."

"There is nothing wrong with a long life. Look at me."

"You are *the Teacher of Righteousness!*"

"I was."

"I am compelled."

Ælfric laughs. "Slow down. You can't save everyone."

"I have to try."

"You have to save yourself."

"This is how I will save myself."

"Do not blame yourself for John's death."

"He is not dead."

Ælfric understands. He has lived a long life. He has proselytized, but only to those who would hear. What Douglas proposes to do is a harder thing. He will whisper to the deaf, cast shadows for the blind, write for those who will not read.

"Will I see you again?" asks Ælfric.

"I don't know," says Douglas. "I hope so. I'll come back to the Holy City. When the time is right, I'll be back."

"Be careful that you are alive to come back."

"That's part of the plan."

"Do you worry about anything?"

"How will I know if what I'm doing is right?"

"You will know. You already know."

"Do you think a man can know his destiny?"

"Yes. You know this already because you know your destiny. That is why you are leaving today with this good seed. That is why you will not be back."

"I will be back," says Douglas. "I feel there is a question I have not asked you."

"There is a question only you can answer."

The mule is packed and Thomas, another priest of the Settlement, stands by to escort Douglas to the river. Ælfric signals Thomas and pats the mule on its rear. "Plant the seed we have given you," he says. "It is good seed."

Loki watches Douglas from his place of hiding.

The Crew

It is almost midday. Andy sits on his father's boat staring at the shore. The boat is anchored. The nets are in. There is nothing more he can do but daydream. Staring at the shore he sees a familiar form. "It's Trigger," he says, springing to his feet. "Peter, look who's here!"

Douglas and Thomas are unloading the mule by the dock.

Peter stops what he is doing and joins Andy at the side of the boat. "Now we can get out of here," he says.

Douglas looks out on the river and sees Peter's boat.

"He sees us." Peter waves to him. Douglas waves back. Andy, Philip and Barty also wave to Douglas. Bobby is also on the boat. He is hitching a ride back to Swifton. They do not see Loki, who has followed Trigger from the Settlement.

"Let's pull in our net," says Andy. Philip and Barty move to the side of the boat.

"We just put it in," says Peter. "We got a late start as it is."

"That's the point," says Andy. "We won't be losing anything. We'll just take the day off."

"Take the day off?" screams Peter. "Are you crazy? You've been off for weeks!"

"What's one more day? The fishing's not as good here anyway. The sooner we get back home the better."

"I don't believe this," says Peter. "Look, if you want, we'll go ashore and the others can stay on the boat."

"Alright," says Andy. He goes to where the rowboat is tied up and gets in.

Peter turns to Philip and says, "We'll be back."

He gets into the rowboat with his brother and they push off from the main boat. Andy is rowing and Peter is speaking.

"You're still under that *Medicine Man's* spell, aren't you?" says Peter. "Have you forgotten what work is? Trigger isn't going anywhere. He'll be back fishing with us after the planting."

"I don't think so," says Andy.

"What do you know that I don't know?"

"John always thought that Douglas had a future," says Andy. "He was with John at *the Settlement*. He knows what John knew. How can he turn his back on that?"

Peter lets out a snort of disbelief. "You know Trigger," he says. "He's one of us."

"I don't think so."

"No? Then who is he?"

"He's like John, *the Voice* of nature. His is *the Voice* that is hidden in us all."

"And I suppose if Trigger asks you to go with him, you will?" says Peter.

"Yes."

"And what about the business?"

"My way is not the business. It is not your way. It was our father's way."

"Now you're including me in your scheme," says Peter. He looks at Douglas on the dock. The seed is unloaded and the priest is departing with the mule. "And what if Trigger just wants to fish?"

"Then I would be wrong."

"I'm not gonna have you be the undoing of our father's business."

"Times are changing, brother. What was important yesterday will not be important tomorrow."

"I wish it was more important to you. I worry about you, little brother."

"You shouldn't worry about me," says Andy.

"I'm worried about my share of the business."

Andy laughs. "You should worry about me."

"The world *is* changing, little brother. You're right. It is becoming more competitive."

"Then it must be returned to its natural state."

"Its natural state? Its natural state is life feeding on death. The fish eats the worm and the man eats the fish and the lion eats the man. This is a miserable world."

"Men seek to rule what cannot be ruled."

"Nature? Is that what *the Medicine Man* said?"

"That's what Trigger said."

"I don't remember him saying that."

"He did. Man cannot rule the world. He may seem to rule, but that is only an illusion."

"An illusion?" says Peter. "I'm not so sure I get your meaning." He looks over and smiles at his old friend, Douglas. They have reached the dock.

Andy and Peter step out of the vessel and onto the dock.

"How are you doing, buddy?" Peter says, shaking his hand. "You doing alright? You eat anything?"

"Yea," says Douglas.

"You got the seed, huh?" Peter asks with a smile. "We'll help you load it."

"Thanks."

Peter throws his hands up in the air. He isn't ever going to get back to fishing. "What are you gonna grow this year?"

"Same old thing."

"What'd we plant last year?" asks Peter.

"Wheat."

"Oh yea," says Peter. "That's the same thing we planted the year before."

"And the year before that," says Douglas.

"We could go on like this."

"Let's not."

"Did you visit the Temple?" asks Peter. "Did you visit *the Holy Place?*"

"It was empty. There's no amulet."

Peter and Andy are taken aback. They knew the rumor, but

they had been conditioned not to believe it.

"Did the priests see you?" asks Peter.

"Yes."

"What did they say?" asks Peter. "Where is the amulet?"

"That's not a conversation we had."

"What about John?" asks Andy. "Did you ask them about John?"

"No. Let them think they got away with it. He will not be forgotten. What he said has already been heard. The priests of the Temple of the Tribes cannot silence the truth."

"The priests?" says Peter. "Are you still on that?"

"The priests. The Great Chief. The Emperor. They're all the same. All liars."

"You ought to watch that kind of talk," says Peter. "It didn't help John any."

"I'll shout the truth from the tallest building," says Douglas, "and let those who have ears hear."

"I hear you," says Andy.

"Now hold on just a minute there," says Peter. "What are you saying? Are you taking up where *the Medicine Man* left off?"

"Will you proselytize?" asks Andy.

"Yes"

"But we're fishermen," says Peter.

"Your father was a fisherman," says Douglas.

"That's what I told him," says Andy.

"And his father," says Peter.

"You must find your own way."

"Now you sound like Andy, or does he sound like you? They killed John. What do you think they're gonna do to you if you get going?"

"If I get killed, there will be another *Voice.*"

"It is *the Voice* of nature," says Andy.

"Someone like Andy?" says Peter. "I don't mind telling you, Dougy me boy, you're making me nervous."

"As well you should be," says Douglas, "because whatever they did to John, they will do to us."

"Us?" Peter hesitates. "I have a wife. I have a business."

"It's your father's business."

"And his father's and it will be passed down to our sons." Peter looks at Andy. It *is* some kind of conspiracy. He looks back at Douglas. "I can't," he says. "This is all so sudden. You just...you just want us to drop everything?"

"I'm with you," says Andy.

"We got a business," Peter pleads with his brother.

"Peter," says Douglas, "You can remain a fisherman and live an ordinary life, or you can light a fire that will spread across the earth."

"I got a family. This is so sudden. I don't get it. You came with me to rescue Andy from John. Now you're proposing to do the same thing he did?"

"I didn't come with you to help rescue Andy," says Douglas. "I came with you to see John and to get seed. I told you that. You had your reason, I had mine."

"I know you're upset with what happened to John," says Peter. "Everyone is. I mean, I liked the things he said. But...my father'd kill me."

"Forget about him," says Douglas. "This is more important. This is your life. John was a friend of mine. He was killed for a reason. He was killed by the priests of the Temple of the Tribes of the Holy City."

"If that's true," says Peter, "do you think it's a good idea to take up his cause?"

"Somebody has to," says Douglas.

"Nobody has to," says Peter. "What he said is a matter of record. You said it yourself. Let it go at that. Are we a nation of martyrs?"

"I will travel further down the road he was on," says Douglas. "You can come with me if you want."

"You'll make a good prophet," says Peter. "You speak in metaphors."

"Listen to me, Peter," says Douglas. "What happens in this place and time could very well decide if the Tribes will live or die. We have leaders who kill their own people."

"That's how they get to be leaders," says Peter. "They kill people in their own Tribe to rise to the top and then they go after other Tribes. The people are pawns. Look, Dougy, I'm sorry about John and all, but I'm just a fisherman. It doesn't seem that urgent to me. I understand you're a little upset about John."

"I am a *little* upset," says Douglas. "I'm just a *little* bit upset. I will have no peace until all can see what John was trying to show them."

"What do you see?" asks Peter.

"Truth."

The word moves Andy.

"What truth?"

"There is only one truth."

Loki watches silently from a distance, not knowing what to think, and thinking never the less.

Jimmy's Farm

Jimmy's farm is in Swifton, a little inland from where Douglas fishes with Peter. It is not a large farm, but it is not small. Soon it will be the planting season and every planting season, wherever the Trigger brothers are, save Tommy, they come together to help sow seed in the field.

The brothers have not been together since the last harvest. While Jimmy and his wife, Kay, watch after the crops, Joey, the youngest of the brothers, lives on the farm raising sheep. Douglas comes and goes from place to place, none and all of which he calls home. Now it is the planting time. After they have sown the field, Douglas will become a fisherman on Peter's boat and they will not come together again until the harvest.

Douglas, Jimmy, Joey and Kay are eating dinner.

"He's a *Son of Light,*" says Douglas.

"Like my father," says Joey.

Douglas does not tell him about his father.

"He's a terrorist?" says Jimmy.

"I don't think he'd call himself that."

"Is he coming home?" asks Joey.

"I invited him."

"Did he find my father?" asks Joey.

"Yes."

"What did he say?"

"That he was not *his* father."

"Now he knows."

Douglas nods his head.

"Where is my father?"

"Sorry, I didn't ask. He was kind of angry, but I know where to find Tommy."

"That's something," says Jimmy. "We heard about John."

"He didn't kill himself," says Douglas.

"That's what we heard," says Jimmy.

"Don't believe the official story. He was murdered."

"Who killed him?"

"He was set up by the priests of the Temple of the Holy City."

"What?" exclaims Jimmy. "I didn't hear that."

"And you won't."

"That's a serious charge," says Jimmy.

"In addition to the Imperial soldiers from the Great Chief's Guard, there were also Temple Guards."

"That doesn't mean they were complicit," says Jimmy.

"You saw him arrested?" asks Joey.

"Peter and Andy were there. Something else…I went to the Temple of the Tribes of the Holy City. I entered *the Holy Place.* There's nothing there. John knew it. The priests deliberately set him up."

"What do you mean, there's nothing there?" asks Jimmy.

"There's no amulet in *the Holy Place.* It is an empty chamber. There's a big hole in *the Holy of Holies.*"

"Only the High Priest can go into *the Holy Place.* Only the High Priest could know. You could not know."

"You haven't been eating have you?" asks Kay, who is becoming uncomfortable with the conversation. "You look thin."

"I was fasting."

"Eat," says Kay, passing him more food.

Douglas smiles and waves her off.

"Eat," she says.

"Eat," says Jimmy.

Douglas takes the food. "Thanks."

"You look like shit," says Jimmy.

"It runs in the family."

"Tell us more about Tommy," Joey says. "What's he angry about?"

"Everything."

"Are you alright?" asks Jimmy. "Kay's right. You don't look so good."

"I'm okay." Douglas still feels weak. He leans back in his chair.

"What are your plans?" asks Jimmy. "Are you gonna stay this time?"

"No," says Douglas. It worries Kay.

"You gonna fish with Peter and Andy?"

"Probably. Jimmy, do you believe in destiny?"

"Destiny? I don't know. I suppose."

"Do you know your destiny?"

Jimmy thinks about it. "I don't really think about it. What about you?"

"I think about it."

Jimmy looks at his brother. He is worried about him. "All men must go to their destiny whether they think about it or not."

Loki lurks outside on the edge of the field. He fashions a nest for the night.

The Day of Rest

The field is on the edge of the desert. It is the Day of Rest. Jimmy and Joey try to stop their brother from working, but he will not be held back. Peter is hesitant at first, but Andy convinces him to join them along with Philip and Barty. Though Jimmy and Joey will not work in the field themselves, they are curious and follow their brother to watch him plow and sow seed.

Jimmy did not sleep all night. "It is the Day of Rest," he says.

"All days are the same," says Douglas as he hoes the field.

Jimmy and Joey look at each other. They do not want to work on the Day of Rest. It is against the Law of the Tribes.

"You're still intent on planting today even though it is against the Law?" asks Jimmy.

"I told you last night," says Douglas. "Why wait? Everybody's here."

"The priests would say this is a sin," Jimmy says.

"The priests are sinners," says Douglas. "Why do you listen to them? It is nature that makes the seed grow. It is nature that makes the man sow."

"Well, it rhymes," says Jimmy. "Is this what you and John learned at *the Settlement?*"

"You must learn to distinguish between natural law and

Laws made by men to control other men."

"Natural law rhymes?"

Douglas smiles.

"It is the Law of God," says Jimmy.

"The Law of God was made by men to control other men."

Jimmy is taken aback. He has not heard his brother talk like this before.

"Tell us about God," says Andy.

"God is a metaphor for that which we have forgotten. It is not a "thou." It is a "we." It is the thing that is the same in all things. It is *Being."*

"Tell us about *Being,"* urges Andy.

"Being is here," says Douglas. *"Being* is now. *Being* is everywhere, but nobody sees it. *Being* is the good seed that bad men cover in unfertile ground to deliberately starve and control the people. But when good men sow good seeds in fertile ground, it produces a good crop that nourishes all.

"Being is the yeast in raw dough. When the dough is cooked, the yeast makes it rise. *Being* is the truth in all things."

"Truth," says Peter. "What is truth but the absence of lies?"

"That is truth in this world," says Douglas. "This is a world of illusion. *Being* is without illusion."

"What illusion?" asks Peter.

"All the lies we believe," says Douglas. "All the untruths we're told when we're children, the lies of the Temple, the lies of the state, the lies our parents told us, the lies we believe that stop us from *Being."*

"What lies?" says Peter. "My parents didn't lie to me."

"They didn't lie on purpose," says Douglas, "they had been lied to themselves. You must forget all that they taught you. Start again. Clean slate. Seek truth like a suckling baby. Be reborn to innocence. John used to baptize people. I get what he was trying to say. Andy gets it. You already know everything you need to know, if you would just remember. You must return to a pre-birth awareness. Mine your *Self* for a hidden treasure. When death is life, and life is death, when you make the outside like the inside and the above like the below, then you will know *Being.*

"See what is already there, and that which is hidden from you will become plain. Do not let the wants of this world control you. It will fill you with despair. Don't worry about your appearance. Don't lie and don't go against your nature, because it will destroy you and keep you from the truth."

"Should we go into the desert and fast to see truth?" asks Andy.

"You must fast from this world," says Douglas. "Turn your back on it. It is not the outside. It is the inside. *Being* did not become manifest because of the flesh. The flesh became manifest because of *Being.*"

"How will we know when we see the truth?" asks Jimmy.

"You will know. You will feel like you've found a hidden treasure."

"What should we do while we look for truth?" asks Andy.

"Recognize that which is the same in all things. Even a stranger houses your own *Being.* Defend him like the pupil of your own eye. If you have money, do not lend it at interest, but give it to one from whom you will not get it back. If you have two coats, give one to a man who has none. If you have food, share it with a man who has none. We are all interdependent. Lighten the burdens of others if you can, but do not make them your burdens."

"You think a man should weigh himself down with the burdens of others?" asks Peter.

"No," says Douglas. "Do not take on the misfortunes of others so that they become your own burdens. Help where you can but know your own limitations. Don't look for the mote in your brother's eye, until you have cleared the speck from your own. When you see the truth, you will know."

"What should we do when we see the truth?" says Peter.

"Be like the merchant who, when he discovered a great pearl, sold all that he had to buy the pearl."

"The pearl is *Being?*" asks Andy.

"You ought to say this stuff in Temple," says Peter. "You'd make a pretty good preacher."

"Today I will be a farmer," says Douglas. "This is the seed

we will plant." Douglas stops hoeing and reaches into a pouch he has over his shoulder. He pulls out his hand and opens it to reveal some of the seeds from *the Settlement.* He plants some in the row he has hoed.

Jimmy is unsure as he watches his brother and looks out on the field he has sown his whole life. It is a harsh field, made up of a variety of topsoil.

Jimmy knows there are places where the wheat will not grow tall. There are places where the wheat will not grow at all. Still, every season, his brothers and their friends sow the whole field because this is what they have always done.

Loki crouches unobserved.

Parochial

The Temple of Swifton is not as ornamented as the Temple of the Holy City. Douglas has not been there in a long time. In honor of his return he was given a spot in the day's service. The crowd is bigger than normal. There is a buzz about Douglas and some people have even come to hear him. Jimmy and Joey are there. Bobby Tarmac has come to listen. The spy from the Temple of the Tribes of the Holy City is also there.

Douglas stands in the pulpit on the altar of the Temple of Swifton. Samuel, the High Priest and the other priests and elders regard the crowd with unease. Samuel remembers Douglas from his youth. He remembers all the Trigger boys, including Tommy. He remembers when Douglas went to *the Settlement.* He has a pretty good idea what Douglas is going to say. He doesn't like it.

Jimmy, Joey, Peter, Andy, Philip and Barty stand by Douglas's side. James and Johnny Z, two other brothers who also sail their father's fishing boat in the same waters as Peter and Andy, are also with them. Douglas looks out at the crowd before him.

"Today I will tell you about freedom," says Douglas. "Freedom is truth. Truth is freedom. Money will not buy truth. The truth comes to those who seek it. The free see the truth.

The true will find freedom.

"You won't be free if you serve the Temple or State. You must serve *the Self* that is the same in all things. You don't need a priest or a politician to find it. No church or government holds the key. It is *the Self* which pervades all *Being.* When you are alone at peace, you will find freedom."

Samuel still thinks of Douglas as the child that he was, to be corrected and graded. "That's not what we taught him," he says to the other priests.

"That's not from *the Book of the Tribes,*" says another priest, "He's making it up."

Douglas offends many. The crowd is restless.

"Medicine Man rubbish," another priest says. "He should not speak in the Temple. He is a mouthpiece for *the Settlement."*

"Who are you that we should listen to you?" heckles Samuel. He looks at Douglas's brothers and says, "Aren't you just a bunch of farmers and sheep herders? Why don't you go back to your farm?"

"My father was a farmer. I am planting a new seed."

"You're still a boy," says the older man. "Why should anyone listen to you?"

"Don't listen to me," says Douglas. "Listen to your own *Voice."*

"You would have us listen to demons."

"If you are a demon."

The crowd is still. The heckler has nothing more to say. He is shocked by such insolence.

Douglas outstretches his arms. "I want to show how you can be free of these walls," he says.

"These walls are holy!" cries an elder. "Do not blaspheme in here!"

"What I say is not blasphemy," lectures Douglas. "The truth is not unholy."

Douglas looks at the crowd. It is an older crowd. They are not buying it. It is not his crowd. He needs to wrap it up and re-group.

"The truth does not belong to any one sect of people. It is

not the purview of one Tribe or a bevy of priests. It can come to everyone. The only gatekeeper to freedom is an ignorance of *the Self.*"

That's a good enough exit line. Douglas looks towards his friends to signal he's done.

"This is the new seed I will plant," he says.

Samuel, the priests and the elders do not like it.

Bobby decides Douglas sounds like *the Medicine Man.* His revolution is not the revolution of *the Sons of Light.* His fight is with the Temple, not with the Empire. Douglas refreshes Bobby. He is not like Tommy at all. Tommy will not like it.

Douglas is finished speaking and his friends surround him and walk him through the throng. As he passes some of the old men from the Temple, he can see that they do not approve of him. The others can sense the discomfort.

"Tough crowd," says Peter.

"I'm still just a child to them."

"We better go," says Peter.

"Yea," says Douglas.

Their escape takes them to the Swift Sea. They get into a rowboat on the shore and head back out to Peter's boat, where they return to Peter's house for the night. Douglas's brothers go back to the farm. Bobby goes to stay with his parents.

Douglas speaks at the Temple of Swifton again. He learns how to get the crowd on his side. He speaks again and again. The people who come to hear him often stay. When someone hears him once, they want to hear him again. The longer Douglas speaks at the Temple of Swifton, the more people hear about him and the more people come to listen. Each time he speaks the crowd gets larger, until one day he is banned from the Temple. Even so, his words spread throughout the area. A rumor also spreads: 'A prophet has arisen in the land. *The Kingdom of Truth* is at hand.'

Loki returns to the Temple in the Holy City to make his report when Douglas is banned in Swifton. Bobby also returns to the Holy City.

Some of the people who have come to Swifton to hear him

do not leave.

The wheat is growing free in the field, but the tares also grow.

The Mother

The trip from the Temple of Swifton to Peter's house is a short overland route to the *Swift Sea*. Rachel, who is Peter's wife, is not happy to see Douglas. Since Douglas came back from the Holy City, there has been a constant stream of activity in her home. There are always men coming and going. There is constant plotting.

"Did people come and listen to you today?" she says.

"There were a lot of people," says Peter.

"Enough to get Trigger banned," says Andy with a smile.

"Banned?" Rachel disapproves. "Mother hasn't been feeling good since you've been gone."

"She never feels very good," says Peter.

"This time it's serious," she says. "Maybe you should just stay home for a couple of days. Let Andy look after the business."

Peter shudders. Andy? "She's just faking it anyway," he says.

"That's not true," says Rachel. "She's very sick."

"I can hear you, you know," says Rachel's mother as she walks cautiously into the room. She leans on a cane.

"Mother," says Rachel.

Rachel's mother is uneasy at the number of men in the room and the thought of her men becoming a part of them.

Her attention comes to focus on Douglas.

"You," she says, accusing Douglas, leaning on her cane. "I know about boys like you. You're a charmer. That's what you are. A charmer. You have come to take my boys away."

"Is that what is ailing you?" asks Douglas.

She leans toward him with an accusing finger. "You are what is ailing me, boy." The old woman finds a chair and sits down with a sigh of relief. "You have a farm near the desert. Why don't you go there? You are not a fisherman. You are like *the Medicine Man.* You are a rebel without a revolution, a priest without a God. Men follow you, but you do not lead them anywhere. Andrew follows you. And now, God forbid, my Rachel's Peter follows you."

"You make me sound wrong," says Douglas.

"I'm a simple woman," she says. "I would not make such a judgment. Peter is content to limit his sermons to the Temple of Swifton, but you, you want the whole world to listen to you!"

"It is your fear that they will leave you that has made you sick," says Douglas. "You must not try to stop them. You have your own path and they must find theirs. Peter and Rachel have different destinies. They may head in a like direction, but no two take the same path. All destinies meet the same end."

"What makes you so wise in the ways of the world?" she asks with scorn and disbelief. "You are still a young man. What if it is their destiny to walk a path together?"

"Then they will," says Douglas. "Do you still mourn for your husband?"

Her eyes become small. "Every day," she says. "Now I have only the boys to provide for me. Don't take them from me."

"Did you love your husband?" asks Douglas.

She listens to him. The room becomes quiet. "Yes," she whispers. "I loved him very much. I love him still."

"How long did you walk with your husband until you took separate paths?"

"Up until the day he died," she says.

"Now his journey is done," says Douglas, "but yours continues."

"I miss having him with me," she says. "I miss when we

were young."

"Don't look back; look ahead, your journey isn't over yet."

"Isn't it?" she says. "Look at me. I am an old woman. This world is for the young."

"It is for those who are still in it," says Douglas. "And you must let those who are in it, find their own way. If Peter and Andy do not fulfill their destinies, what peace will they have when they are your age?"

The old woman takes this in.

"You must spend the rest of your time exploring your own path," Douglas says. "The world is not just for the young. It is for all who are still in it."

She becomes more relaxed.

"Your path does not depend on Peter or Andy," says Douglas. "You must set your daughter on her own path. Be at peace, mother. It will make you free."

She becomes serene. "You know," she says, "I have probably known these boys longer than you." She is no longer an adversary. "I was always afraid that Rachel would want to marry Andrew. They're the same age, you know, but Peter asked her first. I don't mind telling you it was a relief! Andrew was always such a dreamer." She looks at him. "He still is. Peter is very responsible. He's a good provider. The only reason he went with you to see *the Medicine Man* was to rescue his brother. But now, they both seem to follow you. Now I see your charm."

"You make me seem wicked."

She does not comment. "Where will you lead those who follow you?"

"I will lead them to their own path," he says. "I will lead them to freedom."

The old woman stands up. "This world is for the young," she says. "My fever rises."

Bobby's Report

Tommy walks alone with a pack of stray dogs through the crowded streets of the Holy City. The Holy City reeks of the people who have built and live in it. It reeks from the Empire that has conquered it. The streets of the Holy City are where Tommy lives.

The friends Tommy has are good friends. They are fighting friends. But to be Tommy's friend, you have to let him control you.

The enemies Tommy has are good enemies. They are fighting enemies. But for Tommy to be your enemy, you have to let him control you.

Bobby is walking through the same streets as Tommy. He has just arrived in the Holy City. He scans the sea of faces in the crowded streets like some pop preacher looking out on the crowd he has gathered. He's thinking to himself that Tommy's brother is a prophet, like the prophets from *the Book of the Tribes.*

Tommy is in the sea coming towards Bobby. Four dogs trail Tommy today hoping for handouts. Tommy looks straight ahead. He does not see Bobby. Bobby sees him.

"Tommy," says Bobby. "Tommy."

"Bobby," he says, hearing his name, stopping to talk. "When did you get back?" The dogs also stop.

"Just now. I was looking for you."

Tommy taps Bobby on the back pointing him in the direction he was heading. "Let's keep walking. I'm heading over to Timmy's."

"Sure."

They start walking again. The dogs follow. "How was home?" asks Tommy.

"I went to the Temple. I went to hear your brother speak."

"Oh, yeah? Has he got it?"

"Oh, yeah."

"Like *the Medicine Man?*"

"Kind of. They banned him."

"Banned him?" That's what they did to John. "What did he say?"

"He said that freedom is a matter of seeing truth. He said to know truth is to be free."

"Just like *the Medicine Man.* How can you have a spiritual freedom when you live in bondage? What did he say about the revolution?"

"His is not our revolution," says Bobby. "He *is* like *the Medicine Man.* He talks about truth."

"Whose truth? That's what you fight for. Your truth."

"He says there is only one truth."

"His truth."

"People are starting to follow your brother," says Bobby. "Many of *the Ghosts* already follow him."

"Yea. I could tell that about him. I was right. He would be a valuable man to have on our side. My brother."

"I think he'll be one of the voices of our generation."

Tommy considers it. "Maybe you should go back to Swifton," he says.

"What do you mean?"

"Go back to Swifton and hang out with your friends and my brother for a while. You'll be our man on the inside."

"He's your brother."

"I'm not comfortable with that. There's too much bad blood. If I see him, I have to see them and it just goes on and on."

"I'm not gonna spy on my friends."

"I'm not asking you to spy on your friends. I'm asking you to spy on my brother."

"Why don't we both go?"

Tommy hesitates.

"There's strength in numbers."

"I don't know."

"C'mon. He speaks on the Day of Rest."

"Maybe. He'll be at the Temple?"

"I told you, he's banned from the Temple. The priests don't like what he has to say."

Tommy appreciates that. "Where will he speak?"

"Probably the field of your brother's farm. Do you know where that is?"

Tommy scowls. "I know where that is."

They arrive at Timothy's door.

"Here we are," says Tommy.

The Struggle

There is one man in the Holy City Tommy does not try to control. There is one man he takes orders from. That man is Timothy. He lives in a crowded, dark section of town. It is a distance from the safe house. When Timothy and Bobby come to the door, he is in the middle of making dinner for himself.

"Tommy," he says, "Bobby, come in."

Tommy and Bobby follow Timothy inside. He closes the door.

"I was just making dinner," he says. "Do you want some?"

"Ya, sure," says Tommy. "Thanks."

"Yea," says Bobby.

"Sit down," Timothy says, pointing to the table. "It is all done. I just have to cut it in thirds. Lucky for you I made too much."

Tommy and Bobby sit down at the table as Timothy makes the final preparations at a counter in the middle of the room. He brings three plates of food with him to the table and sets them down.

"You want some wine?"

"Ya, sure," says Bobby.

"Sure."

Timothy gets the wine and sits down to eat. "You just get

back?" he asks Bobby, pouring him a cup of wine. He pours one for Tommy and one for himself.

"We're just going," says Tommy.

"Where are you going?"

"Back to Swifton," says Bobby.

"You are from there too, right?" He asks Tommy. Tommy nods. "What is in Swifton?"

"Ghosts," says Tommy.

"Ghosts? The Medicine Man is dead."

"There is another. They're following a new prophet."

"And he is in Swifton?"

"Yes," says Tommy. "He was speaking at the Temple until he got banned."

"He got banned from the Temple?"

"He wasn't referring to *the Book of the Tribes,"* says Bobby. "The things he knows he knows by knowing."

"The things he knows he knows by…Maybe that makes sense to *Ghosts,* but it sounds like bull to me. What did he talk about?"

"He talked about freedom," says Tommy, who was not there, "but he said nothing about the revolution."

"Then it is not freedom. I thought the crowds would follow us once *the Medicine Man* died. Who is this new prophet? Do you guys know him?"

"He is my brother. He is my twin brother."

Timothy is taken aback. "Twin brother? Since when do you have a twin brother? Since when do you have a brother?"

"I saw him at the river. He was with *the Medicine Man."*

"And he is your brother? What is his name?"

"Douglas."

"Douglas Trigger. What does your brother do?"

"He's a farmer on my family's farm."

"A farmer," says Timothy. "A farmer should not cause so much trouble. You never told me you had a brother. And twin? And a family farm? You have a family? I thought you were an orphan."

Tommy does not smile.

"Will your brother join us?"

"One way or another, *the Ghosts* will join us," says Tommy.

Timothy believes him. "Twin."

"I will lead *the Ghosts* who follow my brother to our cause. This time we'll be on the inside. He's my brother, my twin. He'll listen to me."

"I'm friends with all of his friends," says Bobby.

"We're already on the inside," says Tommy.

"Some of *the Medicine Man's Ghosts* grew up in Swifton. I grew up with them and Tommy's brothers. I knew them before I knew Tommy."

"Tell me about your twin."

"I haven't seen him since we were thirteen."

"Your brother was the guy you stashed at the safe house?"

"Yea."

"He owes you."

"He doesn't owe me anything."

"He owes you his loyalty," says Timothy. "Where does he stand on *the Empire Question?* Is he with us or against us?"

"He's not with us," says Bobby.

"Then he is against us," says Timothy.

"People are following him," says Tommy.

"How many people are following him?"

"Since he was banned from the Temple," says Bobby, *"the Ghosts* have filled his brother's field every time he speaks."

"Do you think you will be able to persuade him to become involved in the Struggle?"

"I don't know," says Tommy.

"That is not like you."

"I really don't know him. I tried to talk to him about it at the safe house. He didn't seem interested. There is something about him, something aloof."

"He is your brother, alright. What else do you know about him?"

"I don't know much. I don't think he was a follower of *the Medicine Man*. I think they were just friends---preachers on the same circuit."

"Was *the Medicine Man* from Swifton?"

"I don't think so. I left when I was thirteen."

"No," says Bobby.

"If they were friends, they may have influenced one another. They may share a similar philosophy. Do you know what the philosophy of *the Medicine Man* was?"

"We only heard him that one time," says Tommy.

"He talked about freedom too."

"What kind of freedom?"

"It wasn't a political freedom," says Tommy. "It's not our freedom."

"What kind of a freedom is it?"

"It's a freedom from…"

"Material wants," says Bobby.

"It's more than that, isn't it?" says Tommy.

"Is this what your brother believes?"

"I don't know."

"Let me know when you do know," says Timothy.

"We shouldn't be out of town that long."

"Let us act on this together."

"Right." Tommy finishes his drink. He takes a bite of the food and looks at what remains on the plate. "What is this?"

"What does it taste like?"

"Do you believe in a *Messiah?*" Bobby asks Timothy.

"I believe every man must save himself."

"You are greater than the average man," says Tommy. "I believe that the average man must follow a great man. The average man would call the great man a *Messiah.*"

"But the great man would know that he is no *Messiah,*" says Timothy. "In the end, every man must save himself."

"From what Bobby tells me, I believe that my brother may be a great man. He may be a very great man."

"He is only a great man if he is on our side. Go to him in Swifton." Timothy takes his last drink. "If there is to be a *Messiah,* comrades, he must come from the Struggle. It would be for the common good to contain any other source. Get him on our side."

"He'll join us," says Tommy.

The Stew

A fire burns in the Garden adjacent to Zacharus's office at the Temple of the Tribes in the Holy City. He is not cold. He is hungry. He uses the fire to warm a stew. Loki watches him from the door unnoticed.

"There is a pilgrimage to Swifton under way," says Loki.

Zacharus is not startled. "What's in Swifton?" he says without turning to face the spy.

"Tommy Trigger's brother. *The Ghosts* have a new prophet."

"How many people are going there?" he says, stirring the stew.

"I don't know. *The Ghosts.* A lot. I never saw so many people going north before."

"Are all of *the Ghosts* following him?"

"It's hard to tell a new *Ghost* from an old one."

"Is he the next *Medicine Man?*" asks Zacharus.

"I don't know," says Loki. "The first time I saw him, I followed him from the river with a bunch of *Ghosts* right after *the Medicine Man* died. I think I told you that. They went to *Sarah's Inn.* I thought they went together. Maybe they went with him."

"I saw him with *the Medicine Man* at the river."

Loki is nonplussed. "What did he do that day in the

Temple?"

"I'll ask the questions around here," says Zacharus. He tastes a bite of the stew.

"He was using the Temple of Swifton to speak."

"What does he say?"

"It's unorthodox. It's blasphemous. It's that brainwashing he picked up at *the Settlement.*"

"Is there anything else you can tell me?"

"Just one thing. I mention it because it's odd. Tommy's rebel friend Bobby was there."

"Where was Tommy?"

"He wasn't there. He probably never left the Holy City. He's not *the Ghost* type."

"Bobby Tarmac was there. Maybe this new *Medicine Man* is a rebel. Maybe they think he's that damned *Messiah* they keep waiting for. And he's got a twin who is a *Son of Light.*"

"I think I should go back there. I think I should keep my eye on this one."

"Keep both eyes on this one. We must have orthodoxy in these times."

Swifton

Douglas is back at the farm, surveying the field. There are weeds springing up everywhere. He does not understand what could have happened. The seed he planted was good seed. He takes one of the weeds into his hand. He does not yank it out. He feels it.

Douglas walks back to the house and is greeted by Jimmy and Kay. Joey is out herding. Jimmy sees it in his brother's face. He has come through the field.

"You've seen the weeds?"

"We sowed the field with good seed," says Douglas, "and yet the wheat is tangled in weeds."

"I guess it's our fault. Me and Joey grabbed the wrong seed. We weren't with you on the first day. We must have grabbed some of the bad seed from last year."

"You kept it?"

"It seemed like a waste."

"You should have worked with us that first day. Then you would have known."

"It was against the Law."

"Whose Law?"

"We should start weeding the field."

"We might also uproot the good seed," says Douglas. "Let the weeds grow. Let them grow together until harvest time.

That's when we'll know the good seed from the bad."

"The weeds will choke some of the good seed."

"The good seed will survive."

Tommy and Bobby pass a lot of people on their way from the Holy City. They stop at many inns along the way. All the talk is of the new prophet. Tommy does not like it. He wants them to be talking about politics, not philosophy.

They see Loki at one of the inns on the road to Swifton. 'Why is he on this road? What is his business?'

When the Temple spy sees the rebels, he leaves the inn. He does not want to be seen. He does not know that it is already too late. He is not as clever as he thinks.

Tommy and Bobby arrive at Jimmy's farm on the Day of Rest without asking for directions. Tommy has not been back in almost twenty years. They approach from the Sea and can see the field that borders the desert. It is filled with people.

"How is anything going to grow in that field?"

"I don't know. Are you gonna go to the house?" That's what Bobby wants to do.

"Let's hear him first." Tommy is not ready for a reunion. "When is he supposed to speak?"

"I don't know."

Bobby feels alone standing next to Tommy, surrounded by people in the field. He is starting to be unsure about the Struggle. He wants to be with his friends inside. He wants to hear Douglas speak again. Something has changed in him. It does not matter that Tommy is his friend, or that he had grown up in Swifton, or that there are hundreds of people also there. He feels alone. He is no longer a boy. He is no longer a *Son of Light.* While he waits for Douglas to speak, he feels like something is ending.

"It's weird to find ourselves here, isn't it?" he says.

"In this field?" asks Tommy.

"In this time. I feel like something's happening here, like we're in the crux of history. It's just this feeling I keep getting, like a wheel in motion."

"I think I know what you mean." Tommy does not know

what he means. He takes out his syrinx.

"It's fantastic! That's what it is!"

"Mmph," Tommy smiles. He looks around at all the strangers gathered in the field. "Along the road people kept saying my brother is enlightened."

"He knows the truth."

"That's what they say." Tommy puts the reed in his mouth and gives it a go.

"He has an authority," says Bobby. "I've seen it. Nobody told him. He just knows."

"Some called him a prophet," says Tommy without removing the instrument from his mouth.

"Some people were calling him crazy."

"What do you say?" asks Tommy.

"I would not say," says Bobby. "I will let you see for yourself."

"How long do you think these people have been here?"

"That one guy said he's been speaking every day since he got thrown out of the Temple. Every day is a Day of Rest. Every day it's like a big party."

Tommy plays nothing in particular. He is writing a new song. Some of the people around them are staring at Tommy. Bobby sees it. Tommy notices. He stops playing. One of the seated campers stands up and approaches.

"You're him," he says.

"Not me," says Tommy.

"Are you one of his brothers?"

"Something like that. What brings you to this field?"

"I came to hear your brother speak last week and I stayed."

"Did he speak yesterday?"

"He answered questions mostly. People asked him things."

"What did they ask him?"

"About life. About death. About what is right. About truth."

"Truth?"

"He said everything we want is here and now. He said we live in a *Garden*. We just can't see it."

"This is a desert. We live in a desert. Look beyond the field."

"How many people were here yesterday?" asks Bobby.

"There are more today."

Tommy looks around him. There are several hundred people lined up to listen to his brother. "Did he say anything about the revolution?" he asks.

"He said we don't need one."

"He said that?"

"He said we were already free."

"That's crazy," says Tommy.

"That's what he said."

The crowd swells and a sound from the house makes Bobby and Tommy turn around. A group of people are emerging.

"It's your brother," says Bobby, nodding towards the group. "He's coming this way."

Tommy turns around and sure enough, it is Douglas. "Who are all those people with him?" he says.

"Those are *the Ghosts.*"

"*'The Medicine Man*'s *Ghosts?*'"

"They're his *Ghosts.*"

"It has already begun," whispers Tommy. "It may already be too late."

"What may already be too late?" asks Bobby. "What has begun?"

Tommy does not hear him. He starts to play again. All his thoughts are of himself. 'What should I do?'

Tommy stops playing when Douglas and his entourage approach, and walk past him and Bobby, without noticing them. Bobby makes out some of the faces in his entourage of *Ghosts.* There is Peter on Douglas's right. There are James and Johnny Z. There are Andy, Philip and Barty. There are Tommy's brothers, Jimmy and Joey. Jimmy A is also there. Tommy stares into the group, but he only recognizes Douglas and a couple of others Bobby had introduced to him. When the group passes Tommy and Bobby, they become a part of the group, following behind. Tommy puts his pipe away. More people join them. The field is crowded with people between the stalks of grain. It seems that each person the mass touches is swept up in its wave.

When Douglas was younger, he had said many of the things he would say this day. When he became older, he put aside his search for meaning in order to make a living. Now that he is thirty-two, he feels young again. He feels afraid. Strangers love him, but he feels alone.

Many of those who are gathered this day have heard him speak before. They have come to watch him break the rules once more. And each time he speaks, the group gets larger. And each time he speaks is another shovelful from his grave.

Though Douglas is banned from the Temple of Swifton, Samuel, other priests, and elders of the Temple have come to see him. Douglas looks out on the throng that has gathered before him. "Let me tell you about truth," he says and he waves his arms up in the air. There are cheers from the crowd and discontent. He is uneasy.

"This world is a reflection of the truth," says Douglas, "but it is not truth. It is distorted truth; distorted by men to control other men. The truth must be uncovered. It is spread out around us, but nobody sees it."

"What truth?" asks someone. "What are you talking about?"

"What are you going to do for us?" a woman asks.

"What are you going to do for yourself?"

"You speak as though you are above the Law!" cries a voice.

"I follow my own law," he says. "I follow natural law. All of man's history is wrapped around a natural law, like a spiral stair. We may not be able to touch it, but it's the supporting column that's always there. You may try to break natural law. You may try to write your own Laws. There is only one truth."

Tommy has a question. "What is truth?" he says.

Douglas sees his brother in the field. "Truth is natural law," he says.

"Oh yea?" says Tommy. "Where does the Empire fit into all this?"

Douglas smiles. "It fits in where all that is temporal fits in," he says, "on the stairs."

"The stairs are twisted," says Tommy.

"They wrap around the truth," says Douglas.

"The Empire's authority is not natural, is it?"

Douglas did not expect to be heckled by his brother. He never expected to see his brother. "No, it's not," he answers. "But it's also not natural to take up arms. The Empire will fall. It is temporal. *Being* is not temporal. The truth is not temporal."

"What do you know about truth?"

"I know that which is the same in all things," says Douglas.

"Where is the truth?"

"It is not outside, it is inside. I cannot tell it to you. You must ask yourself questions. You must find your own answers. When you know *the Self,* you will know the truth of all things. The truth is everywhere. It's right here. Everybody's looking, but nobody sees it."

"But you see it?" asks Tommy.

"Yes."

"But Doug," says his brother Jimmy, who is not in a position to be able to see Tommy through the crowd, "where is the truth?"

Tommy sees him. 'Jimmy?'

"It is nowhere and everywhere. It is in the sky. It is in the grass. It is in the stars. It is in the clouds. It is in the beach. It is in the ocean. It is in the wind. It is in the sun. It is in the food. It is in the drink. It is in every man, woman and child. The truth is everywhere, but nobody sees it.

"The truth is within you. It is all around you. It is in all of you. When you know *the Self,* you will feel your connection to all *Being* and you will know the truth. If you do not know *the Self,* you will live in a poverty you recreate every day."

"What should a man do to find truth?" asks Jimmy A.

And Douglas says, "Love and you will be loved. You will find truth. To find something to love in your enemy is to find that thing to love about yourself. And that thing that you can love in everything is your own *Self* because we are one *Being,* separated by false realities, and what separates us is self-imposed, the manacles re-forged with each passing generation."

"What about wealth? What about money?" Jimmy A. follows up.

"Wealth does not come from money. There was this rich guy, lived in a big house. He had lots of land, money and women. One night he said to one of his women, 'I figured everything out when I was just a kid. Pop had some money. When I turned twenty-one, he gave some to me. I wanted to invest, so that by the time I got to be forty, I would lack nothing. My investments paid off. It's like having a storehouse full of wheat. I lack nothing. Tonight I am forty.'

"That night he died. He died alone. He never had a family, just a lot of money with no one to spend it on."

Jimmy A. says, "What if I search the world over and still can't find truth?"

Douglas says, "You will find it when you return home. You will find *the Self* that is *the Self* in all things. You may feel uneasy for awhile, but it will pass and you will feel contentment and you will be free. You will know the truth. You will command your own destiny."

"What is my destiny?" asks Bobby.

"Only you know that. Someone else can't tell you. You can't follow someone to your own destiny. You will find the answer in *the Self*. Do not regulate your free will to a system of order under which you have no control. You must create your own order. You must rule your own life."

"You're asking us to risk a lot," says Peter.

"What price would you pay for your freedom?"

Peter thinks about it. "I would pay anything, risk everything, to gain my freedom."

"Then that is what you must do." Douglas looks at his brothers and his friends and the rest of the crowd. "That is what you all must do."

Tommy tries to count the number of listeners. There are too many of them.

"What does that mean?" asks James.

"That means that just because you and Johnny were apprenticed into your father's business, you don't have to be fishermen. You have to find your own way. That was his destiny. It isn't yours." Turning to Peter, Douglas says, "And that goes for you and Andy."

"Are you so sure you know my destiny?" asks Peter.

"Only you know your destiny."

"What if it is our destiny to run our father's business?" asks Johnny Z.

"What are you gonna give up?" Tommy asks Douglas.

"I have nothing to give up but the clothes on my back."

Tommy knows it is true. Douglas has nothing. Technically, the farm belongs to Jimmy, privilege of the first born. Like Tommy, Douglas does not have a home of his own.

"When will God fulfill his *Promise?*" Tommy asks his brother. "When will the Nations regain their own Kingdom?"

"The Kingdom is spread out around you, but you do not see it. When you recognize what is before you, the hidden will become unhidden. What you see you will know. Whoever knows *the Self* knows the world."

"Are you *the Messiah?"* asks Andy.

"The Messiah? No. No. Listen for the truth. I am not the truth."

"But your words are not the words of other men," says Barty. "You are like the source of a spring that quenches the thirst of everyone who drinks from it."

"When you hear me, it is only an echo of your own *Voice,* or else why would you agree with me? There will be no *Messiah* to rescue man from man and woman from woman. You must save yourselves. For though you may despoil nature, nature will survive you. And if you do not preserve nature, how then can you save yourselves? Do not take more from the world than you need or you will be unwelcome in it. Do not be sheep. Instead become wolves and scatter the flock. The shepherd is a man who takes without giving. The shepherd cares only for how his flock can comfort him. The shepherd despoils nature for his own gain."

Joey is a shepherd. He does not like his brother's metaphor.

"But wolves eat the sheep," says Andy.

"A wolf may scatter the sheep. Let the flock graze on grass for its own sake, and not grow fat to be sold at the market."

The Homecoming

The last time Tommy sat at this table he was thirteen years old. They were boys then. Now they are men. Jimmy is married. The distance between them is greater than the table. Their mother is dead. The room is crowded with Tommy, his brothers, Kay, and Douglas's entourage. They sit and stand around the table drinking.

"He wasn't a *Son of Light,*" Tommy tells Joey. "He didn't leave to join the Struggle. He just left."

"What was he doing?"

"I didn't care. I didn't ask him."

"How long ago was that?" asks Jimmy.

"Sometime after I got to the Holy City. It took me a couple of years."

"Did you see him again?" asks Joey.

"No."

"Did he want to see you again?"

"I don't think so. I don't think he liked being found."

"Did he ask about me?"

Tommy stops himself from saying, 'no' and says, "I told him about you."

"Do you know where he is today?"

"No."

"You haven't asked about our mother," says Jimmy.

"I don't really care," says Tommy, though it is untrue. He turns to his twin. "We are not so different, you and I."

"I speak the truth."

"Truth is a rebel," says Tommy. "Because the Tribespeople in the field follow you, you must lead them. You must lead them to revolution, to freedom, to the overthrow of Imperial order."

"No," Douglas says flatly. "Mine is not a political movement. That is not what I'm doing here."

"What are you doing here?"

"If you don't yet know, you will if you keep listening."

"Yea, I'll keep listening, if you listen. We must free our people."

"We are already free."

"There must be revolution."

"The revolution is already won. You fight to control a manmade wasteland, built on a *Garden* which has been plowed under. You fight for control of an illusion. What you serve will serve you."

Bobby looks at Tommy and then to Douglas. Twins. It's funny to him. Two faces. Two voices. He remembers the first time he saw Tommy in the Holy City and called out, "Douglas!"

"We're going back to the Holy City," says Douglas. "We're going to sail down the river in Peter's ship. We're going to stop in ports along the way and speak in their Temples. We're going to leave after the harvest. You're welcome to come."

"You're welcome to stay," says Jimmy.

Tommy considers them both. "I may need a ride down the river if I'm still here," he says.

"Good," says Douglas.

"You have a good way with the crowds," Tommy says.

Jimmy and Joey look at their long lost brother. They look at Tommy's face and then at Douglas's face. It is uncanny.

"Welcome home," says Jimmy.

Tommy does not feel welcome. He looks at his brothers with suspicion. His experience has led him to trust no one, especially his family.

Action

Aron waits for Zacharus a long time. It is one of the ways a man like Zacharus treats a man like Aron. Zacharus does not like his son-in-law. Zacharus does not like most of the people in his working life. Aron is also in his personal life. Zacharus does not like his life.

Aron is irritated. The sun moves from one window to another while he waits. One day he will be the High Priest of the Temple of the Tribes of the Holy City. Why is he made to wait? What is Zacharus doing? He is doing it on purpose. Aron knocks on the door again. An attendant comes to the door.

"He knows you're waiting," says the attendant. "It won't be much longer." He closes the door.

Zacharus isn't doing anything. He is outside in the sun. He does not have to watch it through windows. The attendant comes out to the garden and disturbs him.

"My Lord, Aron still waits for you," he says.

"Is he getting anxious?"

"He is very anxious."

"Good. Let him wait. Let him wait a little longer and then you can bring him into the garden." He points to the only other seat that is there. Take that chair away."

"Yes," says the attendant, picking up the chair. "As you

wish."

He retreats from Zacharus with the chair into the darkness of the Temple. He shakes his head when he is out of the sight of the High Priest. He waits a little longer before going to get Aron.

Aron thinks about what he will say to Zacharus. He will say that he has been kept waiting. He will say what he has come to say. The attendant leads Aron through Zacharus's office and points him out to the garden.

Outside it is light and Aron, who has been inside in the dark, has to cover his eyes.

"What is this urgent matter you have come to speak to me about?" asks Zacharus as he approaches.

Aron walks around to face Zacharus. "Douglas Trigger," he says. "He is preaching at the Temple in Swifton. He is gaining a following."

"What following?" asks Zacharus, as if he doesn't already know.

"Ghosts."

This is old news to Zacharus. "Are they *the Medicine Man's Ghosts?"*

"From what I hear he's got them and his own *Ghosts."*

"Do you know what he's saying in Swifton?"

Aron hesitates. "The reports I hear are more blasphemous than anything *the Medicine Man* ever said."

"Does he say anything about truth?" asks Zacharus.

"Yes," says Aron. "I hear that's all he talks about. But his truth is not our truth. It is not our Law."

Zacharus knows what he will do. He will go to Swifton.

The Gauntlet

"Why don't you see the world as I see it?" Tommy asks Douglas as they and Bobby stand in the field. The wheat comes up to their shoulders. The weeds are almost as tall. Some of the wheat has been trampled and will not survive. "How can freedom have two meanings?"

"There is only one freedom."

"Truth is freedom. You said it yourself. Isn't it true that to be free, you must fight?"

"What you fight controls you."

"What kind of bullshit is that? If you do not fight, it still controls you. I'd rather fight. How does a slave become free if he does not fight? What about all the other things worth fighting for? How can I be rich when there are poor? How can I be full when someone is hungry? How can I be sheltered when there is someone without a home? How can we be without war when there's a revolution to fight?"

"There are two distances away from the point, and where we begin is the truth."

"And what is the truth?"

"Truth is without time and meaning. It is knowing the unknown can be known. Truth is seeing without looking, sensing without feeling, tasting without touching."

"Where can I look for truth?" asks Bobby.

"You must look inside yourself," says Douglas. "You must follow the wisdom that is within."

Douglas's entourage has come into the field to water the seed. They take up their task again. They do not know that like the Day of Rest, they are being observed. Zacharus and Aron blend in with *the Ghosts* who have come to Jimmy's farm. The spy is also present, hidden in another part of the field where weeds grow.

"Do you see that?" Aron whispers. "Not even *the Medicine Man* would have the audacity to toil on the Day of Rest!"

'He is a new breed,' thinks Zacharus.

"What's wrong with him?" says Aron.

"Shhh!" Zacharus scolds. He puts his finger over his lips to quiet the boy-man. He walks away from Aron and makes himself known to Douglas and *the Ghosts.* They see him. Aron follows.

"Whose field is this?" Zacharus says as he approaches.

"It is my field," says Jimmy, holding up his hand to stop the priest. "Who are you?"

Zacharus stops. He sees Jimmy's resemblance to Douglas and Tommy.

"How many brothers does Tommy have?" he whispers to Aron when he catches up.

"What is it you want?'" says Douglas, stepping forward. "Why have you come to this field?"

"Don't you know that it is the Day of Rest?" says Zacharus. "This is a day to serve God, not man."

"Man must serve *the Self* in all things," says Douglas. "When you tell me to serve your God, what you really want is for me to serve you."

"This is a double blaspheme," says Aron.

Peter is near the other Trigger brothers. He moves closer to Douglas to listen. The others also go over as soon as they notice.

"I blaspheme *your* truth. It is not *the* truth."

"Do not question the Law," warns Aron.

"It is not for you to judge God's Law," says Zacharus.

"It is not for you to judge me," says Douglas.

"You should fast," says Zacharus.

"I am hungry," says Douglas.

"Look, boy," says Zacharus; "we came here from the Holy City. We know about you. You speak in our Temples. *Our* Temples. You are not orthodox. People are calling you, 'Lord.'"

Douglas smiles. Zacharus shakes his head. "Such disrespect. People are starting to look up to you. And yet today, on the Day of Rest, you are working in a field with these men."

"This is our field," says Douglas. "It is a good field. We planted good seed."

"Son, we don't doubt that you have a fine field," says Zacharus, "and we don't doubt that you planted good seed, but can't you just rest for one day?"

"Why should I rest when I am not tired?"

"Doesn't God deserve your devotion?"

"You have a very needy God."

The priests are not amused. "We will be watching you, Douglas Trigger," says Aron.

"You waste *the Light* when you look at me because you do not see."

By this time, Andy, James and Johnny Z are listening and have come around the group. Barty listens.

Zacharus looks at Douglas. "Alright, let's come to the point. What are you telling these people? Why do they follow you?"

"You have ears, hear," says Douglas.

"Such insolence," says Zacharus. "You must not work on the Day of Rest. You must fast."

"If I can, I eat when I am hungry," says Douglas. "I have fasted. I will fast no more."

Jimmy A. and Philip move in to hear.

"Your disrespect for authority is blasphemy," says Aron with cold contempt. "To break the Day of Rest is blasphemy. To consort with the men you associate with is blasphemy. They are the wrong sorts. You should only spend your time with righteous men."

"My friends are righteous," says Douglas. *"You* need to learn respect."

"You and your men are revolutionaries," says Zacharus. "That's how the Great Chief will see it. You're terrorists."

"Is that what you're gonna tell him?" says Douglas. "How many men have you put in the Great Chief's jail?"

"You don't know when to shut up," says Zacharus. "Leave this field. This is God's day to look down on his creation and rest."

"You also work on the Day of Rest," says Douglas. "You work on my so-called 'soul.'"

"You will have no soul if you continue to blaspheme," says Aron.

"I'll have to look out for that," Douglas laughs. "The Day of Rest was made by man. Man was not made by the Day of Rest."

"Man was made by God!" says Zacharus.

"Each man must find his own peace."

"When you finish working," says Zacharus, "you will eat your harvest?"

"So has it ever been," says Douglas. "We are hungry after a long day's work." He walks away from the two men, deeper into the field. It is starting to be damaged by the multitude of fans. The priests follow. "The Day of Rest is for men like you two," he says, never compromising. "It is for men who would follow other men to discover the nature of their own *Self.* We do not need your Law. We are free."

"You're just an anarchist," imparts Aron. "You're up to no good."

"There must be order," says Zacharus.

"Whose order?" asks Tommy, as he follows the others who are trying to keep up with Douglas. "Your order? The Great Chief's order?"

"Certainly not your order," says Zacharus, taking up after the others. "You would get us all killed."

"There is only one natural order," says Douglas.

"And you know it?" taunts Aron as he almost stumbles.

"Tell me about it," says Zacharus.

"I have shown, yet you do not see."

"You would usurp Tribal order," says Aron. "Not only are you a blasphemer, you're a traitor to the Tribes!"

"You have a flare for the dramatic," says Douglas, "and a flare for rhetoric. Those are very clever slogans."

"They'll work too," says Aron. "They always do."

Douglas stops and turns around. "Go ahead and chant it to the crowds, priest," he says. "There's always someone trying to cover up the truth. It might as well be you."

Zacharus ignores the latest slight. "Trigger," he says, "I came here; I brought Aron here, because I wanted to give you a chance to recant. I don't want to see what happened to John happen to you." It is a threat. "But if you keep running off at the mouth as you do, it will alarm the Great Chief. We fear for your safety."

"That's very...nice," says Douglas. "You guys care about me."

"I'm watching you, boy," says Aron, "I'm gonna push you when you start to fall."

"What an asshole," says Tommy.

Douglas leads his friends back into the field. Zacharus and Aron remain on the edge.

When the priests are behind them, Douglas says, "They don't know what they preach. They know nothing about *Being*. How can they guide anyone else? They are hypocrites." Douglas is shaking his head with a detesting grimace. "They're supposed to be an order of 'spirit,' but they seek political power. They are the power behind the throne. They whisper into the Great Chief's ear...threatening me with his office! Soon everyone will know. The truth is always known. What they preach in darkness will be heard in *the Light*." Douglas stops. The others stand around him. "My friends, never fear the man who would take away your body, for after it is done, there is no more he can do. Don't listen to those priests."

"The priests are the least of our worries," says Tommy. "Our worry is the Empire. We are occupied. There are boys, not yet men, wearing the uniform of the Imperial soldier walking around with weapons and shields. They salt their meat with the sweat of Tribal brows. We must end this tyranny. We must unite. We have nothing to lose but our bondage. It is better to die fighting for freedom than to live a slave."

"How many people believe that is truth?" says Douglas. "How many people will follow you? Will it be enough to defeat the Empire?"

"If we have the right man leading them."

"I am not that man," says Douglas. "The Empire fights wars, Tommy. It is what they do. They're very good at it."

"We must try." Tommy is getting aggravated.

"The moment you take up arms against them, they have won because you have become like them."

"We could beat them," says Tommy.

"You could beat them," says Douglas. "Imperial soldiers do what they're told to do. They never question orders. They will fight if they are told to fight. They will die if they are told to die. But you, you would fight for your own ideal. You would die for your own freedom."

"So would you," says Tommy.

"You waste this life if you use it to fight the Empire. It isn't what's real here. Nothing temporal lasts long. Tomorrow you'll be dead and the Empire will be gone. Don't waste this life thinking about the Empire. That's not what freedom is all about."

"What is freedom all about?" asks Bobby.

"Freedom is about lying down in your own bed each night in a free country," says Tommy.

"Freedom's another name for truth. It's like death," says Douglas. "It's a threshold, an end and a beginning. It's between reality and hope. Freedom comes from within. It is not granted by any outside order. You can be free. I am free."

"You are not free," says Tommy. "If you think this is freedom, then you are one of the placated masses."

"Tommy, we are the Empire. We create our own reality. If we didn't want it, it wouldn't exist."

"Exactly. We don't want it. We have a duty to future generations to get rid of the Empire right now, in this generation."

"Time will be your remedy," says Douglas. "Nothing temporary lasts long."

"History is action based. You have to make history to become part of it."

Promotion

Douglas and his friends gather, talking in Jimmy's house. They do not want to go outside because the field is filled with *Ghosts.*

"You're the talk of the town," says Jimmy, "With all these people camping out, the wheat's getting trampled. It's not gonna grow even in the good ground."

Douglas shrugs. "Sorry. We should just leave."

"We should prepare the way for you," says Andy, "let people know you're coming."

"That will also let the priests know," says Douglas.

"The priests already know," says Tommy. "That is why they came here. You have a following and the priests of the Temple of the Holy City are taking an interest in you. Be careful how you expend your capitol. Lead your followers where they should be led."

"Maybe it is time to go on the road," says Peter. "You've got your act down pretty good."

"You're gonna be big," says Tommy.

"I am not the message," says Douglas. "I am the messenger."

"To sell the message, we have to sell you," says Tommy. "You and the message are one. Don't you want that kind of power?"

Douglas does not answer.

"What don't you like about power?" asks Tommy.

"When you seek power, it controls you. Any man can have power. You can have power. But like the currents of the river, men of power and men without power are washed into the same ocean and only some currents are ever free."

"I don't think I know what you mean," says Peter.

"It is the story of the rich and poor man," says Andy. "I agree."

"But when righteous men of power do not use it, what hope have we?" asks Tommy.

"What hope have we if righteous men use their power?" says Douglas, "Power makes all men unrighteous."

"If that is true, then what are we to do?"

"Do not answer to power, and you will be free."

"And if those who have answered to power encroach on your daily life and threaten to kill you?"

"If that power kills you, you are still free."

"How can you be free if you're dead?" asks Tommy.

"Be free while you are alive," says Douglas. "Time makes friends and enemies, but *Being* is without time. Time is an illusion. Without time, *the Self* has no enemies. Without time, there is no *Self.*"

"I don't know what you mean," Tommy says, "and I don't want to hear it."

"We need to reach more people," says Peter.

"I promised Jimmy I'd stick around until harvest time."

"That crop isn't growing," says Jimmy. *"The Ghosts* have crushed it. Even where it has not been trampled, new campsites are being staked out."

"Sorry about that," says Douglas.

"You can't stay here," says Tommy. "The priests of the Temple of the Holy City are already coming after you. If you're right about *the Medicine Man,* you better gain visibility fast. It'll be harder for them to do anything to you."

"If they're coming here, maybe we should go to them."

"We'll go ahead of you and set up the gigs," says Andy. "We'll promote you, tell people where and when. The word will spread all along the river."

"That sounds like a good way to do it," says Peter. "That way we can do some fishing too."

"You know where all the Temples are," says Douglas, "Those are the ports we should stop in."

"Maybe they haven't heard you were banned in Swifton," says Peter.

"If they ban you, we'll speak in your stead," says Andy. "They will have to ban all *Voices.*"

"If they ban you from their Temples," says Peter, "we'll bring the people out of their Temples!"

"That's the spirit," says Douglas with a smile.

"That's the spirit that will get you killed for no reason," says Tommy.

"It kind of feels like it's time for the next step anyway," says Peter, "or else what was all this for?"

"Things are moving very quickly," says Douglas. He looks at Peter. "Maybe you're right. What does everybody else think?"

"Peter's right," says James. Everyone agrees.

"Alright," says Douglas, "I just need people to listen. If I get banned from the Temples, tell people to come to the river. I'll speak to them from the boat if I have to. Tell people that the truth is here and now. It is spread out around us. The priests of the Temple have locked *the Garden* and lost the key. They have not entered and they don't know the way in. They'll try to keep other people from it, because if they can't find the way in, why should they let anyone else find it? They think it would put them at a disadvantage. Don't waste your time with people who believe in the priests and their Temple, but speak to those who have not been tamed by the myth of the Tribes. They are lost sheep. Turn them into wolves. Don't waste your breath on those who will not hear. There are plenty of people who will listen.

"If they ask, 'Why should we listen to you?' Say to them, 'You should not.' Ring a bell, and some will not hear. Behold a sunset and some will not see. Warm up the crowd. You're speaking in a new dialectic. Don't start out with the most controversial stuff. If you come on too strong, the crowd will become hostile and you will lose them. You'll be speaking to an angry mob. Be gradual with the truth. An unnatural order has power over the Tribes at this time. Those who control that order can take us right out of their game with their own rules.

"For this reason, and for truth, the crowds must not confuse us with what we are saying. We are Prometheus. We are not the fire.

"We will bring a *Light* into the world so bright that even the blind can see it. Speak with confidence. Don't light a lamp and put it under a bushel, or in some other hidden place, but rather, set it on a stand so that everyone who enters will see its *Light*. When you bring *Light* into the world, you repel darkness.

"Watch out for the priests. You know what they did to John. Do not be tricked by their riddles. They will deliver us up to their Councils and denounce us in their Temples and their courts. We will be brought before their Great Chief and Emperor to testify the truth. Do not be anxious about how you should speak or what you should say. You'll know what to say. It is not we who speak, it is truth. It is not our voice; it is *the Voice* of *Being*.

"The truth will not bring peace to the world because there are too many people invested or indoctrinated into the old order. The truth will set a son against his father and a daughter against her mother, and a daughter-in-law against her mother-in-law, and you may be opposed in your own household. Whoever is not able to renounce the beliefs of his father and mother will not see the truth. Whoever is not able to walk a path different from his brothers and sisters will not be able to accept the truth.

"If anyone listens to the truth but does not hear, do not judge them. We're not in this world to judge each other, but to save each other. Those who do not hear the truth cannot save themselves. They are already slaves to an order they allow to control them. Those who reject the truth are like the fool at a wedding reception, who was the first love of the bride. When she was young and awkward, she loved him and he spurned her. He said she had no charm. As she grew older, the fool's friend loved her. He told the fool of her many virtues. The fool dismissed her once again. But after the wedding, the bride's veil was lifted, and the fool fell in love with her, but it was too late."

His parable is over. He pauses so they know.

"Give me a good buildup. Prepare the way for others to see the truth. Remember, even though you're setting up these gigs for me, the rednecks aren't going to know the difference between you and me. One messenger is not safer than another. Those who control manmade order will despise and persecute us when we expose them and their violations of natural law. If they persecuted John, they will persecute us. If the priests went after John, they will also come after us. It's already starting. What they did to him they will do to us. If they quote him, they will also quote us. If they assassinated him, they will also assassinate us.

"If anything happens to me, you guys can carry on because you were with me from the beginning. When people ask about me, tell them what I said, not what people said about me. When you quote me, do so without embellishment. First say that these words are not my words, but only similar. If a man or a woman is to hear my words, he or she must hear them from me. And when my words are known, the truth will be known and the things that they hide from themselves will be revealed. Let no man or woman say they know my words unless they have heard them from me. These are the weeds."

There is a knock at the door.

"We'll meet back here at harvest time," says Douglas.

Another Warning

"What have I begun?" asks Douglas.

The knocking on Jimmy's door continues.

"Friend or foe?" Tommy poses to Douglas.

Jimmy gets up and answers the door. It is Zacharus and Aron. Foe. Up close and personal. "Collecting for the poor?" asks Jimmy.

Zacharus pushes open the door and steps into the room.

"What have we here?" Zacharus says with authority as he moves further into the room to stand against the men. He sees Tommy and he sees Douglas. "It is really quite remarkable," he says. "Twins. A conspiracy of like-minded men. But since when has your revolution become against the word of God?"

"*The Sons of Light* are warriors for the one true God," says Tommy. "We are the enemy of the Gods of the Empire. Who invited you here?"

"Do none of you have respect for our authority?" says Zacharus.

They all laugh. Apparently not.

Zacharus looks from Tommy's broken nose to Douglas. "We've just come to talk with you," he says.

"Talk," says Douglas.

"Let's talk outside," Zacharus says to Douglas, "away from

these *other* people."

"What you say to me you can also say to my friends because, you know, I'm going to tell them anyway," he says laughing.

Zacharus is annoyed. He grunts his disapproval. "We've been hearing about the speeches you've been making in our Temples," he says.

"Did you hear that I'm banned in Swifton?" Douglas says with a sly, boyish smile.

Zacharus does not think Douglas is funny. "We know that your talk is blasphemous," he says. "We want to hear it from you. What have you been saying?"

"Quite frankly," Douglas says, still smiling, "I have no recollection of anything I may have said."

"What about your friends?" says Zacharus. "Maybe they remember."

"We don't remember," says Tommy.

"It's one thing to speak in this field," says Zacharus, "it's quite another thing to speak in the Temple of the Tribes. I had hoped to have a private talk with you. Let's cooperate with each other. You be up front with me, I'll be up front with you."

Nobody says anything.

"If you don't want to talk to me," Zacharus says, "maybe you'll talk to Aron." He points to his son-in-law. Aron scowls.

"What is he, the youth Minister?"

"Someday he will be the High Priest."

"What's there to talk about?" says Douglas.

"Let's start with why you're in Swifton," says Aron.

"I live here," says Douglas. "That sure beats any reason why you're here." He laughs.

"You won't be laughing long, mister."

"Who are all these other men?" asks Zacharus.

"These are my friends," says Douglas.

"You got weird looking friends," says Aron.

"You sound pretty tough," says Douglas, "or is it just your robes that make you think you're tough? Or is it the Temple Guards that wait outside my door?"

Aron scowls. Tommy laughs his silent laugh. His brother has balls.

"When you preach in the Temple, you must preach the Law of the Tribes," says Zacharus.

"What makes you think you can say what you say?" says Aron. "You better start to play by the rules."

"I make my own rules," says Douglas.

Tommy glares. "Why don't you guys take off," he says. "You aren't wanted here."

"The world is zooming right past you, Aron," Douglas says. "What power you have over the Tribes is given to you. It can be taken away just as easily."

Aron is speechless. Zacharus frowns at Douglas.

"Tell me, do you have any other stops to make in Swifton?"

"No," says Zacharus. "We came here to see you."

"No friends? No women?"

"Blasphemy!" says Aron.

Zacharus walks to the door. He looks at *the Ghosts* in the field. He looks at Douglas. "Where are you leading them?"

"I will lead them away from you."

"It is blasphemy to lead the Tribes away from the Temple."

"Leave in peace, but leave."

"Devote yourself to understanding *the Book of the Tribes,*" says Aron. "Become a leader of the pious."

"These are the sheep."

"Who do you think you are to speak as you do?" Aron asks. "We will be watching you, Douglas Trigger."

Aron follows Zacharus out the door. Douglas and his friends laugh when they are gone. They stop when they think about what the priests will do. Douglas looks at his twin. "What do you know about that older priest?"

"He is the High Priest of the Temple of the Tribes of the Holy City. He knows me. That's about all I know. I'm not a regular customer."

"Mark him," says Douglas. "Mark them both."

The priests speak as they walk away from the house and field. They are escorted by Temple Guards.

"What do you make of him?" asks Zacharus.

"He says he will lead the Tribes away from the Temple."

"He's young and cocky. His rise must not go unchecked."

"We have no time to worry about a cure for Douglas Trigger," says Aron. "People are already starting to listen to him. I'm sick of all these 'prophets!'"

"He has a way with words and like his brother, he may be a revolutionary," Zacharus says to mislead him.

"What should we do?"

"*We* are not going to do anything. *I* am going back to the Temple of the Tribes of the Holy City. Someday you will be High Priest. If you want to have a flock to inherit, perhaps you should stay here. Bring him back to the Temple. I am old. Fighting to protect the line that divides one philosophy from another, one generation from another, no longer interests me. But if you wish to maintain some semblance to the order of the Tribes, then you'd better move quickly. Douglas Trigger is young and appealing. The students will follow him."

Aron is chilled. "We must stop him," he says.

"Or he will stop you," says Zacharus.

"He is the cause of great disorder."

"It is your charge to maintain the order."

"It is better to live in chains than it is to perish."

"He will take the students away from you. You must bring him back to the God of the Tribes."

Aron remains in Swifton. Zacharus takes the Guards.

The Revolution

"Can we talk? Tommy asks Douglas after the others are asleep.

"Yea, sure."

"You have a way with the crowds," Tommy says softly, so as not to wake the others. "It's too bad you don't say what needs to be said."

"What would you have me say?" Douglas whispers, knowing Tommy's answer.

"I would have you speak the truth, the real truth. That's what you do, isn't it? I would have you become a spokesman for the revolution."

"One form of government is no different than another. The same men always get power. The only thing that happens in a revolution is that civilians get killed."

"Civilians are expendable. They're not in the fight. They're pawns. They're already controlled by the present order. The Emperor and his puppet, the Great Chief, are a government we need to overthrow."

"Why? So you can have power? What makes you think you're any better than the Great Chief or the Emperor?"

"Because I am one of the Tribe. It is so the Tribes can have power. Only a member of the Tribes should rule the Tribes."

"You just said the people are expendable."

"Only those charmed by this order. They're already lost. They're sheep. Anything is better than the Empire and their appointed Great Chief.   You need an elite group of revolutionaries to shape public opinion, an intellectual, moral group that knows who its enemies are, a group to build a strong defense so that we will never be subjugated again. The people will not free themselves. They must be free. We must be free."

"I am free. You can be free. We are as free as we make ourselves in this world. Do not let the Empire rule your destiny."

"It is my destiny to fight the Empire."

"That is not your destiny. The Empire is of this world. You are not of this world. It only exists in time. It is not real."

It seems to Tommy that Douglas knows something that he does not. He does not like it.

"The Empire is a phoenix," Douglas says. "If you defeat it, it will surely rise from the rubble. You yourself will rebuild it."

"We must gain our own Kingdom."

"*Kingdom* is not a place," Douglas whispers. "It's not a title to covet. It's nothing you have to fight for. Your *Kingdom* is spread out around you, but you do not see it."

"You know what I see, Dougy?" says Tommy. "I see that we are not free. I see that we must fight or die. Men need a leader to make them fight. I think you can become that leader. They want a *Messiah.* Think of it. You'll be the hero of the Tribes. You'll be the sword of vengeance."

Douglas does not trust his twin.

"I'm not going lead anybody anywhere," says Douglas. "I'm going to show them themselves. I'm just going to keep telling stories. I'm a teacher."

"Yea, teacher. You're a preacher. I listen to those stories you tell. You shouldn't come to this town, telling stories like that. They don't help the cause. You need to tell stories about the atrocities committed by the Empire. You need to talk about the guerrilla war. Instead of a farmer, make the hero of your story a *Son of Light!* His crop is freedom."

"The farmer's crop *is* freedom," says Douglas. "It is self sufficiency."

"There are two kinds of people in this world, Dougy: those who lead and those who follow. *You* are a leader. Everyone else is just following you."

"I don't want anybody to follow me."

"Oh, that doesn't matter, brother. It's gonna happen anyway."

"Everybody has their own path."

"It's all in what they believe. If they think you're *the Messiah,* they'll follow you."

"Maybe I don't want to be a *Messiah.*"

"Everybody wants to be a *Messiah,*" says Tommy. "It's out of your hands, buddy boy. Let me worry about it."

"What would you do for power?" Douglas asks Tommy.

"All men grasp for power," says Tommy. "All men want what you can have."

"You don't want freedom. You want power."

"Power is freedom, buddy boy. We're the next generation. How can there be justice if we are inactive?"

"This isn't the time for it."

"If you are not working for the revolution, then you are working against it."

"Is that a threat?"

"Just an observation."

"Man is what he always was and will forever be," says Douglas. "Do not think you can change that."

"I'm gonna start by changing you," he says.

"Yea? Good-luck."

"You speak of a sword. You speak of no peace. But you don't speak about the fight. You don't speak about this generation's Struggle."

"My sword is not a military instrument, Tommy. I don't want to promote violence. I want to promote peace. I want to spread the truth. I want to seed the minds of the young before they become overgrown with weeds. A child will suffocate in his own household unless he breathes with me."

"A house divided against itself will fall," says Tommy. *"Your* words. If you lead the Tribes away from revolution, we will never win."

"What would we win?"

"Our freedom."

"Though freedom is a victory, it cannot be won. We have nothing to defeat to gain our freedom."

"We must defeat the Empire."

"No. Before creation, there is inspiration. There is illumination. This world wraps a false covering on our *Being*. It divides the whole. It separates us from each other. That is why we must bring *Light* into the world. We must find people who will listen and help spread the word, for when we are gone, *the Light* may also fade. Thereafter, those who remember *the Light* we brought into the world will also be gone. Our descendants will have only a memory of a memory of *the Light* that's gone. It will remain like this unless another brings *the Light* into the world."

"Another *'Voice* from nature?' Why is breaking the Day of Rest a part of your truth? Is truth defiant?"

"I am not defiant, but man's order is defiant of natural law. I am not a rebel. When I have food, I eat when I am hungry. Manmade order rebels against nature."

"Why don't the Temple Priests see *the Light?"*

"Perhaps they do, but *the Light* robs them of their power. Perhaps they don't look for it. They look for power. If they were the true *Sons of Light,* and I'm not talking about your rebels, the Empire would not frighten them so. The priests of the Temple of the Tribes follow the letter of their or the Empire's Law. That isn't inspiration, Tommy. It's repetition. It's praying to the dead. Men with vision die. His mourners are weeds in his field. You can't see that kind of *Light* in anyone. It comes from within."

"Then how are you gonna tell anybody about it?'

"I can show them."

"I got my wisdom the way you did, from our mother and her husband. They got their wisdom from their ancestors. I believe in the old truths."

"That ain't the truth, brother. That's handed down knowledge. It's not even wisdom. The world has changed."

"It hasn't changed that much. I may not respect our father or our stepfather, or those priests, but I believe in the Law of the Tribes."

"You're trapped in the old order. That's why you fight it."

"I'm not trapped anywhere," Tommy snaps. "What about you? Why won't you help our people? Come with me. The future belongs to us because we are young. If the Empire will not give it to us, we must take it. The crowd follows you. They will fight for you. Help me. Help your people. Help yourself. Lead the revolution!"

"Tommy, your revolution dies when it is won. You will create a new order that is a caricature of the old order. You will give birth to a new revolution."

"Didn't you say that you are trying to create a new order?"

"I'm trying to reestablish natural order."

"The world according to Douglas Trigger. That's a strange concept."

"Not so strange or dangerous as the world according to Tommy Trigger. You epitomize modern man. You make friendships through common enemies. You draw borders to separate the whole. You build fences and decorate your walls. Separation is false. We are one. This is the natural order. This is how man will survive, with no division, with no enemies, with no Empire, no separate Tribes, one Tribe. We will survive as a whole, we the living. We'll live for each other."

"Universal brotherhood. You sound very naive."

"If you could see what I see," Douglas marvels, "If only you would look. I can show you. I've tried to tell you. If only I could find the right combination of words, what was unseen would be seen and the truth would be revealed to you like a curtain rising. You would see a *Kingdom of Truth.*"

"Do *you* see what *I'm* talking about?"

"You're not talking about anything new, Tommy. I see it. I see beyond it. Seeing through the old order is the window to the natural order. In the natural order we are free."

"Free? How can we be free as long as the Emperor keeps sending more troops?"

"His soldiers are not free, nor are your comrades."

"You don't make any sense to me," Tommy says, shaking his head. "You talk about freedom, but you care nothing for the Struggle. Don't you care about freedom?"

"I'm not talking about your kind of freedom. You won't be free if you get rid of some soldiers. You won't be free if you gain your own Empire. Freedom is not tangible. It does not exist in any government's rule. Freedom exists under self-rule. When you are free, you will shed the Empire like a lizard sheds its skin."

"Don't you see what the Empire is doing to you?" he says, exasperated.

"The Empire has no power over me unless I give it to them. To fight the Empire, is to give it power over you."

"The Empire already has power over you. They tax you. They can jail you. And since you are not a citizen, they can chop off your head. I have been to Skull Hill!"

"They can't tax me because I have no possessions. I have no land or money. The Empire may jail me. I have given my life to the truth. We pass through this life briefly, Tommy. I'd rather die trying to make this world better, than to live a slow, passive life. This life is just a masquerade. We pass out of all that seems real in this world. Your body will die and you will leave the carcass of illusion. You aren't your body, Tommy. When you are taxed, the Empire merely takes back what it has given you. It is a parasite feeding off itself. It is the thing that lets the Empire control you. There is no value in a coin of the Empire unless you attach a value to it. The Empire mints its coins and throws them to you. And like a beggar, you pick them up. You pay back only if you have taken."

"We must fight the Empire. We must unite father and son, mother and daughter, brother and sister, against the Empire."

"Tommy, the Empire and the Tribes are brother and sister already divided."

"I don't get you, Dougy. You talk about freedom, but you don't get it. You talk about the Empire and the Tribes, but you're apolitical. You're a rebel with nothing to say about the revolution. You could become *the Messiah*, but you won't lead anyone!"

"I'm not a warrior, Tommy."

"You are not *the Messiah*. *The Messiah* will be a warrior. *The Messiah* will do what must be done. You will not. You won't make any political waves."

"This is not a political movement."

"You could lead the tide of the Tribes to the Emperor's home shore."

"Politics is a game of the old order. Your revolution shouts, *'We are yelling at the warlords! They would not listen and so we will fight for what is ours until it is won. We will keep what is won and call it God's Promise.'* The Emperor's war cries, dripping in blood, *'The revolution must be put down or surely we will be undone. We must keep what is ours---God's Promise.'*"

"What makes you think you can just stand outside it all?"

"This is the great revolution, a revolution without armor. We have it in our power to restore the natural order. That must be our purpose in this time. That is why we were born here. That is why we have come together here. That is why we will all die here. Do you think this happened by accident?

"We live in an age of destruction, Tommy. We will all die soon if the natural order is not restored. Your hatred of the Empire will kill us."

"I don't get you," says Tommy. "I don't know if I should stay with you."

"I want you to stay, brother," says Douglas. "Besides, this is where the action is."

"Very likely."

The others sleep soundly.

The Father

The business Peter has is his father's business. It was his father's father's business. It would be the business of his and Andy's sons. Peter is home before he departs for the tour. He has to have a talk with his father, John.

John is filled with disappointment as he hears his son. He feels Peter is letting him down. He feels he is letting down the next generation.

"Welcome back," John says facetiously. "Staying long?"

"That's what I want to talk to you about."

"Why do I know I'm not going to like what's coming?"

"Andy and I, we're gonna take a break from the business. We're gonna take the ship up the river and speak in the Temples."

"You're gonna what?"

"We've been going up locally. Trigger's already starting to get a following," says Peter.

"Yea, I heard," says John. "He's banned from the Temple. You think that's a good thing?"

"That's what's wrong with the Temple," says Peter. "A holy man should be able to speak the truth in it."

"You think Trigger is a holy man?" exclaims John. "He's a fisherman, a hired hand! First Andy, now you. You're both crazy."

"There's more to life than making money. The world is changing."

"You're naive. Money is one thing that will never change."

"I'm not gonna live my life for it."

"What are you gonna live your life for, Trigger? You have a wife. You should be having children."

"People are starting to follow him," says Peter. "We're gonna help him."

"Help him do what? Blaspheme in the Temple? I've heard about him. Help him do what? This man is your hired hand. He is an apprentice fisherman."

"He is a prophet," says Peter.

"He's a loss," says John. "He's taken four master fishermen from this town away from their duty. What about James and Johnny, what are they gonna do?"

"They're coming too."

"What about the business?"

"They'll leave their ship here. We can combine our crews."

"What about our ship?"

"I was gonna take it down the river."

"Oh, you were, huh?"

"You gave it to me."

"I gave it to you for the business."

"I have a new business."

"We have a lot of steady customers. What are you going to tell them?"

"I'm gonna leave that to you. I'm giving it back to you. It's yours and Zebedee's business. It's not my business."

"You can't give it back to me, at least not without a ship! How can you turn your backs on your future? How can you reject what we've given you? How will you support your wife and family?"

"We have always managed so far," says Peter.

"So far? You've always had the business. You've managed so far because of what I've given you. You have a responsibility to me to lighten the burdens I've carried for you."

"My responsibility is to my own *Self*. Let that also be your responsibility."

"Selfish youth. You need to learn some respect. You must

provide for me as I have provided for you. You must provide for your wife and someday for your children."

"You do not need your sons to provide for you," says Peter. "Your business will provide for you."

"Who will provide for you? What joy is there in a business if a man cannot pass it on to his sons as his father passed it on to him?"

"I don't want it anymore."

"You don't know what you want."

"For the first time in my life I do."

"What happened to you?" asks John. "You used to want it."

"I didn't know what I wanted."

"And now this man, this Douglas Trigger, has shown you?"

"I have seen for myself."

"When are you going?"

"After the harvest."

"Will you stay and fish until then?"

"No. I have to do some advance work along the river."

"Advance work? What kind of advance work?"

"I have to help prepare the way for Trigger. I have to set up places for him to speak, stuff like that. I have to let them know what he's going to say. He's speaking in a new dialectic."

"Is he paying you for this?"

"No. I'm doing this because of the things he says. It's important that people hear him. He's changed what I say when I speak in the Temple."

"Then maybe you should not speak in the Temple. You're not a priest. You're a fisherman! And what about your unborn sons? Think of them. What will happen to them if they have no trade?"

"I will think about my sons when they are born."

"Your brother should take a wife and you should stay with your wife, or you'll never have sons."

"I want to be with my wife," says Peter.

"Good. A man should be with his wife. He should not travel far from his home. It's not good."

"This is something I must do."

"And when it's over and you have no business, no wife, no sons, what then?"

"Let me go into it blindly," says Peter. "I have seen the way you showed me and it was wrong."

"What magic does this farmer use on you?"

"Don't try to talk me out of it."

"You're still young, boy," says John. "You just don't know it yet. Don't blow your future. I've heard about your friend, Trigger, and I've heard about *the Medicine Man*. What I've heard is that they are both blasphemers. That is not good. You shouldn't be hanging around with this guy."

"You've heard rumors. You've heard the propaganda of the priests."

"Propaganda? You must not talk like that," says John. "Don't forget what the priests mean to us."

"We can afford to lose a customer," says Peter.

"Now you sound like a child," says John. "These are not the words of a man. If you want to give up the business, I can't stop you. I'm just trying to prevent you from making mistakes while you're young that you'll have to live with when you're old."

"My destiny is manifest," says Peter.

"What happened to you? Just the other day you were going to rescue your brother from that other prophet, now you're both following Trigger."

"I was wrong to try to get Andy away from John."

"What if we give Trigger a raise in salary," says John, "would he still work for us?"

"He's not a fisherman," says Peter. "He is not a farmer. Some say he's the reincarnation of a great prophet."

"A reincarnation?" John says with disbelief. "I don't get this reincarnation, or whatever you kids are into today."

"It's just a metaphor," says Peter. "It just means he's possessed with the same spirit as the great prophets."

"You make him sound like a demon," says John. "You're talking about possession."

"I'm talking about God," says Peter, "whatever God is."

"God?" says John. "You must not even say the word. It is blasphemy."

"Yea, I know," Peter says with a smirk.

"You must not mock the Almighty. The only ones who can

talk about our Lord are the Priests of the Temple," says John. "We are simple men. We are fishermen. This is what we are. We are not priests to be speaking in Temples. We must be content with our lot. It is with divine grace that we have all that we need. We must not question the Creator."

"I don't think Trigger's content," says Peter, "I don't think John was content, and I don't think I'm content."

The Rebels

It is a hot day in the Holy City. Timothy is hot. Tommy is hot. Bobby is hot. Their drinks are hot. Tommy's dogs are hot outside. It is hot in the sun. It is hot in the shade. It is a sweaty day. Staying inside to drink is no bunker from the sun. It bakes right through the walls.

"So let us hear it," says Timothy. "Is your brother *the Messiah,* or is he just some mad prophet?"

"He's not mad," says Tommy, "not yet."

"How many people are following him?"

"A lot," says Tommy. "They've ruined my other brother's crop. They've trampled the field. There are some people that are camped out on our farm, just waiting for what he will say next. It's the oddest thing. He had to stop speaking to try to disperse them. That wheat's never going to grow. He has followers but he's not leading them anywhere. Right now he and his friends are setting up gigs between Swifton and here. He plans to be in the Holy City for Festival."

"His plans are our plans," says Timothy. "If he is not *the Messiah,* what message does he bring?"

"He brings *Light* into the world," says Bobby. "He brings the word. He brings truth."

"Truth," says Timothy. "What truth?"

Tommy has no answer. "They're just words," he says.

"The truth is natural order," says Bobby. "It is a world without illusion, without separation."

"What do you mean?" asks Timothy. "Illusion? Is your brother a magician? Separation? What about the revolution?"

"He won't take a stand on the revolution," says Tommy. "He is not bothered by the Empire."

"What kind of man is this brother of yours? How can he be a man and not be bothered by the Empire? Does he care nothing for his Tribe?"

"Yes," says Tommy.

"What sort of man is he?" Timothy whispers.

"He says that the Empire does not exist," says Tommy. "It is, he says, as Bobby pointed out, an illusion."

"An illusion?" exclaims Timothy. "It doesn't exist? What the fuck does that mean?"

"He won't listen when I tell him about the revolution," says Tommy.

"Is he intelligent?" asks Timothy.

"Very," says Bobby.

"How can this be? If he were intelligent, he would fight for freedom."

"He believes in freedom through truth," says Bobby. "He says a man need not fight for truth. Truth needs no champions."

Timothy boils. "That is bullshit! Truth would disappear without champions! This kind of talk is dangerous," he exclaims, rising. "Your brother will divide us."

"Yea," says Tommy, "that he may. He talks about freedom without a fight. He says a man can be free under the Empire's occupation."

"That does not even make sense," says Timothy, sitting again. "People are listening to this shit?"

"Yea," says Tommy.

"He will not join the revolution?"

"No."

"While you and Bobby have been in Swifton, I have been hearing about your brother from other sources."

"What have you been hearing?" asks Tommy.

"That he is a prophet, a teacher, a man-God. These

reports are not good."

"He's not a man-God," says Tommy.

"Of course he is not a God!" Timothy yells, kicking a chair. "He is your fucking brother!"

"He is a teacher," says Bobby.

"Does he have his own church?"

"No," says Tommy, "but the people who follow him, *the Ghosts,* have more reverence for him than a church."

"It is another *Medicine Man* cult. That is what it is."

"Yea," says Tommy.

"Bad news," says Timothy.

"Perhaps."

Bobby listens.

"So he is going off in a whole different direction?" says Timothy.

"He's at the other end of the spectrum," says Tommy.

"Is he divisive?"

"Very. He takes the fight out of our people."

"What will you do?" asks Timothy.

"I'll stay with him," says Tommy. "I'll keep after him."

"And if he will not be moved?" asks Timothy.

"I will move him. I will help him realize his potential to lead this fight. He has a way with the masses. He is very clever with words. He tells people what they want to hear."

"What does he tell them?"

"He tells them there can be peace without revolution."

"That is not good," says Timothy. "The revolution will come whether he wants it or not. The question is, when it does come, will we have the momentum to win it? We are counting on the pilgrims to join the fight. He would be an unimportant man, Tommy, except the crowds follow him. He commands strangers. He is an important man to control. One way or another, we must control the message. It would be better if he would join us."

"I don't know if he will," says Bobby.

"The priests have already begun to move against him."

"Stay with him," says Timothy. "Be his brother. If he is the next *Medicine Man,* you can be the next him."

Tommy hesitates. "What about him?" he says.

"Hey, if he is going to go around spouting that *Settlement* shit like *the Medicine Man,* the same thing is going to happen to him."

"Maybe I should try to stop him."

"Maybe so. Your brother should not die for nothing. If you cannot get him to join the Struggle, maybe you can get him to shut-up."

Resolve

It is night in the Temple of the Tribes of the Holy City. Zacharus is being debriefed by Loki and is disturbed by a knock. He looks up from behind his desk. He looks over at Loki who is sitting in a chair before him and motions for him to get behind a drape. When the curtain stops moving, Zacharus says, "Come." The door opens and Aron steps into the room. "You're back," says Zacharus. "Sit down." Aron sits down in Loki's seat.

Aron wastes no time. He has been thinking about things and he is bubbling over to tell Zacharus his plan. "Let us call together the Council of the Tribes," he says. "Douglas Trigger is a danger. He is a challenge to our order. It is a great blasphemy. It is as if *the Medicine Man* has risen. There are those who are saying just that. We are already fighting the Gods of the Empire. We do not need internal debate. Douglas Trigger must be silenced."

"He scared you."

"He should be scared."

"How do you propose to silence him?"

"We will ban him from all the Temples of the Tribes."

"And if he goes and speaks at the river like *the Medicine Man?*"

"We must do something."

"Do nothing," says Zacharus. "What must be done you should not do. The spiritual future of the Tribes will soon be in your hands. I am the High Priest now, but soon you will be. Think about what I said. Take heed. Do not become overzealous. Know that sometimes what a man wants most is what he loses, what he can never get back. Before you deal too harshly with Douglas Trigger, think about what will happen to his *Ghosts* when he is gone. Will the sheep scatter, or will there be a new leader?"

"Who else would lead them?"

"Maybe his brother. Maybe somebody else. Maybe no one. Find out before you take any action."

"I will go back to Swifton."

"Very well then. Be cautious and deliberate. Do not move too quickly."

Aron stands up. "I will not do anything before I know the consequences,"

Aron opens the door. "That's all I ask," says Zacharus.

Aron nods and is gone. Loki comes out from behind the drape. "I don't know about his brother," he says. "I've never heard him speak. I've heard Peter speak."

"What does he say?"

"He kind of opens for him. Some of the other ones too. They all open for him. They're all basically starting to sound more and more like him as they go along. Douglas Trigger is always the headliner."

"What about Tommy?"

"I've never seen him speak. He's not the get up at Temple kind of guy. He's a *Son of Light.* I think he may have his own cell by now. He is not a follower. I don't know if he'd pick up another man's sword, even his brother's. He does have the same face. "

"But what if the sword were malleable? Would he not forge it in his own image? A rebel does not alarm me as much as a prophet. Now is not a good time for a prophet…unless he's *our* prophet."

"It is times like these when prophets do arise. What if it turns out that these times are endemic to the perpetuation of prophets? What if the voice of the prophet cannot be stopped?"

"Then it is the voice of God, but only then."

"Aren't the voices of all prophets the voice of God?"

"The Priests of the Temple of the Holy City are the voice of God, Loki. Is there anything you can add to Aron's report?"

"Yes. He seems to have a consistent entourage. They're with him wherever he goes."

"The men in the farmhouse, who are they?"

"One of them is Bobby Tarmac, another *Son of Light.* He's probably in Tommy's cell. I don't know the others---yet."

"Does he speak?"

"I haven't seen him speak."

"You must also return to Swifton. You must find out who the others are. Keep an eye on Aron."

Tares

Douglas's friends return to the farm, as do many who have heard them speak at ports in the Swift Sea and along the river. Some in attendance never left. The field is dense with camped out *Ghosts* waiting for Douglas to speak again, even though he said he would not until after the harvest. Aron also returns to the field.

It is the Day of Rest. It is dawn. It is harvest time. Douglas waits. He sits at a table with his twin. The others are sleeping, save Peter, who is outside.

"I didn't know if you'd return," says Douglas.

"Me either," says Tommy

Peter walks in from outside.

"What's up?" asks Douglas.

"The priest is outside."

"Which one?"

"It's Aron, one of those priests from the Holy City. What should we do?"

"Let's go talk to him."

Douglas walks outside. Tommy and Peter go along for the ride. It is a nice day. The sun is rising. They stand outside the door. Barty is awake and runs out after them.

"There he is," says Peter, pointing him out. "He looks like a predator."

"Humph," says Douglas.

When the priest sees Douglas outside his brother's house, he walks towards him. Douglas and his friends see him coming with Temple Guards.

"What's going on?" Andy asks groggily, coming out of the house.

"It's the bad man," Douglas says facetiously.

Andy sees the priest with his entourage. "This is how they came for John," he says.

Jimmy comes outside. He sees the priest coming. He looks at him and he looks at Douglas. "Hold it right there," says Douglas. The priest stops. The Guards are brought to a halt.

"I come in peace," says Aron.

Tommy looks with defiance at the priest. *'You gonna fuck with me, asshole?'* he seems to say.

"There was a great landowner," Douglas says. *The Ghosts* in the field begin to wake. "He kept a great deal of livestock grazing on his land, though he lived a great distance from his livestock. He had built a big house on a hill.

"This landowner was so rich, that he hired some shepherds to look after his sheep. As long as the shepherds did what was best for their flock, their authority over it grew.

"One day, the shepherds found a sheep that would not eat what they fed their flock. Rather than try to discover why the sheep was not eating, the shepherds decided to kill him before the other sheep stopped eating too.

"One day while the sheep slept with the flock, the shepherds were able to kill it. The death cries of that one sheep scattered the whole flock.

"The shepherds tried to reassemble their flock using the same food as bait, but the sheep would not be fed of the landowners graze. The sheep were never the same."

Others are awake. James and Johnny Z come out of the house. Joey comes out.

Aron looks around him with unease. A crowd is starting to listen, which he had hoped to avoid. He knows that the story has been told against him. He does not like it.

"Why do you and your *Ghosts* transgress the traditions of your elders?" he asks, formulating a plan.

"We mean no offense by it," Douglas says. "We simply will

not be controlled by other men's ideas of what we should do or be."

"You work in the field on the Day of Rest," Aron says. "I have seen it."

"And we will work today. It is your Day of Rest. In my philosophy, one day is the same as another. I work when there's work to be done. I rest when rest is won. Today there is work to be done. It is harvest time."

"There are Laws, Trigger," Aron says. "You will do what the Law tells you to do."

"I will do what my law tells me to do."

The Ghosts who are awake begin to applaud louder. This wakes most of the other people up. There are people with bedrolls planted like tares in the field, waiting for the possibility that Douglas might speak.

"My Lord," says one who is just coming awake, "Bless me with your word."

"Good-morning," says Douglas.

The man feels blessed. Aron is taken aback. The title, 'Lord,' is reserved for priests.

Douglas looks around at the path from his brother's house. It is festooned with people who are just waking up. Aron and his Guards are still watching. Bobby comes outside and joins Tommy. Douglas decides to walk into the crowd.

As he passes them, some of the people are afraid to speak to him. He waves to them all. He says, "Hey."

Philip comes outside. Jimmy A comes outside. Loki is also in the field. Douglas only sees strangers when he looks into the crowd to speak.

"Freedom must have a face," he says to *the Ghosts* in the field, "it must inspire those who see it to be something. I know that face. I have seen it. But it is hard to describe it to you. I may speak my truth, but how can you see what I see? How can I see what you see? How do we come to a common vision? If you hear the words I speak, do not hold onto them, or you will not be free. My words can help you seek truth, but they will not buy your freedom. You must seek your own truth. You must find your own freedom. You must form your own words.

"Freedom is not in any government, for governments, no matter how they begin, end when men gain power over other men. They become greedy and their every move becomes a play for more power. When they speak of truth, they often tell lies and somehow we continue to believe in them. We allow them to continue to rule us. A man can have power over other men only for so long as they give it to him.

"Freedom has a face and its face is truth."

"What is truth?" asks one from the crowd. "Is it God?"

"Truth is *Being,*" says Douglas.

"Man has a covenant with God," says an old man.

"Your God is a metaphor for that which is the same in all things. It is at the center of everything that lives. You must make a new covenant with yourself. There is no separation between your metaphor and man. We are one mind, separated by different experiences."

Douglas looks into the crowd. He watches *the Ghosts.* They sit transfixed. They wait for instructions. They love their master. Scary stuff. Jimmy and Joey are uneasy.

"Who is most likely to see the truth?" asks Johnny Z.

"An innocent child," says Douglas, "who has not yet been put in order. There are two kinds of innocence. There is the innocence of a child. There is joy in it. There is also the innocence of the ignorant that have been told falsehoods, which, when they grow, they count for truth. These innocents are a danger because they propagate their lies for truth. They believe their lies. Sometimes they become overzealous promulgating their lies. When they substitute manmade Laws for natural law, they are tricked and wasted."

"What kind of lies?" asks Peter.

"It may be an earthly order," Douglas says.

"Would you trap an innocent in your own order?" asks Aron, who has decided to heckle him.

"A human being must seek after his or her own nature," says Douglas. "A human being must establish his or her own order. A human being that is constantly run down by the world cannot be free. A human being must learn to make a trick out of it."

"How will we know when we are free?" asks Bobby.

"When you don't have to tell me. When nothing anybody can tell you or do to you in this world can disturb you."

Tommy does not like another man's audience, even if it is his brother's. "Speak to us about the revolution," he says.

"We're already separated. Those kinds of emotions just widen the gap."

"I don't know if I know what you mean."

"You have to stop trying to be what other men are. You have to stop wanting what other people have. You must find peace and walk your own path."

"But if everyone walks their own path, isn't that separation?"

"All rivers empty into the same ocean."

"I don't know if I understand what you mean," says Peter.

"Each man walks his own path, Peter. It does not pay to try to overtake someone who walks his own way."

"But aren't you trying to get people to walk the path you're on?" says Tommy.

"You're corrupting these people," shouts Aron.

Douglas looks at the people. "This is the world," he says.

Douglas looks at the crowd. Some of them may be getting it. Some of them may just be stoned. Douglas wonders if what he is saying will be remembered when he is gone and if it is, how it will be remembered.

It is harvest time, but there is little wheat to harvest. *The Ghosts* in the field crushed and choked it during the growing season. Only the weeds survive.

Set Sail

It is a new dawn. Many campers have spent the night in the barren field. So many are gathered, in fact, that there is no longer room for them, not even about the door. It is time to move on.

"This is getting weird," Douglas says, peering outside, "I have nowhere to go, nowhere to hide, nowhere to be alone. Look at all those people in the field."

"The good seed did not grow," says Jimmy.

"Only the weeds," says Douglas.

"Let's go," says Tommy, "before *the Ghosts* wake up."

Douglas scowls at his brother. He does not like the derogatory term, *Ghosts.*

"There will be no harvest," says Tommy.

"Let's go," says Douglas. "What we have to do is get from where we are now to the Swift Sea."

"Do you think most of the campers are still sleeping?" asks James.

"Let's just do it," says Tommy. "Let's not talk about it. Let's go."

"Everybody grab your gear," says Peter.

They spring into action, save James and Johnny Z. They are not sure if they are going. Peter knows this.

"What about you guys?" asks Peter. "What have you

decided?"

"How far are we going?" Johnny asks.

"All the way," says Douglas.

"What do we get if we go with you?" asks James.

"If you get anything," says Douglas, "I will not have given it to you."

The two brothers consider this. They consider their friendship with Peter and Andy. They consider their friendship with Douglas. They consider their business and families. They consider the Tribes. James and Johnny Z will go.

Douglas and his friends withdraw to Peter and Andy's ship undisturbed by *the Ghosts,* as if charmed. Once they realize what is happening, many follow Douglas to the Sea. Others remain camped out in the field in the hope that Douglas will return.

Douglas stands at the shore. His entourage surrounds him. They look at him. He looks at them. He silently wishes them well along their journey.

They load the boat with supplies.

"I wish I could go," says Jimmy.

"I know," says Douglas. "I understand that you must tend to the field."

"And to Joey's flock. It's going to be a tough winter without a harvest."

"I know. I'm sorry about that. I wish there was something I could do."

"I know. It's not your fault. People just don't think. Take care of Joey."

"I will."

Jimmy and Douglas hug.

"And Joey, you take care of Dougy."

"I will."

Jimmy hugs Joey.

"Who's gonna take care of me?" laughs Tommy.

Jimmy sticks out his hand to Tommy. "I think you can take care of yourself," he says with a smile. "That's been your burden. It was good seeing you again. I hope I'll see you again soon. You're always welcome here."

"Thanks," says Tommy, who does not feel welcome, not

because of the present, but because of the past. "I'm obliged to you, brother. Perhaps I will be back."

They shake hands. Jimmy tries to hug him, but Tommy stiffens up.

Tommy, Douglas, and Joey step into a rowboat. The others all squeeze in, except for Peter, who shoves the boat off. Peter jumps in as it launches.

Ghosts begin to appear on the shore behind Jimmy. The men in the boat watch their numbers grow.

"This is gonna be a weird trip," says Douglas.

"I wouldn't miss it for the world," says Tommy.

Peter and Andy steer the craft alongside their ship and jump out and tie it off. Douglas is the first to embark the vessel. He and the others unload the remaining supplies and are ready to depart.

"Let's weigh anchor," Douglas says to Peter. "Let's begin."

"Weigh anchor," says Peter.

Andy goes to the anchor.

"Set sails," says Peter.

James and Johnny Z go to the sails.

The crowd on shore perceives that Douglas is leaving and they begin to sing songs. They continue singing as the boat pulls up anchor and sets sail. Douglas and Joey wave to Jimmy as they go. Tommy is not watching the beach. The crowd thinks Douglas and Joey are waving to them.

James has the main sail raised, and a light breeze fills it. They can feel themselves starting to move.

Peter sits down next to Douglas.

"What are you trying to do with the stories you tell?" he asks.

Douglas can still hear the singing from the distancing crowd as they sail along the shore.

"Get people to hear the wisdom that is already within them."

Cody

James and Johnny Z did the advance work in Cody and are the first to go ashore to set the stage. This is one of the towns where they sell a lot of fish and they know a lot of people. When the natives learn that Douglas is in port to speak in the Temple, some go to the shore to see him. Some go right to the Temple. The people know about Douglas Trigger. James and Johnny Z have done a good job. For some townspeople, it will not be the first time they have heard him.

Douglas arrives on shore with his entourage that includes Tommy, Bobby, Peter, Joey, Philip, Andy and Jimmy A. People offer Douglas and his friends food and drink as they pass on their way to the Temple. It is like a celebration. Some do not even know who he is. There is just a festival atmosphere in the air. Douglas and his friends eat and drink with whoever offers them anything.

Some of *the Ghosts* from the field have followed Douglas along the shore or by sea. The spy, Loki, is also there, hiding in the crowd.

Douglas and his entourage arrive at the Temple of Cody and it is teeming with Tribespeople who have come to hear him. Before Douglas is ready to address the crowd, a familiar priest from the Temple of the Holy City calls out a question. "Is it lawful for a man to divorce his wife?" he asks him. Aron is flanked by Temple Guards from the Holy City. He is hoping to entrap Douglas the way he entrapped John.

Douglas sees who it is and knows that it is a trick question. He is surprised to see the priest from the Holy City. The question is the same he posed to John. He wants to entrap Douglas. He wants to try and pull the border audience to his side. He wants to divide the crowd. He wants to usurp Douglas's teaching.

Douglas answers, "While there can be love without marriage and marriage without love, love does not need marriage. It is love that bears fruit. Only the State needs marriage. Marriage is a creation of State Law. It is just one of the ways the State tries to control you. It is a legal contract no different from other legal contracts. There are remedies to legal contracts."

The crowd is silent. They are listening.

"So you're saying that a man should divorce his wife?"

"That is not what I said. That is what you said I said. You try to entrap me, priest, but you're not that clever. I don't know if you believe what you say or if you just think people are so stupid that they will believe you, in your priest robes."

"You are saying that the Great Chief's second marriage is illegal."

"That is what you are saying I am saying. I am not John. I will not parley with you, priest. The prophets spoke of you when they said, 'They honor truth with their lips, but their hearts are far away. They worship in vain, teaching as divine the conceit of men.'" Douglas turns to the rest of the crowd. He says, "The truth is like the sovereign in this story about a farmer: There was a farmer who needed help during the harvest season. He rose up early that morning. The sun was just coming up, and he went into town to hire some workers to help him harvest his field. The people he hired agreed to be paid one sovereign for one day's work before he sent them into the field.

"Though the field was full, the farmer still wanted more workers to lighten the loads of the fine workers he had. Three hours later he found several more to work in the field. He agreed to pay them each one-sovereign for one day's work. He found more field hands in the sixth, ninth and eleventh hours. He agreed to pay them each one-sovereign for one day's work and then he sent them into the field.

"When the sun went down, the farmer called his laborers to his office and gave them each a sovereign. Those who came in the eleventh hour made as much as those who had come in the first hour. When the others were gone, the spokesman of those who came in the first hour protested, saying, 'These last have just worked an hour, and yet you gave them the same sovereign which you gave us who have borne the burden and the heat all day.'

"The landowner said, 'Some people can earn a sovereign in an hour, for others it takes a day. At the end of that day, everyone has a sovereign. You are all equal. The field is not a marketplace.' And when the workers spent their sovereign in the marketplace, they spoke of the farmer's field."

The crowd is silent for a moment. When they realize the bit is over, they start clapping whether they understand it or not.

Douglas feels that Aron is moving in on him again. And it is true. Aron has a plan to entrap Douglas with his own words. But this time it is not Aron who speaks to Douglas, but one of the priests of the Temple of Cody, who says, "Why should a Tribesman pay taxes to the Emperor?"

Tommy likes the question. Aron smiles because he wrote the question. Once again, he is trying to entrap the new prophet.

Douglas hesitates for a deliberate answer. "I am not here to discuss manmade Law. I am here to discuss natural law."

"It is treason to refuse to pay taxes to the Empire," says Aron.

Douglas isn't playing. James and Johnny Z step up to either side of Douglas to join the others.

"Why do you surround yourself with indigent sinners?" says the judgmental voice of Aron.

"These are my friends."

"They're sinners," the priest says.

"What is their sin?" asks Douglas.

"You punk. Don't think you can trick me. These men are

unclean. They are not pious."

"Go away, priest," says Douglas, "no one wants your judgment."

"How dare you talk to me that way?"

"How dare *I*?" Douglas laughs. "How dare *I*? How dare *you.*"

"Your time is better spent with the pious."

"You want a piece of my piety?"

"You blaspheme. You are responsible for what will happen to you."

"Don't threaten me, little man," says Douglas.

Aron is amazed. No one has ever spoken to him like this since he became a priest. "Why do you transgress the traditions of your elders?" he says. "Why don't you be like the other young preachers and teach the Law of the Tribes?"

"I'm not a preacher. I'm Douglas Trigger."

Aron is annoyed by what he perceives to be insolence. "You consort with sinners, dirty street crawlers, the homeless, the poor and the wretched."

"Don't judge these people by what you see of them today. Some of them are not having their best day."

"You break the Day of Rest," says Aron, "and you provoke others to break the Day of Rest."

"We've had this talk before in front of a different crowd. Your act is coming along."

Aron is not amused. "You cannot break with tradition."

"Traditions are for fools who cannot rule their own lives."

"Am I a fool?" asks Aron.

"You are not wise," Douglas says, borrowing his twin's smile.

"You must watch what you say about a man such as myself."

"You are a man, like all men. You have some of man's strengths, but I think more of his weaknesses. You are not more than other men are. You are not less than other men."

Aron's anger boils at Douglas's lack of respect for his authority. He decides to assert it.

"I am a Priest of the Temple of the Holy City," he says up close and personal, in his face, so that only Douglas and those who are near him can hear. "You just made a mistake."

"No more, no less," says Douglas.

"You made a big mistake."

"Hey, Doug," Tommy says to try to rescue him, "we must embark. The sun rises."

Douglas considers an escape. He looks up and the sun isn't that high up in the sky. It is barely midday.

"You are not being orthodox," says Aron before he can go. "In our troubled times, we need orthodoxy. We must be conservative. The Empire is already moving against us. Would you rather worship their Gods?"

"I would rather not worship a God."

"This is the greatest blaspheme. You must recant all that you've said. You must be pious."

"Is a human being any less sacred if he or she does not do what you tell them?" asks Douglas.

"The covenant is between God and the Tribes. It is not between God and every dirty street crawler who can scrape up the courage to beg. These people are not in the covenant. The citizens of the Empire are not in the covenant. It's just the way it is. It's not their fault. It is only the Tribes who are the children of God."

"We have to be going," Tommy says, looking at Aron, tugging on Douglas.

"These people are unclean," says Aron, regarding the crowd. "They are drunks. They are lechers. A lot of these people are not even in one of the Tribes. They should not be in this Temple. It is against the Law."

"Your Laws are for men who would follow them. I am not such a man."

"Who are you?" says Aron. *"Who* do you think *you* are?"

"I am Douglas Trigger."

"Are you *the Voice the Medicine Man* spoke of?"

"Not me, my Lord," he says with sarcasm.

"Are you a new *Teacher of Righteousness?"*

"Not me."

"Are you some other prophet?"

"Not me," says Douglas. "You priests are of a brood of vipers. You look at *Light* and see darkness. When you see

Light, you cover your eyes and you try to block *the Light* from others. Your power over other men is only transitory. It is not real. All are equal. You live in darkness and choose to remain in darkness."

"You would try to corrupt a priest," says Aron. "You are the devil himself."

"We really have to go," says Tommy.

"If you continue to break the Law, you will be charged with blasphemy," says Aron.

"Blasphemy of your manmade Law? Your Law is an abomination. You blaspheme against natural law."

Aron is taken aback. "I don't know if you know what you're saying," he says. "The Laws of God are written in stone. You cannot change God's Law."

"Is your God a lawyer? There is only natural law. Your Law is man forged to control other men who will not rule their own lives."

"You are a disturbingly dangerous man," says Aron.

"A man who does not rule his own life, but allows himself to be led, is a truer danger."

"You're a liability to the Tribes."

"You're no asset," says Douglas.

"We have to go," says Tommy. He pulls Douglas away from Aron. They walk into the crowd, followed by the rest of Douglas's entourage and some new fans.

"You pissed him off," says Tommy, walking away with Douglas and his friends, unaware that Loki is following and watching. Aron also watches them disappear into the crowd. The gathered start to follow him out of the Temple.

"He pissed me off," says Douglas, picking up the pace once outside.

"You shouldn't piss off the Temple priests like that. They've taken a personal interest in you."

"The Temple priests are puppets of the Emperor. They're like the Great Chief. They will fall when the Empire falls."

"You talk of the fall of the Empire, but you will not help to accelerate it. Aron feels like your target. That will make you his target."

"I'll be ready for him."

"I think he believes you want to replace them."

"Why would I replace them? That would be like planting weeds in my own field."

"Leave that to Jimmy," Tommy jokes.

"I would not replace the Temple priests. They would just happen all over again."

"You just want to get rid of them entirely. The whole class. Tread lightly. The priests are respected members of this community. They wield power. The Temple of the Holy City is a sacred institution. You will offend many people. Know what you are doing. You are clashing with the power structure. You are upsetting the order. You're heading for trouble."

With an amused disbelief, Douglas says, "Are you warning me?"

"Yes," answers Tommy. "Don't be stupid. Of course I'm warning you. Somebody might try to kill you. You might hang yourself in your cell. They might find you after you've fallen from a high place. They might stone you. Yes, I'm warning you."

"I guess I knew all this when I started," says Douglas.

"Well, then I'm not gonna be responsible," says Tommy. "I tried to warn you. I tried to stop you. I tried to save you."

Tommy looks behind them at the crowd flowing from the Temple. He sees Loki. It stops him. Douglas stops. The entourage stops.

"What? What is it?" Douglas turns to look.

Tommy taps him. "Start walking," he says. "Everybody's doing what you do."

Douglas looks back in the crowd and it's getting congested.

"It's Loki," says Tommy when they start walking.

"Who's Loki?" asks Douglas.

"Just somebody Bobby and I know. He's that spy from *Sarah's Inn.* I think he's following us."

"There are a lot of people following us."

"This one's different. He tried to become a *Son of Light.* We thought he was one of us. He was some kind of spy, some kind of infiltrator."

"I didn't expect to attract so much attention so fast."

"Yea, well, you did."

"Let's get out of here."

"There's the boat," says James.

"I'll be right with you," says Tommy. "Hold the boat. I want to check out the crowd." He takes his syrinx from his belt and begins to play. Tommy knows a lot of songs.

Bobby stays with him. The others go with Douglas. They return to the rowboat.

One of the campers approaches Bobby and Tommy. "You guys hang out with him?" he says.

"Maybe we do," says Tommy, resting his syrinx. "Why do you want to know?"

"What's he like?" he asks.

"There's nothing I can tell you," says Tommy.

"Is he *the Messiah?*" asks the camper. "Is he God?"

"What kind of a *Messiah* are you expecting?" asks Tommy.

"One who will free us from the Empire."

"Yes, brother, he is *the Messiah,*" says Tommy.

"You guys are lucky to be with him," he says to Tommy and Bobby.

"I guess," says Bobby.

The camper looks at Tommy. "Are you his brother?"

"No," he says facetiously. Bobby looks at him.

"You look like him," says the camper, not getting the joke. "That's a blessing. Thank-you for talking to me."

"Thank-you," Tommy says politely.

When the camper leaves, Bobby asks, "Should we be telling them that?"

"Sure," Tommy answers. "Tell them what they want to hear." He pauses. "Let's go back to the boat with the others. I've seen what I wanted to see."

A crowd surrounds the rowboat. Tommy makes his way through it and boards the dinghy. Bobby pushes the vessel off the shore and jumps in. Tommy sits down next to Douglas. Bobby sits next to him. Peter and Andy row the boat.

Douglas looks at the shore. It is a campground of *Ghosts* from many different towns. "Why me?" he says.

"Why you what?" says Tommy.

The others listen.

"Why me?" he repeats.

"Andy was right," says Peter. "You are a prophet."

Douglas looks at Peter with resignation.

"Some people say that you're *the Messiah,*" says Tommy.

"Who says that?" Douglas is aghast.

"Everybody says that," says Jimmy A.

Pointing to the crowd onshore, Douglas says, "That's who *they* say I am?"

"Yea," says Bobby.

"But I'm just a story teller," says Douglas.

"To them you're a preacher," says Tommy, "a priest, a *Messiah.* You're a leader. Use the power you have! You control the crowd on that shore." He points to them. "You picked up all of *the Medicine Man's* supporters. These people will bark if you tell them to bark. They will fight if you tell them to fight. They will die if you say it's alright. Turn them against the Empire. Teach them what to do with their hate."

Everyone on the rowboat is watching Tommy get red in the face. Peter and Andy continue to row.

"I don't think anybody hates as much as you do," says Douglas.

"I only hate the Empire," he defends.

"You hate more than that," says Douglas. "You hate everything. You hate me. You hate Joey. You hate Jimmy. You hate our stepfather. You hate our mother. You hate the father we never knew. You shouldn't hate anything. Love. It'll lighten your world."

"I can't risk that," says Tommy, not listening to his brother. "You seem to be a man with vision. Can you see nothing at all? This is the generation of Struggle between good and evil, between the Tribes and a corrupt alien Empire. Can't you sense it in the air?"

"There is no struggle there. It is only imagined. You're both on the same side. One is an Empire and one would be an Empire."

"Doug," he says, not listening, "We have to free our people."

"Let's free everybody."

"That takes a revolution," Tommy claims, "That takes fighting."

"Why is there always someone who wants to start a revolution?" Douglas asks the others. He looks at Tommy. "You don't understand what I'm trying to say, do you?"

"Maybe not," Tommy admits.

"Perhaps I am wasting my time with you," he says. The others gaze at him dumbly. He says, "Perhaps I am wasting my time with all of you."

Nobody says anything as the rowboat touches up against the larger vessel. Andy jumps out to tie her off.

"Let's get out of here," Douglas says as they embark on the mother ship. "Soon we will be on the river."

"How quick do we want to get to the Holy City?" Peter asks, still tying off the rowboat.

"Not too quick, Peter," Douglas says, "as long as we're there for Festival."

It fits in with Tommy's schedule.

And the word spreads up the coast of the Sea to meet by its shore. Other vessels also follow. The priest and spy follow by land.

Power

Douglas wakes up on the boat with a start, as if from a bad dream. His shock wakes up Peter.

It is almost light. Douglas stands up in the boat. It is anchored off the shore of some port town on the Swift Sea. Douglas looks at the beach. There are campers everywhere. Tommy is in the rowboat, rowing back from the shore.

"Where are we?" asks Douglas.

"Shacktown," says Peter.

"When did we get here?" he says, staring off into space.

"During the night. You were sleeping."

"Where did all these people come from?"

"I don't know," says Peter, seeing Tommy nearing the boat. "Tommy's the only one who went ashore. Everybody else was on board the whole time. Somehow, word got out."

"What's in Shacktown?"

"Tommy's girlfriend."

"I guess that's as good as any reason to stop here."

Everybody else is waking up. James is waking up.

"Look at all those people," Douglas says of the campers on the shore. "Are they homeless? Do they live here?"

"They came to hear you."

"Maybe I shouldn't do this."

Bobby is awake. Tommy pulls up next to the boat. He ties

up. He hears them talking.

"Why would you want to stop?" he says.

"I don't know." Douglas turns to him.

"It's too late," says Tommy, climbing back on the boat. "It's what you're good at."

"At such a cost," says Douglas.

"What cost?" asks Peter.

"The cost John paid," says Douglas, "I'm pissing off the wrong people."

"You knew that you would," says Tommy.

"If you think you can help save the world," Bobby says, "don't you think you should try? Isn't it worth the risk?"

"You ask an awful lot," says Douglas.

"Bobby is right," says Tommy.

"How many people do you think are out there?" asks Douglas.

"Hundreds," says Peter.

"Thousands," says Tommy. "They're still coming from the town."

"What did you say?" asks Douglas.

"I didn't say anything," says Tommy. "Some people thought I was you. They knew you were coming. It's known all the way to the river. They must know what we look like."

"I don't want to do this anymore," says Douglas.

"It's too late," says Tommy. "It is in motion. You knew what you were doing."

"Maybe Tommy's right," says Peter.

"We better move quickly," says Douglas. "That seems to be what the opposition is doing."

"They'll try to stop us before we get to the Holy City," says Tommy.

"Maybe we should just forget about stopping and head straight for the Holy City," says Peter.

"No," says Douglas. "We'll stick to the plan. We'll be there for Festival. I'm not ready for the Holy City. Nobody's gonna make me panic. What will be will be."

"Do you seriously think that the priests of the Temple of the Holy City would try to kill you?" Peter asks Douglas.

"Oh, yeah," says Tommy.

"Like I said before," says Douglas, "they killed John."

"I agree," says Bobby. "The priests of the Temple of the Holy City are men of power. They are escorted by soldiers."

"Their power is Earthly," says Douglas.

"They could take you off it," says Bobby.

"That's why I can't give up."

"Alright!" says Andy.

Tommy smiles his silent laugh and touches his chin.

"What?" says Douglas.

"You're funny," Tommy says.

"What?"

"I was just thinking, you're funny."

"Why am I funny?"

Tommy looks at the shore. "Why are you funny?" he says. "You're funny 'because you could control all these people, but you don't. Why? Why don't you control these people?"

"I can, but I don't. You don't because you can't. Just let it go."

Maccabees

At an inn that Tommy knows, a minstrel sings a rebel song. Timothy sits at a table drinking, waiting for Tommy. He knows he will come to *Maccabees.* Timothy claps along with the song with some of the regulars. He watches the other people at the inn to see how they react to the rebel's song. He does not see Tommy walk in. Tommy sees him.

Tommy arrives with Douglas, Bobby, Peter, Andy, Philip, Barty, Joey, James and Johnny Z in tow. While Peter and the others look for a table, Tommy tells Douglas, "Hey, I see someone I know over there. I'll be right back. Get me a drink."

Tommy walks across the inn and sits down, saying, "Timothy."

"Tommy. What is up?"

"Trouble."

"What else is new?"

"Where's Mandolin?"

"Searching for her roots," Timothy says facetiously.

"She dreads this place," says Tommy. "I can't believe she came here."

"She came here chasing after you. I cannot believe it myself."

"There are other ports she could have met me in. She

wants me to help her solve all her fucking problems. She wants me to go with her to confront her dickhead father. I got enough problems of my own."

"Your stepfather was also dickhead, was he not?" Timothy says, half-joking.

"My point exactly," Tommy says with a smile.

"I guess she figured if you could go home, so could she."

"Maybe."

"They say your brother is the new *Medicine Man.*"

"New *and* improved," Tommy says with a smile, nodding to his brother, who, with his group, has found a table. "News travels fast."

"Everyone calls him that now. See what I told you?" Timothy is eating. He has a drink in his hand. "I am hearing bad things on the street."

"What are you hearing?" asks Tommy.

"I am hearing, 'Peace.'"

"I'm hearing it too," says Tommy.

"Peace is not a bad thing," says Timothy, "if it is just. When we are occupied by the forces of a corrupt Empire, it is not just."

"I agree," says Tommy.

"People are beginning to listen to your brother."

"My brother is a man possessed by a vision."

"It is not our vision."

"No. He is very difficult to dissuade."

"Do you think it is possible?"

"No," says Tommy. "He's like me. He doesn't listen to anybody."

"You listen to me."

"Oh, yeah," he smiles.

"Soon it will be Festival. Will he be a distraction to the pilgrims?"

"Maybe, maybe not. Even as we talk, the priests of the Tribes are moving against him, just as my brother said they moved against *the Medicine Man.*"

"The priests?"

"He challenges their authority. He challenges their faith.

He challenges their God. I think he's an atheist. He challenges their control of the Tribes. If there is no God, what will the priests do? He will scatter their flock."

"Does he know that the priests are plotting against him?"

"Yes, I told him. One of the priests from the Holy City has been following us. He's been heckling my brother when he speaks. Do you know Aron?"

"Yes. Not too bright. Bit of a kiss ass. Your brother is not intimidated?" Timothy looks across the room at Douglas. Tommy follows his stare.

"No."

"You brother will become a martyr."

"For his cause, not ours. The priests may incite the mob to stone him."

"It is a sacrifice." He looks over at Douglas. "Stay with your brother. Pick up his sword when he is felled."

Tommy follows Timothy's glance at his brother. "Just as he picked up *the Medicine Man's* sword."

"Just like that," says Timothy, "we will be the next to control *the Ghosts.* It will be easy. Look at your face. It is the same as his. It is simple."

"Simple."

"I do not mean to sound callous about the path your brother has chosen, but ours is not a Struggle about the next life. It is a Struggle about this life. His death should have meaning. Why do people listen to him? What is his message? What does he say?"

"He speaks with the authority of divine wisdom."

"That doesn't mean he's right. What divine wisdom?"

"He says that the Empire isn't our enemy. He says it's a transitory illusion and that we're actually brothers with all of the Empire's citizens. He says we're one."

"I never had a brother," says Timothy. "Tell me what brothers are like."

Tommy looks at his brothers across the room. "There is competition," he says. "One is usually dominant."

The innkeeper brings Tommy a beer. "Thanks," he says.

"Who was dominant in your family?" asks Timothy.

Timothy thinks about it. "I guess Jimmy was by default.

He's the oldest. Me and Dougy made a pretty good team. I don't know who would be now."

"I think I do." Tommy gets his vote. "How close are you to your twin?"

"Pretty close for guys who haven't seen each other in almost twenty years," laughs Tommy. "I think he trusts me more than I trust him."

"Good," says Timothy. "What are his plans?"

"He wants to be in the Holy City by Festival. He wants to get there before he's stopped."

"Good," says Timothy, "so do we. It is perfect. He will get a following going. You will be at his side."

"I am already at his side."

"Are you sure you cannot convert him?"

"Yea."

"Has he converted you?"

"No. Maybe *you* could persuade him. Let me call him over here."

"There is no way to nationalize him?" asks Timothy.

"He's not big on tribalism," says Tommy. "He doesn't believe in division. He won't choose a side. Every side is the same to him."

Timothy takes a drink. "He will not choose a side? Do you know what the talk is on the streets?" Tommy does not answer. Timothy takes another sip of his drink. "You do not know the streets anymore."

"Peace," says Tommy. "You told me it was of peace."

"There cannot be peace with the Empire, Tommy," says Timothy.

"There cannot be," Tommy agrees.

"Of course not," says Timothy. "He is turning the Tribes into pacifists, just waiting to be stepped on."

"He talks about love," says Tommy.

"Love," says Timothy. "Love? Do you love your brother?"

"What do you mean?"

"If you have to kill your brother for the sake of the revolution, will you?"

"He's my brother."

"Will you kill him for the good of the cause?"

"Are you kidding me?"

Apparently not.

"Nobody in the movement touches my brother," says Tommy. "If the priests interfere, that's one thing, that's something he chose, but no *Son of Light* will murder him. I warned him about the Temple. He knows what will happen."

"Maybe you should warn him about *the Sons of Light.* You must think about your Tribal family first."

"Blood is blood. He may not be a fighter. He may not be a warrior Chief. He may not be *the Messiah.* He is my brother."

"He is not *the Messiah,*" says Timothy, pushing away an empty plate. "I told you that when this whole thing started. But too many people think he is *the Messiah.* That is why we must control his followers when he falls. You will become *the Messiah.*"

"Thanks for the promotion."

"Do not blow it."

Timothy's mug is empty. He looks to the innkeeper and signals for more.

"He doesn't want to fight the Empire," says Tommy.

"What does he want?" asks Timothy.

"He wants us to love the Empire."

"Love the Empire? How can a man love his enemy?" Timothy shakes his head in disgust.

"Punish the Empire like an errant child," says Tommy.

"How do you punish a child who is bigger than you?" asks Timothy.

The innkeeper arrives with another pitcher. He fills their mugs. Timothy pays him with a nice tip.

"We must unite the Tribes," Timothy says. "Your brother divides us. It must be our voice that speaks to the pilgrims at Festival. How can we be free without revolution? How can there be peace without war?"

"That's not the way he sees freedom," says Tommy.

"Whatever he says is rhetoric," says Timothy. "It means nothing. What does not help us hurts us. We need the young people he is attracting. If he does not bring them to us, then he takes them away from us."

"Let me call him over here," says Tommy. "See if he'll listen to you. You may find yourself listening to him."

"I will do what must be done," says Timothy, "but I will not listen."

Tommy signals to Douglas, who sees him, acknowledges him, says something to the other guys and walks over. Joey looks after his brothers.

"Doug, this is somebody I want you to meet," says Tommy. "This is Timothy. Timothy, this is my brother, Douglas."

"Nice to meet you," says Timothy.

"Likewise," says Douglas. He extends his hand. When he takes Timothy's hand, he sees the rebel tattoo on the fleshy part of his skin between his thumb and index finger. "Are you also a rebel?"

Timothy looks at Tommy. He is amazed by Douglas's candor. "Yes," says Timothy. "Are you a *Son of Light?*"

"Yes, I am," says Douglas.

Timothy is surprised and looks at Tommy.

"Different *Light,*" he says.

"Different revolution," says Douglas.

"There is only one revolution," says Timothy.

"So Tommy tells me," says Douglas. "Let me tell you about my revolution. Mine is a revolution with no armies, a revolution with no enemies, no countries, and no borders. It is a revolution of truth and freedom. All that separates us dissolves until we are one mind at peace. We are one mind separated by different experiences in a self-imposed reality. If we see that truth, we are free."

"In peace, there is only defeat," says Timothy. "For every sovereign you make, the Empire takes a share. For every grain you grow, the Empire takes a share. Even your seeds are taxed. We allow the Empire to control our lives. And when we're alone at night, we pray to some God and ask for mercy. We ask him to be free."

"Praying to some God won't make you free," says Douglas, "because if you're not at peace, if you are not one with yourself, then you are not free. We're not being occupied because we sinned, or because we broke some covenant. Whatever we are experiencing is a self-imposed reality."

"We are occupied because we allow it," says Timothy. "We have to free our people. We have to make the Empire free us!"

"The Empire cannot free you."

"If we are ever going to be free of the Empire," continues Timothy, "We have to fight for it. We need a leader to make them fight. From what I hear, you could be that leader. Look at all these people who follow you. They are looking for a *Messiah.* I am not just talking about throwing some rocks at a couple of Imperial soldiers. I am talking about the return of Tribal Lands and the rebirth of our Nations. It will be the fulfillment of *God's Promise.* I want every member of every Tribe to be able to look at his or her reflection in the river and say, 'I am free!' Once freedom catches on, it will spread like wildfire."

"You don't need me to lead your revolution," says Douglas.

"We need a leader the people can rally around."

"Someone like you," says Tommy.

"The more lands the Empire occupies," says Douglas, "the more Nations they bring under their control, the thinner they spread themselves, the sooner they will defeat themselves. Let them build their war machine. Let the Empire defeat itself."

"It will not happen without intervention," says Timothy. "Think of the injustice. I saw the crowd gathered on the shore this day. You have a responsibility. Do you realize the power you have over these people?"

"I don't want to use it," says Douglas.

"You use it every time you open your mouth to get people to look at you."

"And everywhere we go," says Tommy, "the crowds get larger."

Peter looks across the room and sees Douglas. He heads over. Joey follows.

Banned

It is dawn. The campers on the shore are waking up. Tommy leads Douglas, Timothy and the others through the crowd to the Sea.

"These people are sheep," Tommy whispers to Timothy. "They would do his bidding."

Tommy looks through the crowd for a familiar face as they walk.

"This is what I mean," Timothy whispers back. "Look at all these people. This is what we need."

"Many of these people who have come to see him have already heard him. They follow him. They are the new *Ghosts.*"

"They are *Ghosts,* alright," says Timothy. "They are the living dead. How many people do you think are here?"

"There are thousands," says Tommy, "and they're all here to see my brother, my twin."

"That is some kind of power."

"You have to hear him," says Tommy.

"I did not expect such a crowd," says Timothy.

"It has grown since we arrived," he says, and then louder, to Douglas, "You ready to go on?"

"Yea," he says. "It's showtime."

Douglas climbs up a hill so the crowd can hear. His friends

surround him. "The word travels fast," he says, looking at the throng.

Douglas's entourage keeps the crowds back. Mandolin is in the crowd. She is looking for her Tommy. He is keeping his distance. He does not want to see her until he wants to see her.

"Teacher," says a timid girl who has the courage to walk up to Douglas, "can I walk with you?"

Douglas motions for her to come along.

Some of her girlfriends, who are waiting in a tent to see what would happen, feel at ease. They giggle and chase after him.

Other fans join in the following.

"Is this how it always happens?" Timothy asks Tommy.

"How what always happens?"

"When your brother walks through a crowd," says Timothy, "Does it always press up against him like this? Do others always want to walk with him?"

"Yea, I guess," says Tommy. "They want to be on the path he's on."

"They are as sheep," says Timothy. "They adore him."

"They are his sheep," says Tommy. "They will do what he tells them to do."

"Yes," says Timothy.

Douglas stands on a hill with people all around him. He sees his friends. He sees his brother's girlfriend. He sees Timothy. He sees Aron. He sees Loki.

Douglas hears his name throughout the crowd. They start chanting. It starts softly at first, like a far off rider in the desert:

"Trigger! Trigger! Trigger!"

It is crazy.

"Trigger! Trigger! Trigger!"

The chanting swells nearer.

"Trigger! Trigger! Trigger!"

It becomes like thunder in the desert.

"Trigger! Trigger! Trigger!"

Tommy and Timothy watch the crowd. They do not like another man's audience. Joey is amused. Bobby and the others chant, leading the crowds:

"Trigger! Trigger! Trigger!"

It is very scary.

Aron is also in the crowd watching. *'This is subversive,'* he thinks.

Loki is thinking a spy's thoughts.

The crowd swells like no other Douglas has seen before. He raises his hand to silence them. They are silent.

Douglas speaks: "Listen to me!" he shouts to quite them. "Listen to me! Listen to me! Awake! Unleash the wisdom that is within you!"

The crowd cheers.

"Take responsibility for your own destiny. You will only be at peace if you take charge of your own life. You must find your own way."

Douglas is saying one thing and Tommy and Timothy are hearing another thing. They hear *'revolution!'*

"If you are passive in this world, it will pass from you. You must become caretakers. You must be willing to take control. It's time to grow up. You are the inheritors of the Earth. Hunger and fight for what is right. Lay down your precious life for what is right.

"Peacemakers will survive. Warriors will die. A man of peace must be willing to die to defeat a man of war.

"Those who seek truth will find it. Those who demand righteousness will have it. Those who are persecuted for righteousness will know peace. Ask, and you will be given; seek and you will find; knock and it will be opened to you.

"We are one mind separated by different experiences in an illusion of time. We are one. Be truthful. Don't lie. A lie is a sin against the truth. The truth is always known. The truth is *the Light* that may not be hidden in dark places. Be pure in heart and you will know truth.

"I don't want to renounce the old prophets," he says, eyeballing Aron, "I have come to say what has already been said. What can be known is known. There is nothing new here. There's only one truth.

"Do not condemn one who seems evil. These are the ones who do not know truth. There is no evil in the world, only lesser degrees of good. But everyone may not see what you see.

"Don't do good deeds just so somebody might see you. The thank-you is not your reward. Rather, when you help someone who needs your help, sound no trumpet that others may praise you. Don't tell anyone. Don't let your left hand know what your right hand is doing. The truth is always known. The deed will be your reward. What is given will be given to you.

"Don't pile up earthly treasures, where dust and rust consume and where thieves break in and steal, but share the wealth. You cannot seek money and truth. Money is not truth. Money is what buys you to keep you from the truth. What you do not give will be taken from you. What you take will also be taken. All things die. At the end of the longest life is death. Do not make money your treasure. Instead, gather the treasures that are spread out around you that no one may hoard. Gather your friends into your barn. For where your treasure is, there will your heart be also. You cannot serve two masters, money and truth, for either you will hate the one and love the other, or you will be devoted to one and despise the other.

"Maybe you think you should love your friends and hate your enemies. But I say, 'Love your enemies, and forgive those who persecute you. It will change them. Be filled with *the Light,* because one who is your enemy can become your friend. One who is blind may see *Light.* And when we are all friends, what is divided will be one. The wrong will be right. The bad will be good. The dark will be *Light. The Garden* will be revealed.

"Don't be burdened with your past. Don't worry about what might have been. Every step you take, you take alone. The past is unalterable. Fall into the river and be reborn.

"Don't be anxious about your life. Don't worry about what you're going to eat or what you're going to wear or about where you're going to live. Life is more than food, clothing and shelter. The birds do not sow or reap or gather their harvest into barns, and yet they're never hungry. Aren't you smarter than a bunch of birds? Don't be anxious about tomorrow, for tomorrow will take care of itself. The truth is everywhere. Let the day's own obstacles be sufficient for the day. And which of you by being anxious can add one minute to your life? Don't want after what citizens of the Empire have, seek your own peace, and in righteousness, all these things will be yours.

"Judge not, for that which you judge, will also judge you, and the measure you give will be the measure you get. Don't gossip. Don't think that you're better than somebody else and fit to judge them. You don't know the path another one is on. You don't know their rough ways.

"Not everyone who hears me will listen. And many may speak in my name and still not hear. They'll say, 'I was by the Sea yesterday and he said this…' I did not say 'this.' These are the tares. These are false prophets. But everyone who hears what I have to say can build his or her house on solid rock. The earth may shake, the rains may fall, the floods may come, the winds may blow and beat upon the house, the ground may crack, but the house will not fall because it was built on solid rock. Those who don't listen will build his or her house in the sand."

Douglas is finished. The crowd is dumb. They are used to hack prophets who just repeat passages from *the Book of the Tribes.* Here is a man writing a new book.

He awes Mandolin. Aron wants him undone. Douglas starts to go. His entourage follows and surrounds him. Aron gets in his way at the bottom of the hill. He addresses him on a personal level so as not to include a crowd. His friends hear it all.

"Where are you trying to lead these people?" asks the priest.

Douglas gives him the once over. "Are you following me?" he says.

"Where are you leading these people?"

"If I were to lead them anywhere," says Douglas, "it would be away from you. I would lead them away from your Temple."

Douglas walks away from the priest. Aron and his Temple Guards follow. They aren't keeping up with the group.

"Wait!" says Aron, and he takes off after him.

"I would take them away from anyone who tried to rule them," says Douglas while still walking, heading for the dinghy. "I would show them self-rule."

Aron is closer to Douglas. "You would take them away from the Temple," he says.

"There's no Temple in Shacktown."

"Do not try to lead the Tribes astray."

"I am the Tribes."

"You are one man."

"I am everyman."

"Do you know what you're saying?" says Aron. "You have indicted yourself."

"Your Laws do not interest me."

"You are a blasphemer."

"Every time I see you, it's the same speech," says Douglas. "Maybe what you need is a new writer."

"You blaspheme against God."

"You blaspheme against man and nature. You blaspheme against natural law."

"There is only one Law," says Aron, "and it is God's Law. In God's Law you are a blasphemer. I am leaving for the Holy City. I will not be back. Repent, sinner. Recant all that you've said. If you do not, if you continue this folly, I will surely hear about it."

"You just heard it," says Douglas. "It doesn't get any better than that."

"Stay out of the Holy City then," says Aron. "You are banned from the Temple of the Tribes of the Holy City."

"It doesn't surprise me," Douglas laughs. "It doesn't stop me. Can you ban me from the Temple of *the Garden?*"

"Do not test me, boy," says Aron. "You will not win."

"I'm not trying to win anything," says Douglas. "That's why I can't lose."

He walks away from Aron. He walks away from everybody. He gets in the rowboat.

Tommy looks at Timothy. They are both in awe. They hustle after him. Bobby, Peter, Andy and the others follow Douglas to the rowboat.

The Siren of Shacktown

What Tommy does to women he does without love. It is not his fault. He has never felt loved. He doesn't trust it. What Tommy does, he does without passion. Mandolin is full of passion. She thinks it is enough for both of them. She wants love from Tommy. He has none to give.

Tommy is drunk and naked, lying belly down on a bed in a cheap room at the inn, getting a massage. He does not thank Mandolin for her touch. He does not thank her for her love. He does not want it. He is afraid of it.

"Why did you leave me last night?" she says.

"I don't have to explain myself to you," he says.

Mandolin looks hurt. Tommy cannot see it. He is not facing her. He does not hear it in her silence. She massages him.

"I don't have to explain to you what a man is," he says. "You've been with many before. Don't expect me to be any different."

"I wanted to make love with you when I woke up," she whispers, "But you were gone."

"I'll fuck you again," says Tommy. "I'll fuck you right now if you want."

He starts to roll over. She stops him.

"Why do you say those things and still make love to me?"

"We fuck," says Tommy. "Don't complicate things."

He makes her sad. "Why do you talk to me like that?" she asks.

"I don't know, baby." His eyes are closed in drunken revelry. "Why do you let me talk like that?"

"You're very tense," she says, feeling the muscles in his back. "What do you do that makes you so tense?"

"People that ask questions make me tense."

She feels his butt.

"You got a cute tush," she says.

"Tush?" laughs Tommy. "Nobody calls it a tush. It's an ass."

"You got a cute ass," she says. She kisses it. "Are you following your brother?"

Tommy is annoyed by the question. He turns over on his back and looks at her. "Follow?" he says. "Follow? I follow no man."

Whoops. Mandolin said the wrong thing. She is also naked, with one of her knees on either side of his stomach. Tommy has a nice view. He feels her breasts. She leans down into him.

"You got cute tits," he says.

She smiles. "They're breasts," she says. "How long are you staying?"

Tommy slides up between her legs and sits upright. He takes an arm in either hand. "I already told you that."

She had hoped he would stay with her. "Why don't you talk to me about what you do?"

He gives no answer. They massage one another.

"Are you with him because you're brothers?"

Tommy stops. "It's business," he says, "my business."

"Why don't you trust me?"

"Don't take it personal. I don't trust anyone."

"If we make love again, will you stay the night?"

"No."

"I love you."

He grunts. She puts her arms around his neck and he brings his hands down along her sides. She rests her head on his right shoulder and says sadly, "Don't you worry about growing old alone?"

"I was born alone," says Tommy. "I am alone. I will die

alone. That's how life is." He kisses her again. They fall onto the bed again. "Anyway, I don't think I'll grow old."

Mandolin looks at Tommy with regret. There is no love in his eyes. He does not see her. He is wrapped up in his own world.

"You just come to me for sex," says Mandolin. "We never talk."

"We talk about sex. We talk about how we want to do it. We talk about where we want to do it."

"I love you."

"Yea, well, stop that. It's not gonna do you any good. It's not gonna get you anywhere. It's just gonna hurt you in the end."

Mandolin is hurt.

"Did you see your father?" asks Tommy, trying to talk to her.

"No."

"Why not?"

"I was scared."

"I thought that's why you came to Shacktown."

"I came to be with you. Will you come with me?"

"He's not my father," says Tommy. "If my father did that to me, I'd kill him."

"You'd run away!" she cries.

Tommy frowns.

"I can't kill him," she says. "Why won't you come with me? Why don't you love me? What's the matter with me?"

"Don't cry on me, kid," says Tommy. "There's nothing wrong with you."

"Then why don't you love me?"

"I don't love anybody, kid. I don't even love me."

"Do you love him?"

"Who?" asks Tommy.

"Your brother."

"I don't have a brother. I don't love anybody."

Tommy grabs Mandolin and rolls her over on her back. He spreads her legs apart and uses her again. It almost seems like a chore.

He is done with her. He dresses and leaves her alone. He

closes the door and Mandolin dresses and follows him down to the shore.

During the night, before Peter sets sail, Mandolin sneaks on board the boat.

The Stowaway

Mandolin wakes up on Peter's ship. Andy is sitting nearby watching her. "Who are you?" he asks.

Mandolin squints. The sun is up. She is the type of person who wakes up very slowly. The boards she sleeps on make her body ache.

"Who are you?" Andy repeats.

She rubs the sleep from her eyes. "Mandolin," she says.

Peter sees the girl and goes over.

Mandolin stretches up her neck to look over the boat. It is moving. "Where are we?" she asks.

"We'll ask all the questions," says Peter, moving in to stand next to Andy. "You're a stowaway."

"We're passing through Arteria," says Andy, who is taken by her. "We're about to enter the river."

Peter looks at him. "What are you doing here?" he asks Mandolin.

"I," she says, "I followed my boyfriend on board."

Peter looks at Andy. "Who's your boyfriend?" asks Peter.

She pauses. "Tommy," she says.

The two brothers look at one another.

"I didn't see you come on board with him," Peter says.

"It's a surprise," says Mandolin.

Others are waking up. Bobby sees Mandolin. He looks for

Tommy, who is still passed out. His brain is still soaked with alcohol from the night before. He does not want to be woken up. Timothy is up. He joined the crew for the trip to the Holy City. He looks at Bobby and then he looks at Mandolin. What is she doing here?

Douglas is awake and saw Mandolin while she was sleeping. He goes over to her now that she is stirring.

"Tommy is still sleeping," says Douglas.

Mandolin smiles. "I came to see you."

Peter looks at Andy. "Let's scram," he says.

Douglas laughs. The two brothers aren't leaving. Douglas says, "Well, scram."

They scram. Douglas looks at Bobby. He rolls over and turns away.

Mandolin smiles.

"What're you doing here?" asks Douglas.

"I," she says, "I had nowhere else to go."

"Where is your home? Is it Shacktown or the Holy City?"

"I…have no home," she says.

"Do you live at the safe house?" he asks.

"No. No one is allowed to live at the safe house all the time. It's a place we go to only when we have nowhere else."

"Well, I certainly had to go there." He smiles at her. She smiles back.

"I thought I could face him, but I couldn't."

"Tommy?"

"My father," says Mandolin. "I went to Shacktown to face him but I couldn't. I thought Tommy would help me."

"Why do you have to face him?"

"I have to do it for me."

"What did he do to you?"

Mandolin does not say. She seems like she is about to cry.

Tommy wakes up holding his head. The first thing he hears is Mandolin. *'Shit,'* he thinks to himself. *'I thought I left her last night.'* Suddenly the boat rocks. "What the…?" asks Tommy as he opens his eyes. The first thing he sees is Mandolin. *'What is she doing on this ship?'* he thinks. His head is pounding. He feels like he is going to be sick.

Timothy walks over to his friend to explain the situation.

"She stowed away," he says. "She says she has no place to go."

"I'll give her a place to go," Tommy says, holding his head.

"Be nice."

"I'm always nice. I never should have disembarked in Shacktown in the first place. She's crazy. Sometimes I don't think a piece of ass is worth the price of admission."

Mandolin walks over and smacks Tommy on his lips. When they separate, Tommy is mad. He says, "What the hell are you doing here? I didn't invite you to be here."

"What makes you think I'd wait for your invitation?" she asks. "Somebody else invited me."

"Alright, I'll play your game," says Tommy, "Who invited you?"

She walks over to Douglas and takes him by the arm. "He did," she says.

Douglas shrugs.

"Yea, right," says Tommy. He feels his head. "Where are we?"

"We're in Arteria," says Andy.

"The river," says Tommy, looking ahead. He turns to Mandolin. "What are you doing here? What are you, some kind of groupie? Are you gonna be his groupie now?" He looks to his twin. "Dougy, you got groupies."

"Why didn't you take me with you?" she says to Tommy.

"I didn't tell you to go to Shacktown," says Tommy.

"You didn't tell me not to."

"I don't have time for you. I'm doing something here. It's got nothing to do with you."

"She has nowhere to go," says Douglas.

"Stay out of this." Tommy knows that it is true. She did not confront her parents. She couldn't stay with them unless she did. It was why she left in the first place. With this pack of dogs she will eat sometimes and sometimes she will have a roof over her head. Still, it is none of his brother's business. Mandolin is Tommy's baggage.

"I think I'm gonna be sick," says Tommy.

"Go back to sleep," says Douglas. "We're about to enter the

river."

The River

As they enter the mouth of the river, Douglas looks to the shore. There is a man with long white hair and a beard waving to them with both arms, signaling for them to come ashore. There is a sense of urgency about him. Douglas looks to Peter to see if he sees the man.

Peter sees him. "What do you think that's all about?" he calls to Douglas from the bow of the boat.

"I don't know," says Douglas. "Do you think we should check it out?" The man seems familiar.

Peter walks over to Douglas. "I don't know," he says. "That guy could be crazy."

"You ever look at yourself?" Douglas says with a laugh. "Aah, let's check it out."

"Maybe you're crazy," says Peter. He calls out to Andy, "Let's lower the sails and drop anchor. We're going in."

They get as close to shore as they can with the ship and Peter helps Andy drop the anchor. Douglas can see who it is. It is his old teacher, Ælfric. Douglas waves. Bobby gets up. Philip is already up.

Those that are up go to the rowboat to disembark. Mandolin goes. There are seven on the rowboat. Peter rows.

Ælfric waits on the shore.

"What does he want?" asks Bobby.

"He probably wants to warn me," says Douglas.

"Well," says Peter, "you won't listen to anybody else."

Andy looks at the man on shore. He recognizes him.

When the rowboat lands, Douglas helps Mandolin out. Ælfric wastes no time in coming to him. He splashes into the water with his bare feet and grabs Douglas on his shoulder. The others stop in their tracks. Andy and Philip are still on the rowboat.

Ælfric looks Douglas in the eye. He does not say hello. "It is you I have come to see," he says. "This is a world with one water. This is a river with many currents. Some currents are strong. They take. They are rebuked. Some currents are weak. They become trapped. They become a self-rebuke. The water flows evenly through weak and strong currents. This is the truth."

Ælfric backs away. Douglas follows him to the shore. The others follow him.

"You sure he's not crazy?" Peter whispers to Douglas.

"He's from *the Settlement,*" says Andy.

Ælfric turns to face them again. He looks at Douglas. He says, "The currents of the water contribute to the nature of the river. The nature of the river contributes to the currents of the water.

"Some currents ride a straight, swift path to the ocean. These are safe waters, but the force never changes, and nothing is gained. Some currents zigzag. They hoe their own way. This makes the water seem rough.

"All rivers rest in a different bed. Some paths are short, others long. Some rivers stock death, others life. Some rivers are a joy, others a task. The water has many rivers.

"Some currents flow over a jagged bottom. In strong currents, the rocks become smooth. In gentle currents, the rocks detour the river.

"All rivers flow into one another. All rivers empty into the same ocean. This is a world with one water.

"The water is not a mystery if you have fish-skin eyes." And then, pointing to Douglas he says, "Have you got fish skin on your eyes, boy? Someday you may see what the river shows. Some day you may know why the currents flow. Someday you may get wet as the water goes."

The old man cries out. "This may tempt you!" he says. "You may want to rule the river. But remember an old man must die and a young man must grow old. This the water knows.

"There are men who bathe in the river. There are men who are wet in its water.

"When man was young, he crawled out of the water. He was slime. He was despair. He was the spit of the water.

"Man returned and drank from the river. He returned to fish in its currents. He made his bed in the river. He will return and fill the ocean.

"Woe unto those who once feared the water but now seek to master it. The master does not know the slave. The master does not know the slave!"

Ælfric begins to back away. "If you are traveling down the river, remember the Sea at the end. It is the Still Sea. At the end of the river is death. Are you sure you want to take this journey?"

"The same thing waits at the end of all rivers," says Douglas.

"Be in the world but not of it." Ælfric backs away.

Douglas holds up his hand to stop the others from following him.

When he is gone, Peter says, "He is mad."

"He is not himself," says Andy.

"Do you think there are some people who say that I'm mad?" asks Douglas.

Peter looks at him. "Aren't you?"

"Oh, yeah, that's right."

Everyone laughs.

"I understand him," says Douglas. "Let's get outta here."

"Who was he?" asks Peter.

Douglas helps Mandolin into the rowboat.

"He is *the Teacher of Righteousness.*"

On the Boat

The evening is warm on Peter's boat. "You always knew what you wanted," Tommy says to his twin, "Even when we were kids."

"I guess."

"You always felt like you had a purpose, a destiny."

"We all have the same destiny." Death.

Tommy laughs his silent laugh. He knows what he means. Tommy hands his brother a skin of wine. Douglas takes a swig from it. No one speaks. Douglas hands the skin to Andy. He takes a swig and hands it to Peter. The silence is uncomfortable. "Do the Tribes have a destiny?" Tommy asks.

"Life has a direction it flows like water in the river," says Douglas. "When two streams come together, they join and continue to flow together. This is something men do not do. This, we could learn from the river."

"Now you sound like *the Teacher,*" says Peter.

"Are you saying we should allow ourselves to be subjugated when a bigger body of water alters our 'flow?'" says Tommy.

"I'm saying that we're all going in the same direction."

"Yea, except some of us are getting decapitated."

"I'm not sure if I'm following this whole conversation," says Johnny Z, who grabs the skin of wine from Peter. He takes a gulp and hands it to James.

"Individual destiny is an illusion," says Douglas. "It is a part of the mask of this world. We're all in it together. We'll all get there at the same time because we're already there."

"Yea, but maybe some of us can get there first," says Tommy.

Douglas smiles and laughs.

"Is all that we do an illusion?" asks Philip. "Is this an illusion?"

"It's a collective illusion," says Douglas. "We're all seeing it. We collectively agree on a reality, but the rules we make to enforce that vision are not real."

James passes the skin of wine to Philip. He takes a gulp and gives it to Bobby. Bobby takes a swig and gives it to Joey. Barty also drinks from the skin. Even Mandolin is given some wine.

"Does your destiny parallel the destiny of the Tribes?" asks Tommy.

"Yes," he says. "So does yours."

"Do you think you're *the Messiah?*" asks Tommy. "Is that what you think?"

"No," says Douglas with another laughing smile. He looks into the eyes of his friends.

"What did that old man at the mouth of the river think?"

"He was a teacher of mine."

"I'll bet he was."

"I'm just pointing out a possibility."

"You know how we feel about you," says James.

"We think people in the Holy City are ready to hear you," says his brother, Johnny.

"Where are you leading the people who follow you?" asks Timothy, who does not drink.

"I don't want to lead them anywhere," says Douglas. "I just want to show them something. I don't want them to follow me. I want them to see what I see."

"But they do follow you," says Tommy.

"You cannot be so naive as to imagine that someone could hear you unless they first listen," says Timothy. "For them to listen, they must seek you out. They must follow you."

"If they hear me, they will stop following and find their own way," says Douglas. "When they come to understand this world and find that it is false, they will overcome this world."

"But first they must follow you," says Timothy.

Douglas does not say anything.

"There are two kinds of people in this world, Dougy," says Tommy. "There are leaders and there are followers. How are you gonna set all the followers free? There's only one way."

"And that is to lead," says Timothy.

"And where would you have me lead them?"

"To revolution."

"That's bullshit," says Philip.

"You don't know what the revolution is," says Tommy to shut him up. "And you don't know what he's talking about either," he says, pointing to Douglas. "You let us talk," he continues to Philip. "I'm sick of your pseudo-intellectual bullshit. You're not even a player."

"Fuck-you," says Philip.

"Yea? Fuck-you," answers Tommy.

"Back off," says Douglas.

"See what I mean?" says Tommy, and pointing to Douglas, "Leaders and," pointing to Philip, "followers."

"Fuck-you," says Philip.

"You want to fuck with me?" says Tommy. "I'll fuck you up."

Philip backs off.

"Whatever you do," says Timothy, ignoring what is going on between Tommy and Philip, "you are going to influence a lot of Tribespeople. You are a leader of the Tribes. Do you know what it means to be a leader?"

Douglas locks eyes with him. "It means that when an injustice is done to one man, you feel it as though it were done to you. And you take action, because maybe the guy who was wronged is too weak to take action."

"A natural leader does not shout commands," says Timothy. "He takes action and others follow. Such a man does not make appointments. He attracts volunteers. Some men are natural leaders. Others have leadership thrust upon them after overcoming some societal obstacle or performing a duty. An unnatural authority is alienating. It is not real. It is unworthy of respect. Yours is a natural authority."

"A man must be willing to give up everything," says Douglas, "even his life, or he is not free."

"You must fight for freedom," says Tommy.

"Empires crumble," says Douglas. "The Gods of one era become antiquated and are abandoned for new symbols. Only truth survives. Truth is stronger than all things. The Empire will fall. If we are patient and wise, the Tribes will survive the Empire's destruction. If we are impatient and unwise, the Empire's last breath will blow out the fire of the Tribes. This is a waiting game. If you are impatient, the Empire will fell the Tribes.

"The state is created by men so that they may rule through it. The chief function of the state is to control the masses. Men of state are unnatural leaders. They control the state only for so long as they control the masses. Those with power of the state are fearful men. They know that their power is not real. They know that it is temporal, that they may lose it when a wind blows through the desert, or when the dawn overpowers the night.

"Tommy, Timothy, even if the people do not rise up against the state, the state will die a natural death. It is a child's toy underfoot.

"It may seem that the only path to self-rule is for many to move against the state. But the best path to self-rule is to ignore the state. Better, when you are confronted by the power of state, use it to defeat itself. When the state throws a punch, guide the force of the arm of state so that it throws itself to the ground.

"The danger of the state is that there are many states, forged by different men. To keep power and organize the masses, each state makes enemies of the other states. They create their own order to rule and their own Gods for their subjects to worship. They pit their state against other states and their God against other Gods to distract the masses. The final door to freedom opens when all states fall."

"When all rivers flow in one direction," says Andy.

Tommy looks at Andy with a disgusted scowl.

"That is anarchy," says Timothy.

"I'm talking about free will," says Douglas. "I'm talking about a submersion of ego and revulsion of power."

"We don't have time to wait," says Tommy. "We must defeat the Empire now."

"This is an impatient generation, Tommy," says Douglas. "Everything is now, now, now."

"The Empire is evil," says Timothy. "Surely you must believe that?"

"There is no evil in this world," says Douglas, "only lesser forms of good. When the world started, all was good. When it ends and the world becomes a corpse, all will be good. To return human beings and the world to this natural state of goodness, we must not think we own the world. We must not cling to personal property. It belongs to no one. All in this material world is temporal and illusionary. By pursuing property, we murder the creative and spiritual nature of ourselves. We take the spirit out of our spirit. This is not one man's world. This is one world. *Being* is a portion of itself, as the fire is the spark and the spark is the fire."

"Is there a God?" asks Jimmy A.

"That which you call God is nothing more than a collective consciousness of all living things. There is no separation between man and *Being.* There's no God out there and man here. There's just *the Self,* the truth, the one, *Being."*

"Why do you speak in parables?" asks Tommy.

"It is better to show by example than to preach. If I were just to preach, it would sound arrogant, and no one would listen. Since I would speak the truth, I would sound like what they already know, but which they had not verbalized, and they would resent me for presuming that they do not already know.

"There was a farmer who grew grapes, and his grapes were the purist grapes to be found. His seeds were the best seeds. And he knew that he had the purist grapes. And when it was harvest time, he took his grapes to market and told of their greatness and purity. But his boasts made other farmers jealous and they did not believe him. And the word spread throughout town that his grapes were sour. And so that year, his best year, he sold no grapes and they rotted while he was in town. And when he returned to his vineyard, it was as a desert, because all the vines had been chopped down in the harvest time."

"I see," says Peter.

"To us it has been given to know the secrets of *Being,* but there are many who do not see. Those who have some sight may see more, but those who are in darkness may see even that *Light* fade away, because seeing they do not see, hearing they do not hear, nor do they understand.

"Our eyes are open and we see. Our ears are open and we hear. Many have looked to see what we see, and did not see it and strained to hear what we hear and did not hear it."

Mandolin watches Douglas with growing fondness. She does not understand what he is saying, but she thinks he must be right if so many people are listening. She looks to the shore and there are people watching the boat. Some wave.

Mandolin's Landing

Mandolin wants to find Douglas alone, but he is never alone. Mandolin is always alone, even when she is with someone. That's how Tommy finds her. He sits her down. He sits next to her.

"What are you doing here?" he says in a low tone. "I told you to stay in Shacktown."

"You never want me around," she says. "You only want me for sex."

"Well, maybe if you did what you were told, things'd be different."

"Why should I do what you tell me? You don't love me."

"Is that what you're doing on this boat? Did you come here looking for love?"

"Not from you," she says.

"Oh, I see," he says looking at Douglas, who is with some of the others on the bow. "You know, I don't even know if he likes women." Tommy laughs his silent laugh.

"Very funny."

"I don't want you here," says Tommy, standing. "Case closed. It's nothing personal. Women don't belong in men's business. I want you to get off at the next landing."

"Where would I go? I can't go back to Shacktown. I thought I could, but I can't."

"I'm not responsible for you," says Tommy. "Look at me. I can't even take care of myself. I got nowhere to live when I'm not at the safe house. Just give me a break, will ya? You never should have got on the boat in the first place."

She looks at Douglas. "He said I could come on board."

"That was after the fact. You were already here, what was he gonna say? You're just a stowaway. You don't belong on this boat. This journey began in Swifton."

"What about Timothy?" she says.

"Timothy was in this before Douglas began."

"I'm not getting off," says Mandolin.

"I'll throw you off if I have to. You're getting off at the next landing."

"What if he says I can stay?"

"I don't care what he says. I'm telling you, you can't stay."

"What if I don't listen to you?"

"Don't be a bitch. You'll just piss me off even more. Is that what you want to do?"

"Why don't you love me?"

"Are we gonna go through this again?"

"How many times have we made love?" Mandolin asks with disgust, spitting the taste from her mouth.

"I never made *love* to you," says Tommy.

"Why do you always hurt me?"

Tommy starts to go. "Why do you always let me?" he says. "What do you want? I'm just a guy. That's the way guys are."

"Not all guys," says Mandolin.

"Yea, well, the guys you're talking about don't like girls anyway, so stick a broom in it."

Tommy leaves her alone and Mandolin cries as silently as she can. She looks after Tommy, who is walking to the bow. She looks past him and makes eye contact with Douglas. She shyly looks away.

After a short time of looking at the ground, she hears a voice. "Don't cry," says Douglas. He is standing over her. She smiles. "What's wrong?" he says.

"Nothing."

Douglas sits down where Tommy had been. He touches her on her hand.

"Were you watching?" asks Mandolin.

"I've been watching since you came on board," he says. "Things aren't working out for you two, huh?"

She laughs. It makes them both smile.

"What'd he say to make you cry?"

"He says I have to leave."

"Is that what you want to do?"

"No."

Douglas is silent for a moment. "There's room for you on the boat if you want to stay." he says, patting her hand. "You don't have to do anything you don't want to do."

Mandolin is so happy that she puts her arms around Douglas and kisses him on the cheek.

Douglas smiles. Mandolin is falling in love.

Sedition

Aron paces in Zacharus's office when he returns to the Holy City. He is anxious to tell his father-in-law what he heard along the way.

It suits Zacharus to keep the younger man waiting inside while he is outside. The power is his because the younger man allows him to take it. No matter how long Zacharus keeps him, Aron waits. Zacharus goes in through a secret entrance from the garden.

Aron watches the drapes to the garden blow. He does not know that Loki stands spying behind them. He does not know that while Loki is spying on Douglas, he is also spying on him. Loki has followed the priest back to the Holy City.

Zacharus comes into the office through the door on the other side of the room. He closes it. He looks at his son-in-law. He crosses the room to his desk and sits down.

"Sit," says Zacharus.

Aron sits down.

"So," says the older man, "what have you learned?"

"No 'Hello?'" says Aron. "No 'How have you been?'"

Aron disgusts Zacharus. "What have you learned?" he says.

The son-in-law abandons hope. "He's dangerous. He's getting a following."

"How large is his following?"

"Large. Thousands at some of the spots. People wait for him. They know he's sailing to the Holy City. The closer he came to the river, the larger the crowd grew."

"Is he on the river now? How close is he?"

"I warned him not to come to the Holy City."

"You warned him?"

"I told him he was banned."

"You let him know we were interested in him?"

"It was pretty obvious. He already knew we were interested in him."

It is true enough.

"How close is he?"

"He was in Shacktown when I embarked on my return."

"How many people came back to hear him more than once?" asks Zacharus.

"I don't know. Some, I guess."

"What'd he say?"

"He said that he would lead the Tribes away from the Temple."

"Where will he lead them?

"He did not say."

"Is he a pagan?"

"I don't know if he's a pagan. His philosophy makes no sense. I don't think he believes in any God. He's an atheist."

"Where does he think he came from?"

"I don't know."

"This is blasphemy."

"That's what I told him."

"You told him everything, didn't you?"

"Everything I could think of."

"What else did he say?"

"He compared us to a great landowner. It wasn't to flatter us. He said the people of the Tribes were sheep. He said he would scatter the sheep."

"What else?" asks Zacharus.

"He talked about truth."

"What did he say about truth?"

"He said there was only one truth. He said it was here and

now. He said it was everywhere."

"Who's following him? What are their ages?"

"Kids mostly," says Aron.

"Bastard," says Zacharus. "What else did he say?"

"As I told you before, he spoke with an authority he does not have."

"You told me that?" says Zacharus.

"Yes. We need an angle, an angle like we had on *the Medicine Man.*"

"*The Medicine Man* was a mistake. We don't need another martyr."

"We couldn't have known he'd kill himself," says Aron, not knowing the truth. "How else shall we handle him?"

"Things like this usually have a way of working themselves out."

"What do you mean?"

"With what must be done, we should not talk about it. Wash your hands of this while you can. You are too visible."

"Someday I will be the High Priest."

"Today I'm the High Priest."

Aron is being dismissed. He thinks it is rather abrupt. He leaves anyway.

Zacharus looks at the fireplace. It is dirty. The drapes to the garden move. Loki emerges from his hiding.

"What didn't he tell me?" asks Zacharus, knowing that Aron probably missed noticing something.

"He is definitely coming here."

"Trigger's brother?"

Loki nods.

"To the Holy City?" asks Zacharus.

Loki nods.

"That's bad," says Zacharus. "Tell me about the crowds."

"There were several hundred repeat customers at the shows I saw," says Loki. "A lot of people, I should say kids, went from one port to the next. I kept seeing the same faces. There were some who said that *the Medicine Man* had risen. There were some who said he's the new *Teacher of Righteousness.*"

"It's that same tripe," Zacharus derides. "Bah! Who follows

him?"

"He's got an entourage. There's still a core of about ten guys that are always with him. They're on the boat with him."

"Is it always the same guys?"

"It always is."

"What do these guys do?"

"They're all preachers," says Loki. "They're all prophets. Before they got in the fisherman's boat to sail up the river, they all dispersed and went to different Temples throughout the region. I saw the fisherman and I saw one of the rebels on my way back last time."

"What were they saying?"

"They were all talking about the same thing. They were all talking about truth. The farmer, the fisherman, the rebel, they were all saying the same thing."

"Trigger's the farmer, right?" Loki nods. "Who are the other guys?"

"The fisherman is named Peter. It's his boat. The rebel is Bobby Tarmac."

"I thought you said he wasn't speaking."

"He is now."

"What'd he say about the revolution?"

"He didn't say anything about the revolution. He said, 'the truth is everywhere, but nobody sees it."

"What does that mean?"

"I don't know. I have never seen anything like this. I have never listened to a man like this."

"Would they make him their Chief?" asks Zacharus.

"He is their Chief. He's the Chief of *the Ghosts.*" Loki laughs.

Zacharus is unamused. "What about the rest of his entourage?"

"His brother, Tommy, is one of them. It's the damnedest thing that they're twins. They've got another brother named Joey who is with them. Another rebel, Timothy, was with them in Shacktown. He got on the boat."

"Does he speak?"

"I haven't seen him."

"I don't see Tommy around anymore. Has he been with him

this whole time?"

"Since Douglas Trigger started preaching. I saw them together at *Sarah's Inn.*"

"The rebel bar. How is it we never knew that Tommy had a twin brother?"

"He must not have come to the Holy City before, or maybe he did and we just thought it was Tommy."

"A rebel's brother," says Zacharus. "Is he a rebel?"

"I don't think so. He never talks about the revolution."

"What if I told you he was a terrorist?"

Loki does not hesitate. "Then he's a terrorist."

"What about this other brother, Joey, is he a terrorist?"

"Maybe."

"There aren't going to be any arrests this time. There aren't going to be any more *Medicine Men.* This is the *Temple of the Tribes.* We are not going to give *the Ghosts* any new martyrs to worship."

Loki nods his head.

"I want you to return to the river," says Zacharus. "I want you to pick up his trail. Do you know where he is now?"

Loki thinks about it. "Yes," he says, nodding his head.

"Good. Go there. Come with him to the Holy City."

The Merchant of Commerce

There is a town along the river called Commerce. Douglas and his group stop there at night. Commerce is a greedy town of merchants and traders, almost halfway between Swifton and the Still Sea. John had wanted to save the people of that town and used to baptize them on the river here. Douglas does not stop to speak or to baptize, but to pick up supplies. In his mind he is formulating the parable of the merchant of Commerce.

Many along the river who listen to Douglas once followed John. It is they who anticipate his approach to Commerce and when he and his group disembark, they wait in the harbor for him to speak. He does not stop to speak. He goes into town with Tommy, Timothy, Peter, Andy and Mandolin. Many in the crowd follow.

A man who is not a *Ghost* follows. He is a man in his fifties. He is not like the other people who follow Douglas. He is a merchant and slave trader and a citizen of the Empire. When he sees Douglas, whom he has heard about, he wants to hear him speak. When he does not speak, the Emperor's subject walks quickly to catch up. When the man approaches, Douglas wonders what he wants. He can tell that he wants something.

Tommy looks at him. The man is fat, rich and ugly. His lips are stained with wine, as is the front of his cloak. The man doesn't know what to do when he catches up with Douglas. He takes another swig of wine.

"What do you want?" Douglas says, still walking.

"I have heard of you," answers the merchant, who still follows. "I know who you are."

"What have you heard?" asks Douglas.

The merchant laughs. He says, "Why do all these people follow you?"

"These are my friends," says Douglas.

Tommy does not like the man. He stays quiet.

"You could probably tell these people to do anything and they'd do it," says the citizen, pointing his thumb at the crowd behind them, giggling. "Am I right?"

"You're probably wrong," says Douglas.

"How'd you like to work for me?" says the man. "I could use a man like you to help promote my business to the Tribes in Commerce. I could make you a rich man."

"What is your business?" asks Douglas.

"Slaves," says the man with a smile. "Ætheopian slaves."

Tommy snarls at the man. Douglas looks at Tommy.

"There was a merchant of Commerce," says Douglas, "and he worked all day and night to get money. And when he had so much that it would not all fit in his house, he got a bigger house. And he worked all day and night to get more money to pay for the house. While he worked, others played. He watched his friends get married and have children. And the more money the merchant got, the bigger he built his house. And the bigger he built his house, the more walls he surrounded himself with and the emptier it became. Some of his friends passed away. Some divorced. Some remarried. Some lived happily ever after. And no matter how much money the merchant had, he wanted more. One day he had so much money, that he could not build a house that was big enough, and so he built warehouses for it. On the day that he filled his warehouses, he died."

Knowing the story has been told against him, the merchant

says, "You should not show such disrespect. I am a citizen."

"You get what you give," says Douglas.

"I did not show you disrespect, even though you're just a Tribesman."

"You're a slave trader."

The merchant makes a grunting laugh.

"I feel like I have met you before," he says.

"We have not met before," says Douglas.

"I know you," says the merchant. "You are educated. You think you're better than me even though you're not a citizen. You have not seen this world as I have seen it. I have lived. I have seen this world, my native friend. I practically own it."

"You're just a tourist."

"If I cared to, I could buy and sell you."

"Not me, brother."

"I have a use for a man like you in Commerce," he says. "You ought to be here. This is where you belong. I'll give you a handsome salary. I'll treat you like a citizen!"

"That's very Imperial of you," says Douglas, "but I am not the subject of an Emperor. I am."

Another grunt. "Work for me, and you'll be able to buy the things this life was meant for."

Douglas stops. His friends and the crowd stop behind him. He turns fully to the man for the first time. "I am not worried about this life," he says to the bought man. "I don't think about what I will eat or drink, when I was born or when I will die, will I be rich or will I be poor, will I be brave or a coward. I don't think about my body, or how to cover its nakedness. This life is more than food, clothes and shelter."

"You are a bold man," says the merchant. "I like you. It is too bad we can't do business together."

"I'm not in business," says Douglas.

"Everybody's in business," the citizen laughs. "Everyone has a price. I must tell my friends all that you said tonight."

"You have not heard what I said," says Douglas. "You will plant tares."

He laughs again. "Plant tares? What does that mean? You talk in riddles."

"Then truth is a riddle."

"Truth is a riddle," says the citizen with a laugh. And holding up his skin of wine before chugging it, he says, "Good-day. Have a good stay in Commerce."

The citizen laughs, drinks, and breathes a sigh of envy as he walks away. He remembers Douglas's face. "Youth," he says with lust, remembering his own. He walks back to the harbor. The others wait for Douglas to start moving again so they can follow him.

A False Prophet

It is the Day of Rest. There is a Temple in Commerce. Douglas and his entourage gather with the local Tribespeople, not to speak, but to listen. The speaker is an older man, a priest. "We are all sinners waiting to be judged by an angry God!" he says.

"I'm a little upset myself," whispers Tommy.

"The Lord God is a jealous God and avenging," the priest continues, reading from *the Book of the Tribes,* "The Lord God is avenging and wrathful. The Lord God takes vengeance on his enemies and for them he preserves his wrath. The Lord God is slow to anger and great of might, and by no way will he absolve the guilty of their sins. His way is a whirlwind and it is a storm, and the clouds are the dusts of his feet. He rebukes the sea and makes it dry. He dries up all the rivers. The mountains quake before him! The hills sink! The earth is laid waste before him, the world and all those living in it! Who can stand before his indignation? Who can endure the heat of his anger? His wrath is poured out like fire, and he breaks the rocks asunder.

"'The Lord God knows who takes refuge in him. He will make a full end of all who oppose him with an overflowing flood and will pursue his adversaries into darkness.

"'Behold, I am against you,' says the Lord, 'and I will burn your chariots in smoke, and the sword will devour your young lions. I will cut off your prey from the Earth and the voice of your prophets will sound no more.'

"'Woe to the bloody City, the Harlot City, graceful and of deadly charms, who betrays the Nations with her harlotry, and people with her charms all full of lies and booty---no end to the plunder. And all who look on her will shrink from her and say, 'Wasted is the Holy City. Who will bemoan her? Whence shall I seek comforters for her?'" The priest closes *the Book of the Tribes.*

"And is Commerce any better?" continues the priest. "Repent while you still can! The Lord God is unforgiving. Get down on your knees and beg the Lord for forgiveness! Cry out in the forest of temptation for absolution and God may forgive you."

Douglas's silence is wiser than the fool's oratory.

The Promise

Douglas sits in a corner of the boat alone with Timothy. It is night. They are sailing again.

"Will you fight for freedom?" asks Timothy.

At first Douglas doesn't say anything. Then he says, "What is freedom?"

Timothy smiles. Douglas is already a man who knows about freedom. "This is freedom," Timothy says, motioning at the world around him. "This river, this air, this life is freedom. But there are those who have taken it from us. And we must stop those men. We must regain our freedom. We must take what is ours. We must regain *God's Promise.*"

"*God's Promise...*" muses Douglas.

"It is a place we can call our own. It is a place given to us by God. It is a place where we can be free. It is the restoration of our own Tribal lands, free of this occupation."

"We are free. You said it yourself. And if *this* is freedom," says Douglas, pointing to the world about him, "why must we fight?"

"Because when we step on that shore, we are not free," says Timothy. "It becomes an Imperial shore, an occupied shore. On the river, there is no time, but when we step on the shore we are back in time. We are back in the masses. We are back in the Empire."

"You don't want to be one of the masses, do you?" asks Douglas.

"I am not one of the masses, anymore than you are," says Timothy. "And you can never free the masses, because they will start to follow whoever frees them and then they will be in chains again. The best you or I can hope to do is lead them."

"You want them to follow you," says Douglas.

"No more than you do. If you did not want them to follow, you would not lead them. Where will you lead them?"

"I had this conversation with Tommy," says Douglas. "Why do you want them to follow you?"

"I want this land to be free for the next generation. It is our duty. I want it to be free for me. This is *God's Promise.* Our Kingdom is not somewhere else. I believe it is here and now. I believe we must take it."

"You cannot take freedom by force," says Douglas. "Freedom is truth. Truth is freedom. What investment do you have in the future? Do you have any children?"

"No, I do not," says Timothy. And he points to the far away masses. "But they do."

Douglas smiles. "Do you think it makes sense to die for somebody else's future?"

"It is the only thing that does make sense," says Timothy. "We must fight for justice. We must be willing to die for it."

"These are noble thoughts," says Douglas. "You are an honorable man. Do you do it to be remembered?"

"I do it because I must."

"Do you think you'll be remembered?"

"I will be remembered," says Timothy.

"Will you be remembered with love or scorn?" asks Douglas.

He thinks about it. "Probably with scorn. It is the nature of man to scorn the one they love, to scorn that which they follow to such a point that it takes away their own freedom, their own self. I am getting old, Tommy's brother."

"You're not so old. How long will you fight for freedom?"

"This is a game for the young," says Timothy. "It is for you and Tommy."

"You don't believe that," says Douglas. "You're still fighting.

That's why you're with me, isn't it? You want me to follow you."

"I want you to lead," says Timothy.

"You want me to lead them to you."

"I will not lie to you, Douglas. That is exactly what I want. That is what Tommy wants. That is what you should want."

"Why should I want it?"

"It is our only chance."

"Timothy, what you look for is everywhere, but you do not see it. You are already free."

"Tommy told me about your truth," says Timothy. "You are right, I do not see it. I do not want to see it. I have my own vision. I have my own idea of freedom."

"You are already free."

"This is the Struggle," says Timothy.

"What do you do when your Struggle is over?" asks Douglas.

"You die."

"Are you willing to die?"

"Everybody is going to die," says Timothy "If you die in the Struggle, the Tribes will be free."

"I won't lead the Tribes to you, Timothy."

"Then you will lead them away from me."

"Freedom comes from within. You or I do not grant it. It is not granted by any outside order. We are not subject to anyone. No government can put you in bondage or set you free."

"Under the Empire's authority, there are citizens and there are slaves. It's like that asshole from Commerce. Do you think you are much better off than a slave?"

"You must operate under your own authority."

"I do. I operate under the assumption that you have to be willing to fight for freedom. You have to be willing to die."

"Are you willing to die?" asks Douglas.

"Every day," says Timothy.

"Why?"

"It is better to die a free man at an early age than to grow old in fetters."

"You fight in fetters," Douglas says. "What you fight controls you."

"Why will you not follow me?" asks Timothy.

"You're only a follower yourself," says Douglas. "You follow the Empire."

"I fight the Empire."

"You follow. You're not going to change anything by defeating the Empire. You're just going to start things all over again."

"At least we will be in charge."

"What are you in charge of? This is a temporal life. Nothing is real here. If it is real, then we are nothing."

"The Empire is real. Oppression is real. Imperialism is real. It must be fought."

"What if nobody wants to fight your revolution?"

"They must be made to want to fight. That is what you can do."

"I don't want them to fight. I want them to love."

"Love who?"

"Love their enemy."

"Then they have no enemy."

"Exactly."

"You have to have enemies," says Timothy, "otherwise you do not stand for anything."

"And if you gain power, what will you do to maintain it?"

"This is not about personal power," says Timothy. "It is about freedom. You are too idealistic. You are not practical. This is a dark world in which a man consumes or is consumed. Your followers are not free, and when they realize it, they will turn against you."

"Why do people follow other people?"

"Because they cannot see what we see," says Timothy. "They want us to show it to them."

"Do you see what I see?"

"I do not even want to look," says Timothy. "How do you feel about all these people who follow you?"

"It makes me uncomfortable. I have no personal life. I don't want to make anymore stops on the river. I just want to get to the Holy City."

"I never saw a man in such a hurry to die for nothing. You

have to make trouble, but it is the wrong kind of trouble. You cannot walk away from this, can you?"

"I guess not. Maybe it is my destiny. I started something. I have to finish."

"If you could do it all over again, is there anything you would change?"

"Maybe. Maybe I just would have stuck to the farm. Maybe I would have just been a fisherman. Maybe I would have been a priest. But I don't think I could change how I feel."

"I did not think so," says Timothy. "We are both men of destiny. It is my destiny to lead this Struggle. What I have not figured out yet is why our two paths crossed."

"You think our destinies have brought us together?"

"Yes," says Timothy. "Let me tell you your destiny, kid."

"Go ahead," says Douglas.

"You are the sheep the other sheep follow," he says. "But you do not know where you are going. Someday you are going to lead them all off a cliff."

"That's what you think?"

"Yes. What do you think?"

"Someday you will be defeated. Someday there will be no more Tribes. Someday your sheep will be scattered. Yours is a bloody revolution. Mine is a bloodless one."

"My destiny is to be free," says Timothy.

"I am free," says Douglas. "Are you free, Timothy?"

"Not yet."

"You will never be. Even if you defeat the Empire, you will not be free."

Timothy pats the younger man on his shoulder. "I like you, Tommy's brother. You are an honest man. You are a good man. I can tell. I know you believe what you are telling me, what you tell the crowds. I realize now that we two will not change. I knew my destiny when I was younger than you are. We are not free, Douglas. Unless I try to be free, I can have no pride."

"You cannot gain freedom by changing manmade rules."

"We will live in freedom when *God's Promise* is fulfilled," says Timothy.

"You do not see it," Douglas sighs. He leans his head back

and looks up at the night sky.

"Huh?"

Mandolin watches them from a hiding place. She wants to be with Douglas.

Born Again

The Ghosts gather for Douglas Trigger at the river outside the Holy City. It is where they know he will go. This is where John spoke. This is where Douglas had come out of the desert. This is where he would come again.

"Look at them," says Tommy, as the boat sails by the crowd along the shore, "like sheep without a shepherd."

"There must be thousands of them," says Bobby.

"There are more people than ever came to see John," says Andy.

"*The Ghosts* are yours," says Timothy. "Be a shepherd to your sheep."

"I don't want sheep," says Douglas. "I want wolves. I want to scatter the flocks."

"Wolves travel in packs of hunters. Hunters are fighters. Fighters are warriors."

"They are warriors whose arrow is truth. Freedom cannot be taken by force."

Douglas Trigger stares at the crowd of people on the shore. He remembers an earlier time when John was still alive.

It is dawn. The morning is warm. John and Andy are in the river.

John pushes Andy under the river and the water washes

over him. Andy is submerged and holds his breath in the river. The currents flow around him, though none are so strong that they disturb him. In the water, Andy washes away the world. He goes away from John and all that breathe air. He does not want air. He goes away from the body. He comes to know that which is the same in all things. He is free.

John's hands leave Andy's shoulders and reach under his arms to lift him out of the water. Rising, Andy replants his feet on the bed of the river and starts to breathe again, taking in big gulps of air, as if breathing for the first time. Dripping, he turns to look at the man who has pulled him out of the water. He smiles.

John smiles as he helps Andy out of the river. He waves at Douglas and Peter who are on the shore with Philip and Barty.

John is average looking in a good way. Women are attracted to him, but he doesn't put off men. His clothes are wet and ragged. His hair is fair.

Thousands of people wait on shore for John and Andy. They make a thunderous sound. Some have come from the Holy City to be by the water. Others have come from different parts of the river to be there. Others have come from places farther away. They are applauding, cheering him on. Andy cannot stop smiling. He begins to breathe normally.

Andy looks at the people who have come to hear John, *the Ghosts.* Though the name was first used by the priests of the Temple of the Tribes of the Holy City and meant to be derisive, many of John's followers like it and refer to themselves as *Ghosts.* If these are the dead, then this is Elysium.

Many of *the Ghosts* are camped out and look like they have been at the river for several days. Some of them are playing games. Others are singing and dancing. Some are just arriving. They will probably stay for several days.

The majority of *Ghosts* are very young. Many of them are not yet out of their teens. This, more than anything else, is what frightens the priests of the Temple of the Tribes of the Holy City. It is why they coined the phrase *'Ghosts.'*

"What we do here in this time is important," John says to Douglas when they reach the shore. "We're on a clean-up operation. We don't want to have to come back and do this again."

Peter doesn't know what to think of his brother. He looks at John. He asks, "Why do they listen to you?"

"Because of what I say. I say what they already know, but have covered up. I say what has always been known. There is only one truth."

"What is truth?" asks Peter.

"First, know *the Self*," says John, "then you will know *the Self* in all things, then you will know truth."

Others on shore continue to applaud and cheer Andy's baptism. He feels the water drip down his back.

"So now I'm baptized, huh?" asks Andy.

"You tell me," John says.

Andy laughs. "Yup," he says with a glow. "How many people have you baptized?"

"I don't know," says John. "Not many. Most people just get wet. They go down into the water and come up without having received anything."

"Why are they still clapping?" He points to the crowd, who are still applauding and cheering. As they look around, they can see that the throng is also smiling.

"They're clapping for you," says John. "Wave or something."

Andy waves.

The applause recedes.

"It's kind of cultist, isn't it?" Douglas says with a smile.

"Nah," says John, laughing. He shakes his head. He looks at Douglas. "I feel I've done all I can do here. I sense my end. I'm starting to piss off the wrong people." He points to Zacharus and Aron who are in the crowd. "It will take another *Voice* to travel further down this road."

"Don't talk like that."

"I think it will be your *Voice*," John says to Douglas. "I also sense your beginning."

"You're gonna be around for a while," says Douglas.

Now that the applause has died down, *the Ghosts* begin to surround John and the others. People Andy doesn't know are patting him on his back. "Welcome, brother," they say. Douglas laughs and looks at John, who just smiles.

"Very cultist," says Douglas.

"So's the Temple," says John.

As the applause dies down, John starts to move through the crowd to shake hands and do the schmoozing that is a part of his charm. Douglas, Peter, Andy, Philip and Barty follow him.

People Douglas has never met before all want a piece of John. "Heal me," says one. And John smiles and shakes her hand.

"Help me," says another. And John smiles and shakes his hand.

As the crowd swells around John, it becomes harder for Douglas and the others to stay at his side. Someday, with Douglas, they will perfect the technique of totally surrounding their charge. This is not that day.

Douglas and Peter have sailed down from Swifton to see John. Douglas needed to get seeds from *the Settlement* and Peter wanted to find Andy, who left home several months before to visit *the Settlement,* which he'd heard about from Douglas. Recently, Peter had received a report that his brother had left *the Settlement* to follow John.

Peter wants his brother back on the boat. He wants him back in the family business. He has come to get him. Besides, Peter is curious. He knows John. He has met him a couple of times over the years. He's heard about him. He wants to hear him. You would too.

"You look wet," says Peter, teasing his brother.

Andy is still dripping. "I am wet," he says laughing, "very wet."

"So you're baptized?" asks Peter.

"Yea."

Peter doesn't know what it means to be baptized. He doesn't want to know. He is uneasy.

"You one of *the Ghosts?*" Douglas asks Philip, whom he has just met.

"Yea," says Philip. "I guess."

"I just met him myself," Peter whispers to Douglas.

"He's a new friend," says Andy.

"Definitely cultist," Douglas whispers to John with a smile.

"Are you a fisherman too?" Philip asks Douglas.

"I don't know," Douglas laughs at Peter, "Am I a fisherman?"

Peter smiles. "He's more like an advocate for the fish."

Douglas laughs. He looks back into the crowd who has come to hear John. Some of them are still unpacking their bedrolls. They are settling in for a day or two. They want to be baptized. They want to become *Holy Ghosts*. These are the young ones. This is what their generation is doing. This is their party.

Tommy's Eyes

Tommy and his dogs are also at the river this day. He has come to hear John for the first time and Bobby Tarmac has tagged along with the other strays. Tommy wipes the scowl from his eyes and tries to smile. He sees John. "That's him, Bobby. That's *the Medicine Man.*"

The dogs settle. They are good in crowds. Tommy is not so good in a crowd. He doesn't like being a part of someone else's audience. He takes his syrinx out of his belt and blows into it, his fingers dancing along its edge. Some of *the Ghosts* turn towards him to listen.

Tommy looks out from the crowd at John. He takes the syrinx out of his mouth and looks at it. "Lieutenant," he says to Bobby with a sigh, "I don't know if I want to blow this pipe anymore."

"I don't blame ya," says Bobby. "I don't know if I want to hear you."

Tommy doesn't laugh. He looks like he has come to sheer the fleece off of another man's sheep. *The Ghosts* who have been listening to him turn away when he stops playing. Even the stray dogs plop their heads down and lose interest.

Tommy wets his dry lips and rests the syrinx in his mouth again. As he blows into the pipe, his eyes scan the crowd. He cannot believe how far back the crowd goes. Some of *the*

Ghosts start to listen again. He stops blowing. He puts the syrinx in his belt and opens and closes his right fist in a tightening motion. When he no longer plays his instrument, *the Ghosts* become afraid and go away from him.

Tommy's eyes burn so that they are all you can see. He looks at John with competition.

"Where will he stand on the Empire question?" asks Tommy.

"Where all of his kind stands," says Bobby, "down the middle."

"The Struggle must continue," says Tommy.

"It must escalate," says Bobby. "Now is the time for increased pressure."

"We must find a voice who will lead."

John is about to speak and the crowd starts to settle in. When Tommy looks at John again, he notices he has an entourage. He notices his brother for the first time. It is his twin. It is Douglas. He has not seen him in almost twenty years. It is like seeing his reflection.

Bobby also sees him. "Isn't that your brother?" he says.

"I don't have a brother."

Temple Eyes

Further back in the crowd other eyes watch John. They are the eyes of the priests of the Temple of the Tribes of the Holy City. Zacharus and Aron are both at the river this day, accompanied by Temple Guards. Loki is also at the river in a different part of the crowd. They are all overwhelmed by John's following.

John feels the Temple eyes upon him. When he looks back to Zacharus, the older man turns away. Zacharus does not see Douglas.

"Look at these children," Zacharus says, more to himself than to Aron. "They're mesmerized."

"Doped up is more like it," says Aron, who also seems mesmerized, but for different reasons. *"Medicine Man!"* he says with derision.

Zacharus ignores his son-in-law. As he looks through the crowd, he sees Tommy with another rebel. Aron does not notice them. He has come to the river to trap John. He is a pendent. It is how he maintains control. He misuses the Law of the Tribes for his own purposes. Phantom wheels are spinning recklessly inside his little head. They roll over John. They bring Aron greater glory.

"The crowd is quiet," says Zacharus. "He's about to speak."

"How shall we trap him?" asks Aron, focusing more intently

on John. "What Law shall he break?"

Zacharus is not listening. He is looking at the rebels. Tommy feels the eyes upon him and scans the crowd until he finds the stare. He recognizes Zacharus. He does not acknowledge him. Zacharus stares him down.

Zacharus is uneasy. There are rebels in *the Medicine Man's* movement. And though most rebels are righteous men, there is something about Tommy that Zacharus doesn't trust.

The Son of Light plays his syrinx again and some of *the Ghosts* come back to him. Tommy makes a count of the number of Imperial soldiers in the crowd.

Aron is drawing a blank. "How shall we trap him?"

The younger priest is always asking his questions out loud because he can never come up with the answers in silence. Most times, Zacharus ignores him. This time is no different.

"How shall he indict himself?" Aron asks.

An Imperial soldier is chewing on something and he spits it out. The swill lands near Aron's foot. He doesn't do anything.

Like everyone else, Zacharus waits for the event to begin. Aron keeps asking questions he cannot answer.

Awake

John is reluctant to begin. It is not that he is unsure about what he will say. He has made the same speech before. It is just that every time he opens his mouth, he digs himself in deeper.

The Ghosts who have come to hear John can sense that he is about to speak. They know what he will say. They have heard the speech before. It is why they are here. It is why they are *Ghosts.* John says what they already know.

John's teaching is a call for spiritual change. He preaches for all to take ownership of their past wrongs, to seek amends from those they have wronged, to change course and renounce greed and the material world, to die to this world and be reborn, to become one with nature and to see truth. He says that his won't be the last *Voice* to sing this song. He says nature will always find a *Voice.* It is the song of *the Hierophant.*

The Voice springs up from nature like steam springs up from a geyser. But if human beings live as one with nature, then the pressure is relieved and there is no need for *the Voice.* The veil is dropped and all can see truth and hear the song of *the Self* and live in a *Garden.*

John faces the multitude to speak. The river flows behind him.

"Awake!" he shouts, as if angry, to startle the crowd, to get them going. "The truth is free to all who see. The illusions of this world will melt away! Let me try to tell you what I see." All eyes are on him. John seems like a madman. He is more animated than Douglas will be. He stretches his eyes out to look at the throng. There are all types of people at the river. The crowd is completely silent.

"Born in a sheathe of *Light*," John continues his impassioned oratory, "Shall we bathe in the night? Out of the dark wilderness comes a shaft of *Light!* Out of the dark night comes *the Hierophant*."

The crowd cheers and applauds. This is his audience. But even so, scattered throughout the crowd, there are those who will not hear. There are those who will not listen. Aron is such a man.

"The time has come to stop him," the priest says to his father-in-law. "This crowd is too silent when they listen to him. They applaud when they should be jeering."

Zacharus is not listening to Aron. He already knows what John is saying. He has heard it before, but never like this. He sees Douglas. He looks back over at Tommy. The High Priest is alarmed. Tommy is watching John, or is he watching Douglas?

"This I know," continues John, "because I have lived in the wilderness. And I have lived alone. And I know the oneness which pervades all *Being*." The crowd listens. "Now is the time to prepare for what is to come, the revelation of truth! We live in an immoral society. We live without ideals, without honor, without connection to each other. Such a society cannot last long. Soon, every valley will be lifted up. Every mountain and hill will be brought low. The crooked will be made straight. The rough ways will be made smooth. When the truth is revealed, flesh will melt away. We are one Tribe!"

The crowd applauds.

"Whenever natural law is usurped by the Law of man, then a *Voice* will rise up from nature itself to guard righteousness, to banish all that's not true, to re-establish natural law, age after age. Millennium after millennium, wherever there are lies, only the truth survives. The truth is always known!"

The crowd applauds. They eat it up.

"The time of *the Hierophant* has come," continues John. *"The Voice* is like a door that opens when it speaks and closes when it stops. *The Voice* is an invitation to go through the door and become *Being.* Walk through the door while it is open.

"Who will save the world if you do not save it? Who will save you if not yourself?" John pauses. The crowd cheers. After awhile, he interrupts them again. "Do not be subservient. Always question. I'm talking about a revolution!" They cheer again. Tommy and Bobby look at each other. They look at Douglas.

"Don't do what you're told to do, simply because someone tells you to do it," John says. "Do not bow your head, raise it! If you look into the eyes of your enemy long enough you will see the center that pervades all *Being.* Do not still your *Voice,* raise it! Become aware of it!" The crowd applauds.

"Freedom does not exist under any government's rule. Freedom exists under one's own rule.

"Freedom is not tangible. It does not exist in the lessons of a scribe. It is not in any government document. No manmade religion can give it to you. Freedom is truth. It comes from within. It is not granted by any outside order.

"There are free men and women in the Tribes. There are free men and women who are citizens of the Empire. Freedom exists in undiscovered countries. Freedom exists wherever beings are strong enough to see truth and say, *'I am free. I am Being.'*

"Sovereignty is not gained by changing any earthly order. All orders are the same. All governments are the same. Some may seem to give freedom, and others may seem to limit freedom, but liberty cannot be granted by any government. Governments issue their own truths and thus, limit freedom. Freedom comes to those who see it. Prisoners of the Empire, waiting to die, can see truth and say, 'I am free.' The slaves of the Empire can see truth and say, 'I am free."

"As we grow older, we become caricatures of ourselves. We develop a philosophy and risk drowning in it, becoming increasingly narrow-minded. Let us hope that the young model upon which we base our life is free, for if it is not, we become prisoners in a deliberate world of imposed order which we allow to rule our sacred lives. We live in a time when we must be increasingly willing to take control. Our leadership has brought us to an age of destruction."

Aron looks to the Imperial soldiers to see what they do. They aren't going to do anything.

"This generation is in peril. It's getting darker all the time. We will not survive an extended night. When a tree is rotting, we chop it down with an axe and burn it. Folks, it's time to strike down rotting foundations to build again. When *the Hierophant* speaks, listen. When the word is said, hear. If you are moved, be moved. The farmer goes into his orchard, and to those trees that produce no fruit, he gives the most dung. If you have ears, listen!"

The crowd applauds. John becomes silent. After a moment of quiet, he continues, "Our leaders are corrupt technocrats interested only in the perpetuation of their own power. They care nothing about the people." John sees Aron in the crowd. He points at him. Others follow his stare and his finger pointing. It alarms Zacharus. "Like well-fed lambs, we worship megalomaniacs who control systems of government they do not understand. Such men would have us pledge allegiance to their Empire, or chant prayers to their God. This we will not do."

The crowd cheers again.

"We will not pay tribute to their Empire, or pay taxes to their church, or offer sacrifices on the altars of the Temple of the Tribes. They will not grow fat while we grow lean. Our political and spiritual leadership is fat. The people starve! The Great Chief lacks the moral authority to lead. He's an adulterer and a puppet of the Emperor, who was installed and remains in power through assassination!"

The crowd cheers and applauds.

"He's attacking the Great Chief," Aron says to the elder priest. "He's attacking the Emperor. He's a rebel."

"He's an anarchist," says Zacharus. "It will be his undoing."

Loki wishes he had instructions. He wants new orders.

"Don't be led to your slaughter by outside forces you can

control," John cries out. "Take charge of your destiny. When *the Hierophant* speaks, listen. Every human being can be as free as he or she chooses to be!"

John has said enough. His speech is over. He turns away from the mob and looks at the river. When the crowd realizes it is over, they cheer still louder. There is the sound of thunder from them.

Destiny

It is the last time Douglas is with John. They walk alone along the shore of the river and talk about his destiny.

"What are you gonna do now?" asks John.

"I'm gonna go to *the Settlement,* pick up some seed and head back to the farm."

"Go into the desert first."

"The desert?"

"Your journey begins there." John taps Douglas's chest. "Your journey begins here."

"I know," he says. "My journey began a long time ago."

"Do not think about what you will find in the desert. It will find you. You will find solitude. You will know that which is hidden in plain sight."

"It will be a solitude I have never had," Douglas considers. "It will be a solitude I cannot find at *the Settlement,* a solitude I cannot find with Peter on his boat, a solitude I cannot find with my brothers on the farm."

"A man must turn his back on the illusions of this world. He must shed everything he has been told is true. He must die and be reborn with fresh eyes. Fast in the desert and be one with your *Self* and all that is known will be known. A human being must first know *the Self* before it can see *the Self* in others. A human being must look to *the Self* to know where his or her path may go. While you are in the desert, find your true path and fully know your destiny."

"You think you know my destiny," says Douglas. "But even I don't know my destiny. No man can fully know his destiny."

"I had a dream that you had sprung up from *the Garden,*" says John, "You started speaking and your *Voice* was loud and strong. You were very ordinary, but you spoke like one from nature with a divine wisdom. And when you spoke, people listened. You wanted to free them, but they wouldn't free themselves. They wanted to be your slaves. They wanted to follow you, but you would not lead them. You wanted them to be free. They wanted you to rule over them in an everlasting *Kingdom of Truth.* But there is nothing everlasting in this world. There is nothing temporal when we fall away from it. Those who follow cannot be free and when you would not become their master, the crowd turned on you and stoned you. And in my dream, those who would kill you would come to worship you."

"That's some dream."

"What if it's not a dream? What if your destiny is to walk a path with me? What if you walk a path where others follow you? What if you're *the Voice* I've been talking about? What if you're *the Hierophant?*"

"I don't want anyone to follow me."

"If it is your destiny, it will happen."

"Let them follow you."

"Time is starting to run against me. If it is your destiny to travel the path I'm on, what will you do?"

Douglas cannot answer. The last drops of water are evaporating from John's cloak. Douglas sighs. "What if I don't accept my destiny?" he says.

"If you allow what is in you to come out, you will be at peace. If you allow what is outside you to seep in, then it will control you and you will be in discord with *Being.* Recognize what you already know and that which is within you will be revealed and the hidden will be unhidden and nothing will be covered which will not be uncovered. You must accept your destiny or live without peace. You will not be free. You're the one. You're *the Voice.* You're *the Hierophant.* It's you."

The Rebel's Field

It is almost a year later. A lot has happened in that year.

Douglas stands on Peter's anchored boat and stares at the shore where the crowd continues to gather. He is in a daydream. The audience quiets, waiting for him to speak, just like they quieted for John so long ago.

His friends and Mandolin are sitting away from him, watching him watch the crowd. Tommy wonders what his twin is thinking. He is wondering why it isn't him the crowd is coming to see.

"It is the end," says Peter.

"The end of what?" says Tommy.

"The end of the river." Peter does not look at Tommy. He looks up to Douglas. "This is it. We're almost in the Holy City."

"What do you think he's gonna say?" asks Philip.

"He's gonna say what he always says," says Tommy.

"What's that?" asks Peter.

"He's gonna say that we're free." says Tommy.

"We are free," says Peter.

"Not me," says Tommy. "He has you brainwashed."

"We are all free," says Andy.

"Dullards," says Tommy. "Swifton dullards. Nothing is free."

Douglas leans over the side of the boat and looks at the water. The people on the shore all know who he is. They wonder what he will say.

"He looks like he's about to puke," says Tommy, watching Douglas.

Bobby laughs at the joke.

Douglas stands up in the boat and turns away from the multitude. Tommy gets his attention.

"What bits are you gonna do?" he asks.

"The Rebel's Field," says Douglas.

"That new?" asks Tommy. "Do I know it?"

"There was a farmer," says Douglas, "who raised his sons to be like him---rebels. He trained them like he trained the wheat in the good ground in his fields. As each turned sixteen, he gave them a sword. And they were told that the land was theirs and they should fight for it. And each in turn went off to fight a foreign despot who laid claim to the land. And each in turn never came home.

"The farmer was left with no sons to help him sow or harvest. And he realized what he had done to his sons, what he had sown in them, and he knew that he never should have tried to possess them like he tried to possess the land. He realized that no man could own the land or the sky or the sun or the wind or another's *Being.* He knew he should have raised his sons without expectations and judgment.

"That season, the wheat grew wild in his field. He did not harvest it, not because the task was too much, but because the wheat was not his. The seed was not his. He did not plant it. All that was his he already possessed. That which was not his he could never own."

Douglas is done.

"Good bit," says Tommy, "but why don't you tell another one?" He motions for Douglas to sit down. "Sit down," he says.

The crowd settles. They wait for him to speak. Douglas does not sit down.

"What does that story mean?" asks Peter.

Douglas looks at Peter. He blinks. "There was a farmer who raised his sons to be like him," he says and repeats the story verbatim. He finishes the story again and is silent. The crowd onshore is silent. They are waiting for him to speak to them.

"But you just repeated what you said," says Philip.

"I can't tell you what it means," says Douglas. "I can only show you."

The crowd waits for him on the edge of the beach.

"Why don't you support the revolution?" asks Tommy. He points to the shore. "See the bank of the river?" he says. "It is what keeps the river in. If I was the water in this river, I'd break the bank. Take the theater in the Holy City. Haven't we had enough Games? If I had my way, I'd tear the walls down. I'm talking about a revolution."

"I'm also talking about a revolution," says his twin, "but I'll tell you about my revolution. It isn't Tribal warrior against Imperial soldier. It isn't rock against spear. It is not a game where someone loses. It is not a game at all.

"Power is something the Empire thinks it has, but it is something you give them. It is something you want. You can only have power over someone for so long as they give it to you. If you were not to acknowledge the Empire, it would lose its authority over you."

"I would be beheaded."

"You would be free," says Douglas. "Have you ever felt what it feels like to be free? The Empire is a parasite. Those who maintain it, do so for power and money. They're all parasites, feeding off a parasite. Those who operate governments get power and money at the expense of others. They live off the sweat of their brothers. They rest while others toil. They eat great feasts and waste their spoil. The poor are hungry. A fight will broil."

Tommy wants to say something, but he does not know what. He looks at Timothy.

"Freedom does not come from any government," says Douglas. "It is not in the Gods of the Empire. It is not in the Law of the Tribes. Freedom comes to those who see it. Men of Skull Hill can see truth and say, 'I am free.'"

"Why do you say what you say?" asks Timothy.

"I feel compelled to say what I say. If I could, I would just walk away."

Tommy says, "If you're not gonna help us, do you have to

hurt us? How about not doing that bit today?"

"That's the bit I'll be doing."

Tommy and Timothy exchange a *'How can we stop this guy?'* look.

Douglas walks to the edge of the boat to face the throng. He's going to talk to them from the boat. The river's shore is quieter than if there were no crowd at all. He thinks about what he will say. He thinks about *the Rebel's Field.*

The Swimmer

When they enter the Still Sea, Douglas has Peter dock his boat at the port near *the Settlement*. Douglas stands on the deck and looks at the pier. The others look over the boat with him. There is no one there to greet them. They have come far enough.

Mandolin puts her arms around Douglas to hold him. Douglas holds her too. Tommy watches them with disgust.

"I have to go," Douglas whispers. He turns to say goodbye to the others. "I'll meet you guys in the Holy City," he says to Peter. "I have business in this port."

"Can I go with you?" asks Mandolin.

"No."

"Is it a woman?" she asks.

"No," says Douglas.

The others watch him.

"How long will you be?" asks Peter.

"I don't know," says Douglas. "Just meet me at the inn."

"What inn?" asks Peter.

"I know what inn," says Tommy. "You want me and Timothy to go with you?"

"Thanks, no. I won't need your help where I'm going."

"Are you going to the cliffs?" asks Andy.

"Yes."

"For how long?" asks Peter.

"I don't know," says Douglas.

"Why are you going there?" asks Andy.

"To see Ælfric."

"Do you think he's back?"

"I think he is."

"Do you want me to go with you?" asks Andy.

"No. I'll meet you in the Holy City. I'll meet you at the inn."

"You want me and Johnny to go with you?" asks James.

"No."

Douglas jumps over the side of the boat onto the dock. Andy watches him go. The others watch also. Mandolin watches him.

"What is in the cliffs?" Mandolin asks Andy.

"He's not me, you know," Tommy interrupts.

"I know."

He grunts and walks away from her. *"The Settlement,"* Andy says.

"Well," says Peter, "What are we gonna do?"

"I am going ashore for a drink," says Timothy. "It will be some time before your brother arrives in the Holy City."

The port city is not far from the mouth of the river. Douglas walks through its streets unaccosted. In this port, they are used to such men. He likes the anonymity of it.

Douglas is thinking about what he is doing, without paying attention to where he is going. Somehow, he is guiding himself through the port crowd.

He walks by an inn and hears his name. It stops him where he stands in the street.

"He gets up at the Temple like he owns the joint," someone is saying, "He then proceeds to talk as if possessed, as if he has ultimate authority. It's those priests, I tell you. Nothing good comes out of here."

Douglas keeps walking. He smells fresh bread baking. He follows its direction. He finds a baker. He buys two loaves.

Douglas heads for the cliffs of *the Settlement* where he had come to seek truth and study in his youth. He wants to see his old teacher, Ælfric.

Douglas remembers those days:

"And so," says Ælfric, "what have you learned?"
"I still see the way I always do, but now I know the rules."

The cliffs of *the Settlement* are away from the Holy City, away from the port, in the desert. As Douglas enters the desert, a wind blows through urging him not to go. He treks deeper into the desert, the sand flying in his eyes, blinding him. Still, he knows he must go onward.

The storm grows worse so that he has to keep his face completely covered. He cannot tell east from west, but on he has to go. And when the storm sees that he will not yield, it dissipates as quickly as it arose.

It was in this desert that Douglas had found *the Self.*

He remembers: 'I need no man's bread.'

Douglas holds the bread in his hands. He feels the water. He walks alone. He walks deeper into the desert.

'There is no peace at *the Settlement,*' he remembers. 'There is only academic politics.'

The Settlement is still a journey to go. Douglas looks up at the sun and it seems hotter. He feels a growing sweat on his brow. The only vegetation in this part of the desert is a tree and it is on fire. That's hot.

Douglas stops when he sees the tree. He watches it. He does not approach it. He wonders at it. He moves on.

The Self is the same in all *Being. The Self* in the man looks up and that which is the same in all things becomes a bird sailing above the horizon. *The Self* flies above it all, preying off the flesh of those who crawl. *The Self* also crawls.

The Self flies on to the cliffs. And the first man that *the Self* sees *the Self* becomes. And when *the Self* inhabits the man, there is a hole, a longing, an absence, a missing essence. *The Self* is alone. Ælfric is dead.

The feeling snaps *the Self* out of the man, and Douglas Trigger is himself again in the desert. He stops. The birds that have stayed are there too. He looks ahead to the cliffs of *the Settlement.* He sets himself in quicker motion towards it.

Before Douglas can get to *the Settlement,* there is a sudden hailstorm in the desert. Douglas has never seen anything like it. He covers himself and runs for cover, but there is no cover. And as soon as it starts, it is over. It is man against the sun again. Douglas uncovers his head and slows down to a walk. He looks ahead into the desert.

The cliffs of *the Settlement* are closer. They are visible to him. He continues his forward march. He feels the sun again. He arrives at the cliffs before dark.

Douglas reaches his destination and learns that his teacher died several weeks before, not long after their last encounter. He was found on the shores of the river and presumed drowned. Douglas thinks it is odd. Ælfric was a very good swimmer.

The Judgment

Aron sits waiting outside Zacharus's office. Zacharus is keeping him waiting. Zacharus always does this to Aron. It makes the Temple Priest very mad. All he can do is think about that and Douglas Trigger.

'We should never have let him get this far,' he is thinking. *'Soon he will be in the Holy City. Then it will be too late.'*

Aron listens through the door to what is happening in Zacharus's office. He hears talking. It is muffled. He cannot hear what is being said.

"Is he a revolutionary?" asks Zacharus,

"I don't know," says the spy. "I never heard a man speak like he speaks."

"Are you also deceived?" asks Zacharus.

"No, my Lord."

"You must never repeat what you heard him say."

"Not even to you?"

"Never."

The spy seems surprised.

"You must never question the word of God," Zacharus continues.

"And what if a man were not to question God, but were to question the Temple?"

"You must never repeat what you heard him say."

"Yes, my Lord."

"Find out where he goes when he leaves *the Settlement*," says the priest, "I don't ever want to see him in The Holy City."

"Yes, my Lord." Loki hesitates. "He may be leaving as we speak."

"Do you know where he will go in the Holy City?"

Loki thinks about it. "Maybe."

"I don't want another martyr. We must move quickly, before Aron moves." Zacharus looks to the door. It is quiet out there. "Get behind the drapes," he whispers.

Loki looks to the door and hides.

Aron hears the talking stop. He hears Zacharus get up from his desk. Aron steps away from the door as it opens. "Come in," says Zacharus. He clears his throat as he walks into the room. Aron follows him.

At first Zacharus doesn't say anything. He walks over to his desk and sits down. "Douglas Trigger is almost here," Aron blurts. "He's docked at *the Settlement* port."

Aron looks around to find out to whom he was speaking. He sees no one. "We have to stop him before he speaks," he says, looking towards the garden door.

"Do you have a plan?" asks Zacharus.

"We must find a way to get the Great Chief to prosecute him."

"Just like *the Medicine Man.*"

"Yes. With all the people who follow him, it should be no problem to convince the Great Chief of his sedition. There are some who call him 'the Great Chief!'"

"He is a blasphemer. He should be stoned."

"The crowd will not turn against him."

"We don't need the whole crowd," says Zacharus. Just a few select thugs.

"We should call together the Council of the Tribes. We must also decide what to do with the others, with *the Ghosts.*"

"Don't you worry about *the Ghosts,*" says Zacharus. "When their shepherd falls, the sheep will scatter." Anything Aron does is unimportant. Zacharus's solution is already in motion.

Aron thinks he sees something in the drape to the garden door.

On Alert

There is a spy outside the safe house. Tommy sees him before the others. Loki is snooping. Mandolin, Timothy and Bobby stop when Tommy holds up his hand and places a finger over his lips to silence them. Even the stray dogs that follow Tommy stop. He points to the spy and they take cover in an alley to watch him.

Loki seems to have determined that no one is in the safe house and he's standing at the door, looking around, poised to go in. Tommy and company duck behind a building to avoid being seen. When he looks out again, the spy is gone, apparently inside.

"We may have been discovered," says Timothy.

"Loki," says Tommy. "I always knew he was an infiltrator."

"What does he want?" says Bobby.

"It does not matter," says Timothy. "We have to kill him."

"We should have killed him years ago," says Tommy.

"We will kill him now," says Timothy.

"Right now?" says Tommy.

"We cannot let him tell anybody what he has discovered."

"Shouldn't we find out who he's already told?" asks Bobby.

Loki looks around in all of the rooms. He sees nothing.

"Hold it," says Tommy, pointing down the street. Timothy looks to what he sees. It is an approaching garrison of

Imperial soldiers from the Palace of the Great Chief.

"Damn," says Timothy. "Until another day. The safe house is gone."

When the Temple spy emerges on the street, the rebels have moved out. The Imperial soldiers march past Loki and he watches as they go.

Timothy is running ahead of Tommy and Bobby. Mandolin runs behind them all. The stray dogs are mixed in.

"What do you think he wanted?" Tommy asks Timothy.

"I do not know what that traitor wanted," says Timothy. "He must have been gathering intelligence when he was with us. It does not bode well that he is back."

"Who do you think he's after?" asks Bobby.

"He is after one of us," says Timothy.

"Or all of us," says Tommy. "He was at *Sarah's Inn* that first time I saw my brother. He must have been following us all these years."

"Now we know he is from the Great Chief's Palace," says Timothy. "Those were Imperial Palace Guards."

"We don't know that they were with him," says Bobby.

"Why is the Great Chief bothering us?" asks Timothy. "He never bothered us before. Have they tightened the strings that much more? Do we have to start fighting him too? It should not be that hard to topple a puppet. Strings can be cut."

"Do you think they know about Festival?" says Tommy.

"Maybe we should lay low," says Bobby.

"That is probably a good idea," says Timothy.

"Should one of us double back and follow him?" asks Tommy.

"He is following us," says Timothy. "Let us keep going."

"We should split up," says Tommy to the two men, as if Mandolin is not with them. "Let's meet later back at the inn. Maybe we'll hook up with my brother." Timothy and Bobby agree. Tommy looks at Mandolin. "That doesn't go for you. I don't want to see you there. This is stuff you don't need to know about."

Timothy runs to his dwelling in another part of the Holy City before going to the inn. Bobby goes to *Sarah's Inn* to see if Douglas is there. Tommy goes away from Mandolin. The dogs follow. Mandolin has nowhere to go. Tears fill her precious eyes.

Waiting

It is a busy night at *Sarah's Inn.* Peter sits at a table with Andy, Joey, James, Johnny Z, Phil, Barty, and Jimmy A waiting for Douglas. They have waited there every night since they got to the Holy City. This night the group has no money for drinks. It is starting to wear on the innkeeper, Michael.

"You guys sure you don't want anything?" he says, patting his large belly.

"No, we're fine," says Peter.

"You just want to sit there?"

"We're waiting for someone."

"This guy must be *the Messiah,*" says Michael, "because you've been waiting all night, not buying anything."

"I'll take water," says Philip.

Michael is losing it. "Water?" he says.

"We don't have any money," says Jimmy A.

Michael looks at him. "You don't have any money?" he marvels. "You were buying drinks last night. What happened to your money? What...did you all get robbed?"

"We pool our money," says Peter, "Our treasurer isn't here."

"Your treasurer? That's better than *the Messiah!* You're a big fancy business. Maybe my treasurer should talk to your treasurer. Before you know it, they'll be making you a citizen."

Michael looks at the group. He notices that the only one of the group he knows is missing. "Your treasurer is Tommy Trigger?" he asks.

"That's right," says Peter.

He smiles. "And you gave him your money?"

"That's right."

Michael laughs. "I guess you're not too bright. Did Tommy say he'd be here tonight?"

"Yea," says Peter. "He's coming by later."

"And he's got money?"

"Yea," says Peter.

"Your money?"

"Yea."

"I'll spot you a round until he gets here."

"You can cancel the water," says Philip.

"You were never getting it," says Michael. He goes to the bar.

"When will Trigger come?" Andy asks Peter.

"When he comes," says Peter. "When he comes. The last time he went into the desert, he was gone a long time. We have time. He'll be here before Festival."

Tommy and Bobby get to the inn at about the same instant. Tommy laughs. "It's kind of hard to split up when we're both going to the same place," he says. They go inside.

They look around. "Where's Timothy?" asks Bobby.

Tommy looks. "Not here yet. There are *the Ghosts.*"

They approach the table. There are no cups on it. "Aren't you guys drinking?" he says as he sits down.

Michael sets the first beer in Tommy's hand. Tommy looks at him. "Michael, ya musta seen me coming."

"I heard you were coming," he says with a smile. "I bet your friends here that you had taken off with their money."

"Maybe I did," says Tommy. "I'm the only one who knows how much money there is." He laughs.

Peter looks at Andy.

Michael smiles. He says, "Well, since you're the guy with the money, I'll start a tab."

"Do that," says Tommy.

Michael takes his empty tray back to the bar.

"Have you guys had any trouble since you've been in the Holy City?" Tommy asks.

They look at each other. "No," says Peter. "What is it?"

"It's nothing," says Tommy. "We should take it easy on the drinks tonight. It's been a while since we took up a collection."

Peter nods his head. He's thinking about his business. The others agree. Timothy shows up. Douglas does not. They wait until closing.

Douglas comes the next night. He walks right through the door. Tommy is the first to see him. "There he is," he says to Bobby. It is the same group at the same table as the night before, with the addition of Timothy. Douglas seems fazed. He sees them. He walks to them. They stand to greet him.

"Sit down," says Tommy. "Did you find what you were looking for?"

Douglas remains standing. "No," he says. "What I went for was gone."

"Sorry to hear that," says Tommy. "Let's sit down. Did you eat or were you hanging out in the desert again?"

Douglas doesn't sit. "I'm okay."

"How was *the Settlement?*"

"Ælfric is dead."

"Sorry."

"The Teacher of Righteousness," says Barty.

"What happened?" asks Andy.

"They said he drowned near where we saw him."

"Were we the last to see him?" asks Peter.

"I don't think so."

"How do you feel?" asks Andy.

"Alone."

"Then sit down," says Tommy. "Have something to drink. You won't feel so alone." Douglas sits down opposite Tommy. They all sit down. Douglas looks at the others around the table. "Anyway, we're all alone," Tommy says, "even you and me."

Douglas looks at his reflection in his brother. He looks at everyone at the table. "Why do people come to listen to me?" he asks.

They look at each other. "They like what they hear," says Tommy.

"Some say that *the Medicine Man* has arisen from the dead," says Peter.

Douglas does not react.

"Some say that you are Elijah," says James.

"Some say you are a reincarnation of some other prophet," says Andy.

"Why do people say that? What do you tell people when they say those things? Who do you say I am?"

"You are *the Voice,"* says Andy.

"The Hierophant," says Barty.

"Is that what you tell people?"

"Isn't that what you want us to say?" asks Philip.

"It is what you are," says Jimmy A.

"No," says Douglas. "Don't tell anybody that."

"It's what you are," says Andy.

"Don't say that," says Douglas. He looks at his twin.

Tommy's eyes narrow. He studies his brother.

"Who do *you* say I am?" says Douglas.

Tommy laughs his silent laugh. He says, "You're the second best looking guy in this inn."

It gets a smile from Douglas.

"People recognize something in what you say." says Tommy. "How do you define yourself? Do you want to be *the Voice?* Are you *the Hierophant?* You could be *the Messiah!"*

"Your *Messiah?"* says Douglas. "A *Messiah* of your *Holy War?"*

"Yes," says Tommy.

Douglas looks at his friends who are not rebels. They are men who will do anything they are told to do. He looks at *the Sons of Light.* They will only do what they tell him to tell them to do.

Tommy sees what his twin is thinking. "People will follow you," he says.

"So it would seem," he says with subdued remorse.

"You must lead them where *we* are going," says Tommy.

"You would lead them to murder and terror."

"Each man must face terror," says Tommy. "Every man

must feel the horror of his own mortality."

"Violence is a tool to bring that which will come, come sooner, and that is greedy," says Douglas.

"Sometimes, change must come swiftly," says Tommy, "and such change is always violent. Look around you. People are dying. Though you may not agree with our motives, know your destiny. Yours is a destiny of horror and terror. You are plotting a course in direct competition with the established order. We are a new generation and you renounce all generations that came before you. Now that we are in the Holy City, they will quickly take a greater interest in you." Tommy leans back in his chair. "They will take a greater interest in all of us. We are all watched men."

"I know that," says Douglas.

"If they do not prosecute you as a rebel," says Tommy, "they will stone you as a blasphemer."

"Will it be the Law of the Empire or the Law of the Tribes?"

Tommy grabs Douglas's shoulders. "It will not be your law," he says, shaking him. "It will be written by someone else." He releases him. "Heed this warning and join us."

"You have already warned me once."

"Then listen to me. Just listen."

Douglas smiles and slaps Tommy on the back. It is dark in the inn. Douglas calls for another round.

"Now that we are in the Holy City, what do we do next?" asks Peter.

"We will do what we always do," says Douglas. "We will go to the Temple."

"You're banned from the Temple," Tommy says with a smile.

"Just watch me."

Tommy smiles. "What if they don't like what you say?" he says.

"They won't."

"The Temple is guarded," says Tommy.

"You think they know you are coming?" asks Timothy.

"They know," says Tommy. He turns to Timothy and says, "Maybe the infiltrator was after somebody else."

In a dark, unnoticed corner of the inn, Loki drains his drink and slips out a back door.

The Tax Collector

Jimmy A's Brother, Matty, has a job at the Holy City Customhouse collecting taxes for the Empire, which pays for the cost of their occupation by assessing the Nations they occupy. Douglas, Peter, Andy, Joey, Philip, Barty, James, Johnny Z, Tommy, and Bobby are walking through the street on their way to the Temple. The customhouse is on the way. Other *Ghosts* and Tommy's dogs are also with them. Tommy is playing his syrinx.

"You're not gonna believe what's coming," says one of the Emperor's Imperial soldiers, standing in the door of the customhouse. "It's a mob of people. It could be trouble."

Jimmy A goes to the door to see about the mob. He observes it is Douglas. He smiles. "It's Trigger," he says to his brother, "The one I told you about."

"You know them?" says the soldier.

"Yea," says Jimmy A, "It's nothing to worry about."

"They coming here?" asks the soldier.

"Yea," says Jimmy A. He goes out to the street to get Douglas.

Jimmy A's brother, Matty, doesn't like his job. His father got it for him. He is just a rich kid with connections who doesn't know what else to do with his life.

The way Peter wanted to save Andy for business, Jimmy A

wants to save his brother from business, especially this business. A tax collector for the Empire is the most despised of men. He is a tax collaborator.

Another of the Emperor's Imperial soldiers brings in a young man. It is Martin Collins. He can see that the tax collector is a fellow Tribesman. It disgusts him. "Traitorous scum," he says as the soldier throws him at Matty A's table. Martin Collins spits at the tax collector.

Matty looks down to avoid the young man's eyes. He wipes the spit from his face.

"Are you that worried about the Emperor's tribute money?" says Collins. "It's snakes like you that will be taken out first. Haven't you heard about the underground? You haven't got much time, boy. I'm gonna remember you." He points an accusing finger at Matty. "I'm gonna remember you."

The soldier who brought him in cracks Collins on the back with the butt of his sword. It knocks him down. Collins groans.

"Don't do that," says Matty.

"I'm gonna remember you," Collins says to his fellow Tribesman.

The soldier hits him again. "You got to have discipline," he says. "You got to have order." He looks at Collins. "I'm gonna remember you!"

"Leave him alone," says Matty.

"Don't you fight for me, boyo," says the recovering taxpayer, getting to his feet. "I'll give you your tribute. I'll give you your gold." Collins pulls his penis from under his pants and begins to urinate in Matty A's direction, who jumps out of his chair and manages to sidestep the stream. The soldier butts the young man between his shoulder blades, stopping his flow, and he goes down again.

"How does it feel to be a traitor?" he gasps. "How does it feel to be a marked man?" He tucks himself in.

Two other soldiers lift Collins to his feet and one of them grabs his purse and throws it on Matty's table. They begin to take him away.

"Wait," says Matty. "I need the man's name."

"I'll give ya my name. Remember it well, for you shall hear it again. My name is Martin Collins of Brushire."

Two soldiers drag him away. "You're a marked man!" he screams as they bring him away. "A marked man!"

Matty A tries not to listen. He gets a different chair to sit in and writes the man's name in a ledger, entering the tax he paid. On this day, he particularly hates his job. He stands up. He goes to a washbowl and rinses off what remains of Martin Collins's spit. He dries himself with a cloth. Matty goes to the door. "I'll be out front," he says to one of the soldiers.

"Who's gonna clean up the piss?"

'Good question,' he thinks. Matty A walks out to the street to look for his brother and to get a breath of air. He sees the group of people and is impressed with its size. His brother mixes right in with them. He sees the one man who seems to be the center of it all. This must be Douglas, he thinks. He sees his twin, Tommy and thinks it is odd.

Jimmy A sees Matty and waves him over. He walks to the group and gets introduced. Tommy has been watching Matty since he came out from the customhouse. "What is it you do?" he asks.

Matty looks back at the customhouse. "I am a tax collector."

"You work for the Empire?" asks Tommy.

"It's a private company," says Matty.

Tommy doesn't like tax collaborators.

"This is just a temporary job until he can find another," says Jimmy A.

Tommy looks at the brother. "You call yourself a Tribesman?" he says.

"Quit and come with us," says Jimmy A.

"I'm not hanging out with a tax collector," says Tommy.

"He's my brother," says Jimmy A.

"You think that will save him?" says Tommy. "That just serves to lower my opinion of you."

"Come with us," says Jimmy A.

Matty looks back at the customhouse.

"I quit my job," says Jimmy A. "C'mon!"

"Where're you going?" asks Matty.

"To where we've always been," says Jimmy A.

Matty sees the soldiers at the customhouse door. He looks at the hate in Tommy's eyes. "Fuck it," he says.

Jimmy A. smiles. The group is moving again. Tommy is disgruntled. How unusual.

Robber's Den

Douglas stops when he enters the Court of the Infidels of the Temple of the Tribes of the Holy City. His friends and *the Ghosts* who follow him also stop. Tommy's dogs follow them. There are three today, two big and one small. They are allowed in the Infidel's Court.

It is almost Festival and the pilgrims have already started to crowd the Court. There are moneychangers at the gate. There are more vendors and merchants set up than usual. They are everywhere. It's a bizarre. It's like Festival has already started.

There are more shepherds selling more sacrificial goats and lambs to more penitents than Douglas has ever witnessed. Tommy's dogs bark at the chickens. The Court looks like an Imperial circus. There are beggars and thieves everywhere. It is not a place of repose. It is not a Temple. It is a marketplace. The vendors have purchased licenses from the priests to be there.

"Headdress?" says one as Douglas starts to walk again. "You ain't got no headdress. Get one from me. It's a sunny day." He thrusts the headdress at him.

Douglas disregards the dealer. A beggar confronts him. "Alms?"

He ignores him. The beggar speaks to Douglas's friends. "What about you? Alms?"

Tommy walks close to Douglas to guard him from the crowd. He stands between his brother and the supplicant and gives him a coin to deflect the man's attention from his twin. The smallest of the stray dogs sniffs the man. They keep walking.

"You ain't got no jewelry," says the next dealer.

"He doesn't want any jewelry," says Tommy, pushing the nuisance away.

"What do you want?" says another dealer. "I will sell you anything." He points to a young woman.

They ignore him.

"You religious?" says the next dealer. He holds up a necklace. "Lookit what I got here. This amulet represents the gift of our God. It's just like *the Holy of the Holies.* Isn't it beautiful? That's something you can put around your neck and feel proud about. It's just like the one in the Temple. Women love men who wear amulets."

Tommy grabs the necklace from the dealer and throws it across the Infidel's Court in disgust.

"Hey," says the man, "What's wrong with you? That necklace is *real* gold!" The merchant is angry. He wants to go after Tommy. In his mind, he advances on him, but Tommy has too many men around him, so the dealer's body does not take action.

"Doesn't your Law tell you not to worship false idols?" asks Douglas.

"This ain't no false idol," says the annoyed merchant. "This is the real thing. Genuine gold."

"What you worship is manmade."

The vendor stares at him dumbfounded. "Do you want the necklace?"

Douglas keeps walking. The merchant waits for him and his gang to walk away and then he retrieves the necklace. When he passes a friend of his, another dealer, he says, "Those guys were crazy, man."

Douglas walks up the stairs to head to the inner sanctum of the Temple. He passes through the Court of Women with his entourage. In the next chamber, there is an animal sacrifice being performed by Zacharus. He is poised over the dying lamb. He is covered in blood. The knife is still in his hand. The animal is the offering of a wealthy merchant who is down on his knees, chanting a prayer hoping for forgiveness. Only he knows what he did. Zacharus looks up from the altar when the group approaches and sees Douglas.

"What blasphemy is this?" says the priest, who is interrupted just as he is about to light the pyre.

Douglas stops when he sees the ceremony. The rich pilgrim makes a cash offering as well, trying to buy his way into the next life. His sin must be heavy. The picture of the priest dripping in blood and the rich man down on his knees with his money is almost funny.

Two Temple Guards stand outside the huge bronze doors that open into the inner sanctum of the Temple, where only priests can go, where is *the Holy of Holies,* an empty chamber, hidden behind a veil and an altar of incense.

When Douglas sees that he will not be able to advance anymore, he heads back outside. The group follows him. Zacharus lights the pyre. The dead animal begins to burn. The rich merchant is the most supplicating he's been so far. He is chanting louder and faster. He is kneeling and he is bobbing his body up and down, faster and faster. Zacharus leaves the chamber to follow Douglas. He wipes the blood from his hands.

Outside in the Court of the Infidels, Aron is collecting booth fees and counting money.

"Quite a business they got going here," says Douglas to no one in particular.

"You," another merchant says to Douglas. "You ever heard of *the Medicine Man?*"

"What are you selling?" asks Tommy.

"I have in my possession the collected sayings of John, *the Medicine Man,*" says the merchant, "transcribed personally by one of his followers. This is the genuine article. If I could read, I'd read it to you. Can you read?"

Douglas stops.

"I knew that would get your attention. Sure, I look like an old man, but I know what the young folks listen to today. In my day it was *the Teacher of Righteousness.* These days it's *the*

Medicine Man. Who knows who it will be when you get to be my age?"

"What's the name of the disciple?" asks Tommy.

"The name?" says the dealer. "The name? I don't remember the name. I don't think he gave me his name."

"How many copies of these sayings do you have?"

"How many do you want?" asks the dealer.

"How do we know they're real?" asks Douglas.

"They're real alright," says the man, "Seeing is believing," He picks up one of the scrolls to show to Douglas. Look at the workmanship," he continues, "look at the legibility. Only a gifted scribe could have perfected such a work. Even if you didn't know it was the words of *the Medicine Man,* it would still be a collector's item."

He hands it to Douglas. Douglas takes the scroll from the merchant, and opens it. He reads it. 'God is angry,' it says. 'God is avenging. God will in no way forgive his enemies unless they first worship him.'

"This is bullshit," says Douglas. "These are not John's words." With a sweep of his hand, Douglas scatters the other scrolls of sayings.

"What are you doing?" cries the merchant. He is powerless to stop him. Douglas's entourage is imposing. They keep walking.

Douglas swings his arm against one of the poles that holds up another merchant's tent. That side of his tent comes down.

"Hey-hey...What's going on here?" says the old man.

"What are you doing?" Tommy says to Douglas.

Across the court Aron hears the disturbance. "Look over there," he says to Zacharus as his father-in-law emerges from inside the Temple. "He's banned! I banned him."

"What are they doing?" asks Zacharus.

The dealer is running away scared.

"This shouldn't be a market place!" Douglas shouts with upturned arms as they go. They come to the next peddler. Douglas overturns his table without even looking at the merchandise.

"Hey!" shouts the peddler. "Hey, you have to pay for that!"

"I don't want it," says Douglas.

"What are you doing?" says Tommy.

Aron starts to run towards the noise. Zacharus stops him. "Go get the Guards," he says. "I'll meet you at the disturbance."

Without saying anything, Aron runs to get the Temple Guards.

Douglas goes back to the merchant selling the God amulets. The merchant sees him and flashes Douglas a big smile. He smiles at the prospect of money.

"Alright!" says the merchant. "My man decided he wanted the amulet of God after all. Good decision. There are no two alike with this one, but they all represent *the Holy of Holies.* It's a good thing I retrieved this when your brother chucked it across the court. Normally, that'd cost you extra. But I like you. I tell you what you can have it for...How much were you thinking of paying?"

Douglas smashes the dealer's display case with his God necklaces. He steps on the dealer's goods. He steps off them and continues his stalking.

"Hey! Hey, you can't do that! What's wrong with you, man? You drunk? You smashed all my shit, man. How 'm I gonna sell that shit? How 'm I gonna eat? You're an asshole, man! It's a good thing they're genuine gold!" He looks at his merchant friend. "That guy is crazy!" he says. "They're all crazy! Man…Hey, did I show you this necklace?"

Zacharus walks in front of Douglas to stop him. Douglas stops. Aron sees what is going on and comes over.

"Trigger," Zacharus says.

And the merchants and peddlers repeat, "Trigger." Now they know who he is. They have heard of him. "He's an asshole, man," one of them says.

Douglas looks at Zacharus. "Is this your idea?" he says, gesturing to the marketplace.

At first Zacharus does not get his meaning. Finally, he says, "This is the way of the world."

"Is your Temple about this world?" asks Douglas.

"We must survive in this world if the word of God is to live," says Zacharus.

"Do you think you can take truth out of the world? Do you

think you can change natural law? Truth needs no champions. When all is not right, when we are not one with nature, a *Voice* from the silence will sound out and reveal truth."

Douglas walks away from the priests. His group follows. The priests also follow.

"You could get yourself arrested with that stunt you just pulled," says Zacharus.

Douglas sees a garrison of Temple Guards approaching with Aron. "Is that why you sent for your Guards?" he says.

"No," says Zacharus. "You're not under arrest. Not yet. It would cause too much of a scene to do it here." Zacharus smiles. "These markets get worshipers involved with their Temple. It's a community activity. It's a good thing. It is almost Festival. The pilgrims must pass through this court. They must come to the Temple to offer alms to atone for their sins." He is still wiping the blood from his hands.

Aron arrives with reinforcements. Zacharus shoos them away. Aron does not want to go, but Zacharus gives him an extra wave away.

"Trigger," says Zacharus after Aron has left, "I'm going to be frank."

Douglas stops and faces Zacharus. Zacharus stops. "Please be candid," says Douglas.

"I will speak to you man to man. Do not think of me as a priest."

"I do not," says Douglas.

"As a man," continues Zacharus, ignoring the slight, "I will tell you what I would do if I were the High Priest."

"Go on," Douglas encourages him.

"If I were the High Priest, by now I would be tired of you. Perhaps I'd warn you. Perhaps I'd give you a last chance to change, to recant all that you've said and come back to God. The Temple would welcome you with open arms. But if you did not come back, as the High Priest, I would have to address your blasphemy."

"Just as you dealt with *the Medicine Man*."

"He was in the Great Chief's jail."

"Just like you dealt with Ælfric."

Zacharus is startled that Douglas knows. "I do not know

such a man. You are very insolent. You should show some respect."

"What kind of respect have you shown me?"

"It is written in *the Book of the Tribes* that 'Any who seek to lead the Tribes astray from the Lord, your God, shall be stoned to death.'"

"Do you think that I'm afraid to die?" says Douglas.

"You're either very cool or very stupid," says Zacharus.

"I'm pretty stupid," says Douglas with a laugh. He turns to his friends. He says, "Let's get out of here. There is no truth here. Soon this Temple will be gone. Soon these walls will fall."

"Do you prophesy?"

"Time turns the biggest boulders to dust. These stones mortared together by man will crumble. You may kill me now, but soon we will all be dead."

Douglas and his band walk away from where Zacharus is standing, through the columns of the Temple. Tommy's stray dogs follow. When they are gone, the merchants rebuild their displays and start to trade again.

Zacharus knows that what must be done must be done quickly. Douglas did not speak this day in the Temple. He will be back.

To the Garden

Tommy leads Douglas to the Garden outside the walls of the Holy City. This is where they have been camping. The others follow behind them, along with some *Ghosts.*

"I don't think you have to be a genius to figure out what Zacharus was telling you," Tommy says as they walk along.

"Well, that's good," says Douglas, "because I'm not a genius."

Tommy smiles a knowing smile. "What are you?" he asks.

"An idiot," Douglas says with a laugh. "Look what I got myself into."

"You're on the verge," Tommy says. "You could break right now."

"Or I can still walk away from it. That's what they want. Don't stir the pot. Nobody'd ever know---just a couple of thousand people along the river."

"Is that what you want," asks Tommy, "to lead an ordinary life of subjugation?"

"I don't know what I want," says Douglas. "I don't know if I can walk away from it. I don't know if I could find peace if I did."

"That's just your *Self* talking," says Tommy with a smile, trying to use his brother's terminology. "A man can walk away from anything. That priest just about told you he'd incite the mob to stone you if you keep coming."

"Maybe I'll incite the mob."

"That's what he's afraid of. Blasphemy's a bullshit charge, but people are stupid. They're just looking for an excuse to throw a rock at somebody. I don't understand you, brother. The things you want to die for make no sense to me. I don't know what you want to die for. You have to want to die for something. Either that or you're crazy. You know what I want to die for? I want to die for the Tribes to be free. That's what I want to die for."

"I don't want to die for anything," says Douglas.

"Bullshit," says Tommy. "You're begging to die."

"I don't want to die, Tommy. It's just that maybe I can see my own death coming."

"I could have told you that when you started," says Tommy. "You can go underground. I have friends that will help you. But leave the Law of the Tribes alone. Let the priests rule their Temple. We were meant for something greater. The time for the revolution has come. You can be one of its leaders."

Douglas doesn't say anything.

"You'll be the greatest of all *Messiahs,*" says Tommy. "Men will follow you. They'll name you their Great Chief! There will be a new Tribal Nation of Nations. All you have to do is lead them."

"I don't want to lead them."

"What do you want?"

"To show them."

They come to a level clearing. "Let's set up camp here," says Peter.

"Ya, cool," says Tommy. He turns back to Douglas. "You're a natural leader, more so than me. Join the revolution. Be free! Take a stand. Save yourself and save your land! At least think about it."

Everybody starts to sit down. Some of them unwind bedrolls.

"You're not saying anything new to me," says Douglas as he sits down on a large stone. "I'm not going to lead people anywhere."

"There is nothing that can persuade you?"

"I am resolute," says Douglas. "Where's Mandolin?"

"Mandolin?" says Tommy. "Fuck Mandolin. Many have." He laughs.

"Why do you talk about her like that?"

"She's a whore, brother. "

"What makes you say that?"

"I'm a whore myself," laughs Tommy. "I know. You won't be the first to fuck her, or the last. She's particularly fond of Imperial soldiers. Use her, but don't love her."

"How can you talk about her like that and still be with her?"

"I'm not with her; she's with me, just like the dogs are with me when we're in the city. I didn't think she'd really follow me to Shacktown. But I'll tell you this, if anybody's gonna fuck her tonight, it's gonna be me. I don't care about tomorrow night. You can have her."

"Why do you talk about her like that?"

"She's just a groupie, a *Sons of Light* groupie, nothing more. Don't get involved with her. Don't confuse an erection with love. Use her."

"Is that how you feel about all women?"

"You can't love her," says Tommy. "She doesn't know anything about love."

"Maybe somebody should show her."

"Somebody like you?" Tommy laughs. "You're making a mistake here. Do you want to fuck her?"

Douglas doesn't answer him.

"If you haven't fucked her yet, don't fuck her," says Tommy, "because then you'll want to fuck her again. Then you'll be stuck with her. Take my advice, brother. Mandolin is a woman of the night. When it is day, you will want to roll out of bed and forget you were with her. She is a woman to go to when you are full of drink. She'll never be your girlfriend. She's too damaged."

"Let's not talk about Mandolin anymore," says Douglas. "I'm going for a walk alone."

"Think about what I said. Think about the revolution."

Mandolin's World

Mandolin is face down on the street outside the safe house in the Holy City. Her body is bent so that it looks like she fell forward while kneeling. The blood is still oozing from her skin-torn body. The back of her head is crushed. Her dress is torn and blood soaked. There are blood-red rocks and stones in piles all around her. Her eyes are closed. Her left leg is broken. Mandolin is dead.

Douglas and the others come upon her by accident. They are not really looking for Mandolin. Douglas and Tommy see the body as they approach and it stops and then it starts them again. They do not, but they do know. They run to her. Peter follows at a safe distance. The others follow.

Douglas kneels down and slowly reaches out and touches her shoulders. He rolls her over into his arms. What has been done to Mandolin's face fills him with horror. It is a dirty face soaked with tears and blood.

"Fuck these people," says Tommy. "Fuck the Temple." He picks up one of the blood soaked stones. "This was a stoning," he says. "This is not why we're fighting this Holy War."

A stoning it was, a stoning by sinners and blasphemers all. Who stirred them on?

As Mandolin was dying, she embraced the face of a love

she never had in life.

"Who started this?" asks Douglas. They all look around and at the passersby. There is no sign of anyone who may have done this.

"She never should have come back here," says Tommy. "It wasn't safe. I should have told her. It wasn't safe."

"Why wasn't it safe?" asks Douglas.

"Its cover was blown," says Tommy. "There is a spy watching us."

"What spy?"

"An infiltrator from the past. He was that guy I saw that first day at *Sarah's.*"

"*That* guy? Is he from the Temple?"

"We think he's with the Great Chief."

"This was a stoning." Douglas and Tommy look at Mandolin's dead body. They look at each other. "This was the priests of the Temple of the Tribes of the Holy City. Your spy is a Temple spy. Why did she come back here?"

"She had nowhere else to go," Tommy whispers with almost a hint of emotion.

The people of the Holy City pass by as if Mandolin and the others aren't there. "They're all just passersby," says Douglas. "Not one will stop to help."

"Don't get worked up about it," says Tommy. "That's the way it is. Some of them probably threw stones. We will never know because they feel no remorse. This is the Holy City."

"It means nothing to them," says Douglas. "That is why they're doomed. No one will miss them when they're gone."

"We should cover her," says Tommy. "Are you alright?"

"No," says Douglas.

"Did you love her?" asks Tommy.

"Didn't you?"

"It's not in me, kid. Look, we should get her out of here."

Peter stands away from the body and the other two, unsure what he should do. The others stay back also.

Douglas puts one arm under her knees and holds her shoulders with the other and lifts Mandolin up. Tommy helps to cover her. "Where should we bring her?" asks Tommy.

"To the Temple," says Douglas. "Come with me."

"Do you think that's a good idea?" asks Tommy.

Douglas doesn't say anything. He walks past Tommy with Mandolin in his arms.

"Do you want some help with her?" asks Tommy, taking up after him.

"No," says Douglas.

Peter and the others follow.

"I told her the world was full of *Light,*" says Douglas, "and she believed me. But the Laws of the Tribes are dark and her people are sheep and so accursed is this place, and accursed are its Laws. They came into the world full and they shall leave empty. They will not see truth again in this lifetime, though it was the first thing they saw. They are drunk with a homemade brew. When they shake off their drink, they will forget this place."

"I never heard you speak like this," says Tommy.

No one says anything until they approach the Temple of the Tribes of the Holy City.

"Are you sure you wanna do this?" asks Tommy.

Douglas is silent.

Peter is several steps behind them.

They enter the Court of the Infidels. The yard is empty. The circus is gone.

Douglas crosses the Court and walks undisturbed up the stairs to the Temple gate. The others follow. There are no priests, no pilgrims and no Guards. Tommy opens the gate and Douglas carries Mandolin's corpse into the Court of the Tribes. It is quiet and they cross the Court quickly and pass through the silver and gold plated gate to enter the Court of the Priests. Douglas rests Mandolin on the altar.

"Go get some water from the well in the garden," he tells Peter, who is still at the door. And to Tommy he says, "We will anoint the body."

Peter goes to get the water and Andy goes looking for some sort of cloth to wash her with. When they return, Douglas starts with her forehead, wiping it clean until all the blood is off. He rinses the linen in the water Peter has brought and works his way down Mandolin's body. When the linen he has is blood soaked, he wets another cloth and begins to wash her legs.

"She had a pretty name," says Douglas.

In the Temple, the world seems darker somehow. The walls seem pale and bare.

Douglas's head droops down and he stares at the floor.

"What a fucked up way to die," says Tommy. "This is a fucked up world we live in."

"It must have hurt," says Andy.

As Douglas continues to cleanse her body, what was stained becomes clear.

"What are we gonna do?" Peter asks as he washes the red from her legs. "What are we gonna do?"

"She was lonely," says Tommy. "For all the men she had, she was lonely."

Douglas dunks the blood soaked rag in the water. It is too stained to go on. Tommy hands him another piece of cloth.

"I'll go get clear water," Peter says and he picks up the pail.

The others are silent in the Temple as Peter goes to the well in the garden to get water. No one says anything until he returns. He puts the pail down.

"Fuck this Temple," Douglas says with anger. "Fuck the priests of the Temple. They are like a dog sleeping in a manger of oxen, for neither do they eat nor do they let the ox eat."

"Are her parents in Shacktown?" asks Peter. "Do they worry about her?"

"They don't give a fuck about her," Tommy says with contempt. "They're why she ended up like this."

Douglas motions to Peter and Tommy to help him turn the body. The three of them roll Mandolin over on her stomach. Douglas tries to wash the table under her while they turn her. He begins to cleanse her back.

"Where do we go from here?" asks Peter. "Do we just go back home? Do we stay in the Holy City?"

"We're not going anywhere," says Douglas. "We stay in the Holy City."

They turn her over on her back again. Douglas grabs another cloth and wets it in the water. He continues to clean Mandolin's dead body.

"Where do you think all the Temple Guards are?"

"They're probably guarding an empty chamber," says Douglas. "Andy, can you look around and see if you can find any linens to wrap her body in?"

"Sure." He goes off to look.

"This was a warning," says Tommy.

"Ælfric was a warning," says Douglas. "It's a warning of desperate men trying to hold onto power."

Douglas begins to rip what is left of her clothes off her body so that he can wash away all the blood. "She was so pretty," he says.

"I guess she was," says Tommy. "Do you hear what I'm saying? This was a warning from them to us. This was a warning to you. Maybe Loki is a spy for the Temple. Now you know who you're fucking with."

"They don't know who they're fucking with," says Douglas.

Tommy drops it. "What do you want to do with her once she is anointed?" asks Tommy. "Should we leave her here?"

"We don't have the money to bury her," says Douglas.

"What about her parents?" asks Peter.

"Forget it," says Tommy.

Andy comes back with a drape.

"Where'd you get that?" asks Tommy.

"You don't want to know," says Andy. He starts to tear the drape into pieces, and together with Douglas, Tommy and Peter, they wrap the body. When they are finished, Peter goes to the door to see if there is anyone coming. There is no one.

Douglas kisses her on the cheek and says good-bye. He moves to the door. The others follow.

"Let's go," Tommy says to Andy, taking one last look, as they both walk to the door.

Mandolin is at peace. The dead have no expectations. They have no wants or desires. They have no fear. They have no ego or jealousy. They have no separation. They are *Being.*

Douglas and the others leave the blood soaked pail and linens on the altar with Mandolin, a sacrifice to the God of the Temple of the Tribes of the Holy City. They march across the Court and into the streets of the Holy City. Mandolin is gone.

The Rising

Tommy and Bobby wait at *Sarah's Inn* for Timothy. Bobby is no longer in their revolution, but he knows that if he does not remain quiet, his former comrades will move against him, for they believe that those who are not with the revolution are against it. Though he changed his philosophy on the river, Bobby still has loyalty to the rebels. And for a *Son of Light,* there is only one way out of the revolution. The rebels have Bobby's body, but they do not have his *Being.*

Tommy looks up and says, "There he is." Tommy's back is against a wall. He is facing the door.

A hot air blows into the inn with Timothy. The door silhouettes him as he approaches. "It is another sunny day," he says when he sits down at the table.

"Let's not talk about what kind of day it is," says Tommy.

"It is on," says Timothy. "Is that what you want to hear?"

"Yea," says Tommy. "That's what I want to hear." He says it like they are talking about sex.

The sun shines through the door of *Sarah's Inn* and lights a section of the table where Timothy leans his elbow. A shadow passes and Martin Collins enters and sits down with the other *Sons of Light.* Greetings are exchanged. Michael brings them a round. It is a hot, dry day. It is a day like any other day.

"There will be four groups of pilgrims," Timothy says,

speaking in code. "When the Emperor's I.A. goes into the desert at Festival to play their war games, we will launch several prayer meetings in the Holy City. We will exorcise the military barracks and government buildings. Bobby, you can take a group of pilgrims to worship at the deserted army barracks. Martin is going to lead a garrison of pilgrims to shut down and take up a collection from the tax company. Tommy, you will lead a group to the Temple Fortress. That will be our headquarters. It is the tallest tower in the Holy City. I am going to lead a garrison of pilgrims outside the walls to the edge of the Holy City to wait for the I.A. to return from their games."

"That's the plan," confirms Tommy.

Bobby nods.

Martin listens.

"This will be the beginning of a long campaign," says Timothy. "Will your brother join us?"

"No," says Tommy.

Timothy takes a sip of his beer. Tommy and Bobby drink also.

"He has a nature that people follow," says Timothy. "But he cannot be led."

"No," says Tommy. "He has a strong will."

"He has attracted most of *the Medicine Man's Ghosts.* It would be nice if he would help us," says Timothy, "but maybe we do not need his help to make him a *Messiah.* He is becoming bigger than he is. He is becoming bigger than he can control by himself."

"You think we can control him," says Bobby.

"Or at least those who follow him," says Tommy. "We can control *the Ghosts.*"

"But they follow *him,*" says Bobby. "They are his to lead."

"He's making powerful enemies," Tommy laments. "I keep warning him. Look what they did to Mandolin. Look what they did to *the Medicine Man.* If he falls, we must pick up his sword."

"He's your brother," says Bobby.

"It would be better if he did not speak to the pilgrims," says Timothy. "The time has come to draw *our* sword. We do not need the pilgrims distracted by stories about *'the Rebel's*

Field.' We keep waiting for somebody else to free us. We keep waiting for a *Messiah.* We do not need your brother with us. We just need to make sure he is not against us when we rise. Let the revolution begin. Justice is on our side."

"To Festival," toasts Tommy, raising his mug.

"To Festival," says Timothy.

"To Festival," says Martin.

"It will be a holy day," says Bobby.

"This is a *Holy War,"* says Timothy. "Our numbers are small now, but once the Rising begins, all Tribal Warriors will join in the rebellion. Let it begin while the pilgrims are in the Holy City for Festival."

"What are our numbers?" asks Martin.

"We have righteousness on our side," says Tommy, "And when we rise, all Tribal Warriors will follow. Our numbers will be great. We will have all the Festival pilgrims on our side. Timothy is right. We can't let my brother talk to the pilgrims before we do."

"There can only be one message this Festival," says Timothy, "and that is to rise!"

Two bulky shadows fall on the table. Tommy and Bobby already face the two men. Timothy and Martin turn to see who it is.

"Imperial screw," whispers Timothy.

"They're from the Temple," says Tommy.

Malachi, the Captain of the Temple Guard and another stand at the door and search the room with their eyes. Tommy leans away from the light into the shadow. Bobby does the same.

"They seem like they're looking for somebody," says Bobby.

"Shhh," says Timothy. "They probably are." Timothy feels like a hunted hunter. "Let us slip out of here," says Timothy.

Malachi rests his hand on his sword and leads the other Guard into the room, who also holds his weapon.

The other rebels at the bar appraise the soldiers. They decide to wait to see what develops.

There is no back door. Timothy considers his options. He draws his dagger under the table.

"Was there any rebel activity today?" Tommy whispers to Timothy.

"Just rock throwing."

"Why is anybody throwing rocks when we are about to strike?"

"Do you think this has anything to do with what happened at the safe house?" asks Bobby. "Do you think they're here for us?"

"I do not know," says Timothy. "They were Imperial soldiers. Maybe it is just a coincidence. Still, as soon as they are far enough away from the door, let us get out of here."

Tommy and Bobby nod. The shadows grow larger on their table. Timothy drains his drink. Tommy takes out his own dagger and clenches it under the table. Malachi looks to his left and then to his right. The other Guard follows him deeper into the room and their shadows withdraw.

"Let us get out of here," whispers Timothy when the two soldiers walk away from them. "I do not like this."

The three men get up slowly and walk to the door. Timothy and Tommy conceal their daggers so as to lose no time in battle. They do not look back at the soldiers.

Outside it is bright. Tommy's strays spring to attention. The *Sons of Light* squint their eyes and shield them from the sun with their hands. They walk into the streets and hide among the people. Tommy's dogs follow.

The Resolution

It is the Day of Rest. Aron and Zacharus sit in the older man's office. Zacharus laments that Aron will be unable to deal with a new generation of unorthodox prophets. He laments his heir. 'Why is this happening now?' the older man wonders. 'Why is this happening to the younger generation? If I can serve as High Priest until these prophets are gone, I will lead the new generation back to the Temple of the Tribes. If I die and Aron becomes High Priest, these prophets will lead the younger generation astray.'

Zacharus has decided that Douglas Trigger will have to be eliminated. It will need to happen quickly. He cannot be allowed to speak to the Festival crowd. Perhaps it is his own frustration with Aron, but Zacharus can see no other way. He is a man of action. He is a man who sees what must be done and does it.

Though Zacharus will give the order to kill Douglas Trigger, he rationalizes that he will be guilty of no crime. It is the word of God as recorded in *the Book of the Tribes.* Zacharus has warned Trigger. If Trigger does not recant all of his teachings and return to God, then it will be Trigger who is responsible for his own death. Zacharus is a man of swift action. He looks across his desk through Aron.

"I will gather witnesses against him," says Aron. "I will bring him before the Council of the Tribes."

"For blasphemy?" says Zacharus.

"An example must be set. We will disgrace him before his own people. He will be stoned in the city square like that whore he left on the altar."

Aron will never get a chance to implement his plan. It will take too long. Zacharus has another idea.

"Who will your witnesses be?" he says, encouragingly.

"The Ghosts will indict their Master."

"How do you propose to get them to speak against him?"

"With fear."

"Will you try to get him to bear witness against himself before the Council?"

"If we can, but we do not need him as long as we have witnesses against him."

"Let this be a secret Tribunal. Do not publicize this until it is done. If you are going to bring him before the Council of the Tribes, then do it in the middle of the night, when the pilgrims in the Holy City are sleeping. Right or wrong, his followers see him as a man of honor. The death of *the Medicine Man* in the Great Chief's jail alienated his followers from the Temple. They know we are a part of the Great Chief's Council."

"We are not responsible for what happens in the Great Chief's jail."

Zacharus is silent.

"Isn't the point of stoning him to make an example of his blasphemy?"

"It is better to make the example without the interference of his followers."

"You speak of honor," says Aron, "but what has honor to do with a heretic? And why should we worry about what his followers think? They should fear our judgment!"

"You are a man without honor, so I would not expect you to know, nor would I be able to tell you. Your charge, Aron, was to bring Douglas Trigger back to the Temple, but you have turned him away from it. And now, other men follow him. You couldn't accomplish your task and so it has come to this."

"I warned him," says Aron, "I scolded him."

"Now you must discredit him," says Zacharus. "He must not

die a hero. He must not be a martyr."

"Already the crowds call him 'the Great Chief.'"

"He is not the Great Chief. Soon you will be the High Priest. Let this be your final test, Aron. Do not fail again. I will not always be here to get you out of these things. You must resolve problems without involving the Great Chief or the Empire. The more help you ask for, the more power you will give away."

"Don't worry, father. When the Temple belongs to me, I will not lose it."

"Somehow, I don't believe you. Be careful. Now is the time of prophets. Beware of false prophets."

"Don't worry. It will never come so far again."

"You must make his blasphemy clear. It was a mistake to put *the Medicine Man* in the Great Chief's prison. You must not involve the Great Chief or the Empire. That would hurt us more than if we allow him to go on. We would lose them forever."

"How could I know the prophet would kill himself? We will not lose his followers. When Trigger is buried, he will be forgotten. We will regain control of *the Ghosts.*"

"Will they forget him?" Zacharus wonders out loud.

"He's a rebel, father. He's a blasphemer. We must preserve our priestly order. We must control the Temple of the Holy City. That is our chief task."

"Is it?" Zacharus says with resignation.

"It will be a priority of my administration."

The room seems darker. There is no *Light* in the Temple.

They both hear an approaching crowd in the Court of the Infidels.

Epitaph

Aron is the first to reach the Court of the Infidels. The future High Priest and current High Priest of the Temple of the Tribes of the Holy City watch as Douglas leads a growing number of pilgrims into the Temple's first court.

"I don't believe it," says Aron. "What nerve."

"He must have a death wish."

"Let us arrest him here and now," says Aron.

"No. Let us do it quietly at night when there are no crowds to rally around him."

"We can't just stand here and let him blaspheme in our own Temple! It is almost Festival. Look at this crowd!"

"It will make what must be done more palatable to the Tribes," says Zacharus. "His affront to God will be undeniable."

"We will trap him with his own words."

"If that is your plan, then you must find witnesses to his blasphemy."

"I fear there will be no lack of witnesses."

The two priests make their way out to the Court slowly at first, standing at the top of the stairs to the Temple. To their great shock, they are standing where Douglas has decided to make his speech. The onetime farmer and fisherman climbs the stairs while his entourage surrounds him on all sides.

Tommy's dogs take up the rear.

The two priests back away from Douglas and his group, as Douglas centers himself at the top of the stairs. His entourage clears from the stairs as Douglas turns to face the crowd. Tommy's dogs lie down on the stairs the humans have abandoned. Douglas raises his hands to silence the crowd.

"He's banned," Aron says to Zacharus.

"Shut-up."

"Awake!" says Douglas. "The word I bring is truth."

"That's what *the Medicine Man* said," Aron whispers to a wiser man. Zacharus hardly listens.

"We are all equal parts of the whole," says Douglas. "We live in a *Garden.* We are one mind separated by different experiences in physical reality. When we come together as one, these Temple walls will fall, as will all that has separated us. When you seek the truth, when you shed your individual ego and become part of the whole, when you stop worshiping manmade Gods, you will have a revelation. The truth will be revealed to all who seek it."

"This is the greatest blaspheme I have heard," remarks Aron.

"Let me tell you about truth," says Douglas.

"We must stop him now," says an anxious Aron.

"No," says Zacharus. "Let him hang himself."

"Truth is not angry. Truth is not happy or sad. Truth is not judgmental, because judgment is a thing of this world. Truth is not vengeful, because vengeance requires judgment. Truth does not choose sides. We are not being punished because we strayed away from some written manmade Law. And yet, the *Being* of every citizen is darkened whenever a son of the Tribes is oppressed and subjugated. Truth is not out there," he says, pointing to space, and then pointing to his chest, he says, "Truth is in here."

The crowd is quiet. They are not used to such talk. Aron looks to Zacharus for permission to end it. Zacharus's face is unmoving. He does not look away from Douglas. There is no permission granted.

"There are no dichotomies in *the Garden.* There is no he or she. There is no black or white. There is no right or wrong.

There is no inside or outside. There is no man or God. There is no good or evil. There is no Empire. There is no Temple. There is no Heaven or Hell. There is only truth. The truth is a collective consciousness of the whole. We are creators and we are created. In this life, we can divide or come together. When we are one, we will overcome the world."

"Are you *the Messiah?*" shouts one from the crowd.

"What does your *Messiah* do?" asks Douglas.

"Free me," says the man.

"No," says Douglas. "I'm not your *Messiah*. You must free yourself. You must be your own savior. Only you have the power. No one else can save you. You are your own Temple. When will you listen to the wisdom that is within you? When will you ask questions of the invisible within you? When will you know your *Being?* When will you see that we live in a *Garden?*"

"We live in a desert!" shouts one from the crowd.

"We live in a *Garden* and you do not see it."

"Where is *the Garden?*" says the man. "All I see are Temple walls!"

"It is not a place. It is not in these Temple walls. These walls are impermanent. Just as your body masks your *Being,* these Temple walls hide the truth from your eyes."

"They're still listening to him," an agitated Aron whispers to the older man.

Zacharus makes no answer.

"This is a story about a man who could not overcome the world," says Douglas. "It is a story of a poor man whose hard life had left a hole in his *Being.* From the time he was a young man, he was taught to believe that the only way to overcome this world was to become rich. He worked hard and long to accumulate wealth. He worked so much that he never had time to take a wife and have a family. He became richer and richer, but he distrusted the future, and though his house was a mansion, he still thought he was poor, and the more he reaped of the material world, the more he invested in things that would make him richer. Everything he bought became an investment. He filled his mansion with ornaments of gold and silver. His attic was full of the things he'd buy. He had so many possessions that he filled a storehouse so that he should lack nothing. This, he thought, would fill the hole, but the richer he became, the larger became the hole. This man never knew *the Self* in all things.

"You create your own reality," continues Douglas. "This is all an illusion. When all are one, the distinction between *Being* and this world is overcome. You will be free. You will fold back into eternity."

"How do you look into the future?" asks one from the crowd. "How do you prophesy?"

"I do not prophesy by looking into the future. All of the answers are in the past. All that can be known is known. I'm not saying anything new."

The crowd pauses. Aron makes his foray, though it is against his father-in-law's counsel.

"Who are you to speak of truth as you do?" he says. "What do you know of truth? God is truth!"

Douglas turns his head to his right where the priest is standing. Douglas looks disgusted. "Who am I?" he asks. "I am one who has confidence in his own knowing. What do you know? You are blinded by darkness, not *Light*. You would lead those blinded by *Light* into the dark and hope they turn to you to see."

"Tell me," says Aron, "Is it proper to kill a goat by bloodletting?"

"Are you kidding me?" answers Douglas.

Some people laugh.

"You don't like to answer questions, do you?" says the priest.

"I answer my own questions," says Douglas. "Yours do not interest me."

"But you must answer them," says the priest. "Everyone waits for you."

"You wait to trap me," says Douglas.

Aron is startled to be discovered. "I just want you to answer a question."

"About goats? The question is not an honest question, it is meant to trap."

"If you won't answer that question, then answer this: Do

you agree with *the Medicine Man* that a man should not divorce his wife?"

"You brood of vipers," Douglas says to both priests with a laugh. "You want me to make a judgment? I'll make a judgment. You do not know *the Self.* You are not at peace. How can you pretend to speak for your God when all you care about are the trappings of this world?"

He turns to the crowd and says, "Behold the priests, who like to go about in long robes, who devour widows' houses and for a pretense make long prayers. They pass judgment on others for things they do themselves. Out of the abundance of the heart the mouth speaks. The righteous man out of his righteous seed brings forth good fruit. What the jealous man plants produces tares. In this world, it is by your actions you will be justified, and by your actions you will be condemned. They honor truth with your words, but their actions are lies. Their words break up when they leave their throat. The gap between their words and their deeds is a hoarfrost moat.

"Beware the bread of the priests, for it is stale," Douglas calls out. "They preach righteousness, but they do not practice. They are without vision. The bread of the priests is another man's dough. Beware of those who plant tares when men of vision die. John is dead. Beware of those who would tell you what he said. The priests bind heavy burden, hard to bear, and lay them on men's shoulders, but they themselves will not move them with their finger. They do all their deeds to be seen by others. They shout their prayers so that others can hear how righteous they are. They love the place of honor at feasts and the best seats in the Temples and at the Games, and salutations in the market place, and being called 'Lord' by men."

He turns to his right and looks at Aron and Zacharus again before continuing to the crowd. "Behold the priests who believe they are the gatekeepers to *the Garden,* but they neither enter themselves, nor do they allow those who would enter to go in. They cleanse the outside of the cup and plate, but inside, they are full of extortion and rapacity. First, they must clean the inside of the cup and plate, that the outside may be clean. They are like whitewashed tombs, which outwardly appear beautiful, but within they are full of dead men's bones and all uncleanness. They outwardly appear righteous to men, but within they are full of hypocrisy and iniquity."

The crowd in the Court of the Infidels is shocked that a man would speak in the Temple as Douglas is speaking.

"Truth is not in this Temple," Douglas says. "You will find the truth within. It is not outside. It is inside. Know *the Self.* We are one."

Douglas's speech is over. He walks down the steps and into the crowd. His entourage and Tommy follow. Tommy's stray dogs jump up and spring to attention.

The audience doesn't know what to do. They do not applaud. They begin to talk amongst themselves.

The chanting is a couple of people at first, but it becomes louder: "Trigger! Trigger! Trigger!"

Douglas and his friends look at each other. "It's time to go," he says softly.

"Me and Bobby will meet you back at the camp," says Tommy. They have a meeting with Timothy and Martin. *The Festival Rising* is almost upon the Holy City.

"Alright," says Douglas already walking.

Outside the Temple's walls they can still hear the sound: "Trigger! Trigger! Trigger!"

Zacharus stares at the crowd with a resigned resentment as they follow Douglas Trigger and his entourage through the gate. Aron is anxious.

"Douglas Trigger is even more dangerous than *the Medicine Man,*" says Zacharus. "They think his is the voice of God."

"I shall call a meeting of the Council of the Tribes. Let us do what must be done."

As Tommy and Bobby watch Douglas and the others fade away, Aron sees Tommy and motions to Zacharus to get his attention. "A witness," he says.

Zacharus nods his head in approval and Aron signals to some nearby Temple Guards, who quickly surround the rebel, ignoring Bobby, who backs away. One of the Guards relieves

Tommy of his dagger and syrinx. Another Guard puts his wrists in shackles.

Tommy looks to Bobby and motions for him to leave while he still can. Bobby turns around and walks away.

"Where are we going?" Tommy says with a smile to the scowling Guards as they drag him away.

The stray dogs follow Tommy.

The Council of the Tribes

At night, Aron gathers the Council of the Tribes in the Great Courtyard behind the Temple to make his case against Douglas Trigger. The Council is comprised of rich old men, Tribal priests, scribes and elders of the Temple of the Tribes of the Holy City. There are no priests from *the Settlement.* The group meets periodically as a court to pass judgment on major religious and political cases. This is religious and political.

Aron stands in the Courtyard next to his throne looking out at the galleries that line the hill. The seats are all empty, just as Zacharus wants it. No witnesses. Loki watches from a shadowy dark place. Aron cannot see him. Zacharus sits at his place behind a long table. Other priests are there, some of whom Tommy knows. There are Zacharus and Aron, but there is also Sean Tracy, a rich priest and a co-conspirator in Tommy's revolution.

The Temple Guards bring Tommy into the Courtyard and make him stand on a raised platform in the center. He is chained to escorts, who sit on either side of him. The stray dogs that follow the rebel are no longer with him. They were put outside the Temple where they wait for Tommy.

Zacharus signals to the Guards that the chains are not necessary. All exits are blocked. The Guards unchain his wrists. Tommy thanks Zacharus with a nod of his head. *The*

Son of Light does not like what is happening.

Tommy looks at the panel of older men as they begin to file in. He does not recognize most of them. He feels outnumbered. He's right. Tommy wonders what he will do. He wonders what Bobby is doing. He feels sure of one thing: what this Council will decide has already been decided. The rest is dressing. All that he can do has been done. The body Tommy uses will be used by the priests of the Temple of the Tribes of the Holy City. He is their prop now. He knows how his brother feels.

It is a cold night. Some of the Guards and other servants are making a coal fire in the middle of the courtyard.

Aron waits for the other members of the Council of the Tribes to arrive. Several members are being stirred from their beds.

Nicodemus, another priest, who is not likely to support anything the other priests do, is the last member of the committee to enter the open Courtyard. He is of Zacharus's generation, and he eases himself into a chair between the High Priest and Sean Tracy. Once they have gathered, Aron moves to take his place as the Chairman of the Council by settling into his throne and banging a gavel on its stone arm. He looks straight ahead without emotion. He does not look at Tommy. Zacharus does not look at Tommy. No one looks at the rebel but Sean Tracy. They are all playing the same game.

"What do you want?" says Tommy.

The Council members are shocked. "You will be quiet until you are told to speak," says Aron.

"Why have you detained me?" Tommy asks. "You must want something."

Aron bangs his gavel. "This Council of the Tribes will now come to order," says Aron. He looks at his witness. Tommy scowls.

"As most of you know by now," says the priest, "another 'prophet' has arisen in the land. This one's name is Douglas Trigger. He's from Swifton. I don't think I have to tell you what he said today in the Temple or about the incident in the Court of the Infidels this week. The question we have to ask ourselves is what do we do about this man? He is leading the Tribes away from the Temple. He says the Tribes don't need the Temple. Such talk is blasphemy. This man is against God. He is against the Temple. He is against the Tribes. This blasphemer is not some zealot attacking the Empire. *We* are his targets. He is zealous for his own ideas. What are *we* going to do?"

"What would you have us do?" asks Tracy.

"Our path is clear," says Aron to the assembled group. "Some are already calling him *the Messiah.* Not only does he take men away from the Temple, but he also gathers them against us. If we let him continue, there will be anarchy amongst the Tribes. The Empire will come down not only on him, but on us as well because we could not control our own people. What we do, we must do quickly, for it is almost Festival. He will move the pilgrims away from us. The Empire and *their* Gods will gain control over them. He is perilous. We must not allow this man to influence the thousands of pilgrims who are already flowing into the Temple. This man could foment an institutional revolt. How can we unite against the Empire if he divides us? How will the Tribes survive if they turn their backs on God?"

"You've brought me here to testify against my brother?" asks Tommy.

Aron looks at him and smiles. "You are a witness," he says.

"I didn't see anything," he says.

"Please state your name for the record," says Levi, one of the scribes.

"I have no name."

"His name is Tommy Trigger," says Aron. "Tell us about your brother, Tommy."

"I have no brother," says Tommy. "I'm an orphan. Everybody knows that."

"Tell us about Douglas Trigger."

"Douglas Trigger?" Tommy says. "I don't think I know that name."

"Do not play games, Tommy," Aron says. "Tell me what you know."

"I don't know anything."

Aron is becoming agitated.

"You should answer his questions," Zacharus says. "Don't you realize the power this Council has over you?"

"Yes." He laughs his silent laugh. He understands what his brother means about freedom. The Council is waiting for more of an answer. "You have power over me only if I give it to you."

"You must want to live," says Nicodemus. "You must fear death."

"I want to live," says Tommy. "I don't fear death."

"I can tell you about this man, Douglas Trigger," says Nicodemus. "I met him once and he talked about a second birth. He talked about a birth of *Being.* 'The wind blows where it will,' he said, 'but you do not know from where it comes or to where it is going, so it is with *Being.*'"

Nicodemus is on his own spiritual quest and is also a secret fan.

"This is blasphemy," says Aron.

"This is dialogue," says Nicodemus. "I have never met a man who spoke like this. He did not simply repeat tradition, he used his own words. He spoke of what he *knew.* He spoke of what he'd *seen.* He showed me his *Being,* and in so doing, he showed me my own."

"What he spoke was blasphemy," says Aron. "I have seen him too. This radical wants to bring down the Temple with his blasphemy. He would have the crowds call him 'the Great Chief of the Tribes' and in gaining his Chiefdom, we will lose ours."

Nicodemus leans back in his chair.

Tommy laughs. Douglas doesn't want a Chiefdom.

"What's so funny?" asks the High Priest.

"Nothing is funny," says Tommy.

"Nothing is funny," says Aron. "It is already happening. Your brother is a very deliberate young man. He knows what he's doing. What are you going to do about it?"

"Do?" says Tommy. "What will I do? I will plant flowers on it and let them grow. I will not do anything. What do you want from me?"

"I want your support."

"Against my brother?"

"Tommy, your brother is out of control."

"He is out of your control."

"He is out of control, Tommy. I don't know if you realize the seriousness of what's happening here. The crowds are larger in the Holy City and more dangerous." Tommy smiles. "This was his second disruption after he was banned. It was his first sermon. He already has a reputation. Your brother incites the mob. He challenges order."

"Your order?"

Aron ignores his comment. "The time has come when we must stop him," Aron continues. "The time has come when we must regain control of order."

"Why must *you* rule order?" Tommy asks.

"Whatever he has made you think..." says Aron.

"No one makes me think," says Tommy.

"Of course not," says Aron to humor him. "Whatever...*you* think of us, we are responsible for the destiny of our people. We stand between the Tribes and their total subjugation by the Empire."

"What if he is *the Messiah?*" asks Nicodemus.

"There is no *Messiah*," says Aron. "There is only survival under this heretical occupation."

Sean Tracy shakes his head at the High Priest. He does not like what is happening.

"This is not true," says Nicodemus. "A *Messiah* will come."

"Douglas Trigger is not *the Messiah*," says Aron. "He's just a rabble rouser who talks with an authority he does not have."

"He has an authority that no man can grant," says Nicodemus. "It comes from within."

"That is not authority," says Aron. "Authority is granted. It is earned. Respect the authority I have earned."

"That is a different kind of authority," says Nicodemus. "It is an earthly authority. I have listened to this man, Douglas Trigger. He would respect your authority only so long as you followed natural law. You would fold natural law into your own image to gain power."

"Nobody on this Council cares what Douglas Trigger's opinion of my authority might be" says Aron. "Natural law?

There is only God's Law."

"It is natural law."

"And what about you?" Aron says to Tommy. "Is that what you say?"

Tommy's answer is silence.

"He is finished," Aron continues. "The decision is already made. Don't make a fatal mistake."

"Are you threatening me?"

"I am telling you what will happen. I'm prepared to offer you immunity if you will testify against your brother in front of this Council."

"Immunity from what?"

"There are a variety of things we could charge you with. How will it serve your cause if you are jailed and he is left free?"

"I don't want to hear this talk," says Tommy. "You disgust me."

"We will get a witness against your brother."

"It's not me."

"He has already indicted himself. We just need confirmation for the record. We already know that your brother is guilty of blasphemy. You better answer my questions or you will receive the same judgment as your brother."

Tommy is silent.

"Do not fall with him," says Aron. "Just answer some simple questions."

"I have no answers," says Tommy. "If I'm your only witness, you guys are in a lot of trouble."

Tommy looks for an escape. He doesn't want to miss the start of the revolution. There is no escape.

"Tommy," Aron says flatly, "we are moving against your brother. We are bringing him before this Council. You can join us, or you can fall with him. You can help us and help yourself."

"I will not be your witness."

"Somebody will talk and they'll be rewarded for it. It may as well be you."

"It may as well be somebody else."

"I will not take 'no' for an answer," says the priest.

"Then you better ask a different question."

"I don't think you understand the gravity of your situation," says Aron. "I don't think you understand the power this Council has over you."

Tommy laughs. "You have no power over me," he says.

"Of course we have no power over you," says Zacharus, playing along with the trial. "We know that your own death is not a threat to you. Indeed, you are willing to die for what you believe in. You are willing to die for the Tribal Nations. You are a patriot. We know that a strong man cannot be threatened."

"This is getting you nowhere," says Tommy. "Why don't you go bother somebody else?

"Know this, Tommy," says Aron, "If this *'Hierophant'* legend of your brother is allowed to flourish, we will all die. I'm not talking about some brief fascination, or one life thwarted by time. I'm talking about the death of our race and the end of the Tribal Nations. Have we survived since recorded history began to be stopped by one man? We survived enslavement. We were deported and banished from our homeland and survived to return to survive and flourish under another occupying Empire. We will survive this Imperial occupation. Our past is done. Our time is done. Our lives are done. Shall all that we've done since the first tale of the Tribes was told be undone? There is a reason for our Nations. We are *God's Favorite.*"

"I won't help you."

"Your brother will die anyway," says Aron. "Save yourself."

"I will not help you," says Tommy. "I do not know the man."

"The destiny of our people is greater than the destiny of one man. The individual is expendable. The Tribal Nations are not. Our Council, offering guidance to the Great Chief, is the only thing preventing the Empire from launching a campaign of Tribal genocide."

"You got it all wrong," says Tommy. "The Nations are expendable. The individual is not."

"Individuals make up the Nations."

"The Nations do not make up the individuals."

"Think of your future," says Aron. "You're throwing it all away."

"I have no future," says Tommy.

"Be a witness. Think of the Struggle, Tommy. This is survival. Don't you see whom he is striking out at? He is not attacking the Empire. He's not like you. *We* are his targets. He is attacking his own people. He is attacking the Tribes. In these times, the Law must be obeyed if we are to avoid the death of our culture and our assimilation by the Empire. How can we stand strong if he divides us? How then can we overcome the Empire?"

"Do you think that's what he wants?"

"Think about what you want," says Aron. Tommy grits his teeth. "If he rules the mob, the Tribes will fall. If we continue to rule them, as we must, we will survive until the fall of the Empire."

"Why must they be ruled at all?" Tommy muses out loud.

"What kind of a question is that for a *Son of Light* to ask?" says Aron. "We know about you. We know about your…comrades. If you care about your Tribe, if you care about all the Tribes, if you care about the Struggle, you must help us."

"What makes you think I'm a *Son of Light?*"

"I'm not after you, Tommy," says Aron. "I want your brother."

"I don't have a brother."

"Help me," says Aron. "Help your Tribe."

"You're not in my Tribe, priest."

"Neither is he," says Aron.

"He's my brother."

"We serve the Tribes. He divides us. He scoffs at the Law, Tommy. The Empire will view him as a malcontent. They will not tolerate him. He will go eventually. If he incites enough citizens, we will all be persecuted. Isn't it better for one man to fall than for our whole people to suffer?"

"You would allow the fall of a man because it is easier than saving him, wouldn't you?" says Tommy.

"If you do not cooperate with us," says Aron, "maybe you'll cooperate with the Empire when we lose our authority over him."

"You have no authority over him."

"Do you respect the authority of the Empire? He will be a martyr for your revolution."

"I have heard he is a man of peace."

"Men of peace usually die in violence," says Aron.

Tommy laughs. "How do men of violence usually die?" he asks.

"Of old age," says Aron.

"There are so many martyrs already," Tommy says. "I know too many men who are dead or dying."

"His revolution is done," says Aron. "His life is done. Shall all that we've done be undone? Join us."

"I don't like the game you're playing," says Tommy.

"It isn't a game," says Aron. "Help us regain control of the Tribes. It's over for your brother."

"Maybe it is over," says Tommy. "Maybe his revolution is done. Maybe my revolution is done. Perhaps the time has not yet come."

"Does that mean you'll help us?"

"No."

"Do you know who you're talking to?" says Aron.

"You're just a mercenary like me," says Tommy.

Aron lets it go.

"If there's nothing else," says Tommy, "I'll be leaving."

Zacharus looks at his son-in-law.

"Let him go," Tracy says with authority.

"Aye," says Nicodemus, "let him go."

Zacharus nods his head. Aron looks at the older priest then back to Tommy. "Think about what I said, and know that the Temple or the Empire will not long endure a 'prophet.' Do not be with him when he falls."

"He will not fall."

"If he does not fall," says Aron. "We will push him."

Zacharus shakes his head.

Tommy does not get back his dagger. Loki already has it. He does not get back his syrinx. Outside the dogs wait for him. Their numbers have grown. Tommy takes off at a quick pace to go to Timothy's. He missed the meeting. Loki follows him at a distance. Malachi, the Captain of the Temple Guard watches Tommy from his post.

Aron leans back in his chair. "Douglas Trigger has conspired against the established order," he says. "He has further conspired to take control and form his own order." Aron looks up and down the table of men. "This is blasphemy. This is blasphemy against the Temple and against God. I implore the members of this Council to vote that Douglas Trigger be given the opportunity to defend himself against the very serious charges made against him here today."

"Is that a formal motion?" asks Levi.

"Yes," says Aron.

"So moved," says Zacharus.

"If there is no further discussion," says Aron, "I will call for the vote." He pauses.

"This is an outrage," says Nicodemus. "This was not a hearing."

"Is this why we are meeting at night?" asks Tracy.

"All those in favor say, 'Aye,'" says Aron.

All of the priests and scribes save Tracy and Nicodemus say, "Aye."

"Opposed?"

"Nay," say the same two.

"The 'Ayes' have it." Aron shoots an 'I'll remember that' look to the two priests. "That being the only matter before the Council of the Tribes, I order that we are in recess until we can bring this man before us. I summon the Captain of the Temple Guard to tail the witness to locate Douglas Trigger. Upon learning his location, you shall return to the Temple for reinforcements and we shall move to arrest him."

Aron bangs his gavel. It is over.

The Conspiracy

The two spies follow Tommy and his dogs to Timothy's house. The rebel does not spot them. The spies do not spot each other. Tommy knocks on the door. He looks around him while he waits. The dogs settle. They do not see the spies. The door opens.

Timothy is surprised. "They let you go," he says. "Bobby told us what happened."

"Is he here?"

"He went to tell your brothers. Martin's here. What happened?"

"Let me come in."

"You brought the dogs."

"They like to follow me."

"They make you easy to follow."

"Meet me at the rendezvous."

"Do not bring the dogs."

Tommy nods and Timothy closes the door. Tommy takes off. The dogs and the spies follow him.

Tommy meets Timothy and Martin in the Holy City square, which would have been crowded at the appointed hour, but is now empty. Tommy is still trailed by the dogs. "I couldn't get rid of them," he says, though he never tried.

"What happened?" says Timothy.

"There're after my brother," says Tommy. "They wanted me to be a witness against him. They gathered the Council of the Tribes to charge him with blasphemy."

"No doubt the same conspirators who gathered against Mandolin," says Timothy. "What did you tell them?"

"Nothing."

"What're they gonna do to him?" asks Martin.

"Kill him."

"A member of their own Tribes," ponders Timothy. "Next they will be conspiring with the enemy."

"They are the enemy," says Tommy. "That's what my brother says. He may be right. He says they're no different than the Empire."

"He is right," says Martin. "Order is order."

"Power is power," says Timothy.

"Why do we fight this Holy War?" says Tommy.

"We do it for God, not men," says Timothy.

"Soon it will be dawn," says Martin.

"Aye," says Timothy, getting back to business. "It is on, Tommy. Everything goes as planned. There will be more people in the Holy City today than at any other time of the year. Your mission is confirmed. In addition to your assignment, we need you to rally *the Ghosts.* We need you to make sure your brother is not around to make any speeches."

"I don't think you have to worry about that. After what I've just been through, I don't think it'll be too hard to convince him to lay low during Festival. I'm going to him right after I leave you. I have to warn him. He may not agree with our cause, but he's still my brother."

Timothy nods his head. "Did you get any sleep?"

"Sleep is for the weak."

"Where's that taxman?" asks Martin.

"I don't know," says Tommy. "He's probably in the Garden with the others."

"Is that where he is right now?"

"He quit that job."

"Not soon enough."

"Do not kill anyone before it starts," says Timothy. "It starts this morning. Tommy, you have to keep Douglas from speaking before then. You have to speak in his name."

"Aye."

"That is it then," says Timothy. "Go to your brother, Tommy. To Festival!"

"To Festival!" says Tommy.

"To Festival!" says Martin.

Tommy leaves the dogs in the Holy City Square, but he does not shake off the spies. Timothy and Martin separate and go to their homes. The dogs prowl the Holy City Square. Martin burns with rage to think of the taxman.

The Garden

It is night in the Garden. Tommy comes back and everyone is sleeping, save Douglas, who is standing alone, looking out on the Holy City. He is surprised by his brother's return.

"Are you alright?"

"Yea."

"Bobby told us what happened. We were gonna go in the morning when there would be a lot of pilgrims around."

"You couldn't sleep?"

"Yea. Bobby told me about your plans for tomorrow."

"He shouldn't have done that; unless you want to join us?"

Douglas laughs. They both laugh. "I'm surprised you returned," says Douglas.

"I had to. I figured I owed you that. You're my brother."

"I'm glad you feel like that."

Loki is hiding in the bushes watching. *The Ghosts* are waking up listening to voices.

It will be hard to kill Douglas Trigger. He is never alone. The assassin plans to kill him while he sleeps. It is almost morning.

Malachi, the Captain of the Temple Guard, also followed Tommy and is now on his way back to the Temple for reinforcements. He never saw the other spy, nor had Loki seen him.

Douglas and Tommy walk away from the others, who are falling asleep again. Loki moves into a better position.

"The reason they detained me was because of you. They're coming for you, brother. They're gonna kill you."

"Is that what they said?"

"They said that. They said it. They're gonna kill you."

"All I wanted to do was lead a normal life," says Douglas.

"It doesn't always work out the way you plan," says Tommy. "Besides, what is a normal life?"

Tommy sits down on a rock. He has a doomed expression on his face. He is looking at Douglas.

"They offered me immunity if I become a witness against you."

"Immunity from what?"

"From what they're going to do to you. They're gonna keep coming after you until they get you."

"I'm just a philosopher."

"It's not their philosophy. They have a word for people who don't agree with them---blasphemer. It's probably what they called Mandolin. It's probably what they called your friend, John. It's what they're calling you. You're a pacifist philosopher during an Imperial occupation of *God's Promise.* Maybe you're not looking for power, but you're looking to take it away from a group that has it."

"It's not your philosophy either, is it?" says Douglas.

Tommy doesn't answer. "They had a hearing against you tonight. The Council of the Tribes was assembled. They tried to get me to testify."

"What did you tell them?" asks Douglas.

"I told him you weren't very funny."

"At least you were honest."

Tommy laughs his silent laugh.

"What?"

"I was just thinking I do have a different philosophy. I mean, we're twins and everything, twins, and I might think that you see my point of view and you might think I see yours, but man, you don't know me and I don't know you. And it's not just because of all those missing years. It's a crazy world, isn't it? I thought you were listening to me. You thought I was listening to you. Crazy world."

"What now?"

"Stay low. Don't make any more speeches. Let me take over for a while. Less talk about religious things and more talk about political things."

"Well, I don't see any reason to change anything."

"I think it's almost over. You took a lot of men away from the revolution. I should have killed you myself." Tommy laughs.

"Deep down, you know I'm right."

Tommy still smiles. "No," he says. "No, I don't think you are right. I know what I know. That's enough. I don't need somebody trying to change my mind, even you. I just can't figure out why so many people are listening to this pacifist crap. We're being occupied."

"If we were to play it your way, there would be no Tribes," says Douglas. "The Empire would wipe us out."

"At least we'd die proud. You talk like a coward."

"No. I'm not a coward. I'm not afraid to die."

"Well, that's good, 'cause you're gonna."

"Do you know when?"

"Soon. They are already moving against you. You should consolidate power. You should arm *the Ghosts*. It is the only way you will survive. Join the revolution. You could be the Great Chief."

"I am a philosopher."

"Why can't a philosopher be the Great Chief?"

"It's not a good idea. It is the greatest temptation of even the wisest of men to seek to rule those with lesser ability--- whether his motive is selfless or selfish. Such men fear only themselves. They do not fear other men. They do not fear retribution. They do not fear life. They do not fear death. They sense the immortal. A philosopher should be an advisor to politicians. He shouldn't be one. He shouldn't live so much in this world. Politics is the dance of illusion. Philosophy is the dance of *Being*."

"Brother, I don't understand you, but I know that we must fight for what is ours."

"When we die, Tommy, the inert and the mortal will outlive

us in this world. But the Empires of men are like so many birds scattering. When we are dead, men will call the Nations something else. It is the land of all human beings. It is the land promised to all beings. It doesn't matter who claims it or in whose name. The Empire that rules today will be called something else. The priests of the Temple of the Tribes of the Holy City will be called something else. *The Sons of Light*...who will you be? The deeds are constantly changing hands. What are you fighting for? You will die, only your terror will survive. At *Harvest Time* the people who live in this world will have the same concerns we have. There will be two brothers talking in a Garden one day. One will take joy in its beauty and say, 'What a lovely day.' The other will see the same Garden and say, 'Someday I must own it.'"

"I wish I knew what the fuck you were trying to say, Dougy, but sometimes, I just don't get you. You make no sense. If this were another time and place, I might support you. But this is here and now and I can't support you in this time. I can't allow the Empire to control me."

"What you repel controls you. How many must die before you learn the lesson? One man? One army? One people? One Empire? One world?"

"There can be no peace for an oppressed people. Damnit, Dougy, are you blind?"

"Tommy, you are misled. Your revolution dies when it is won. Eventually the masses will rise up against it. My revolution gains new champions every day."

"I will be remembered."

"So what? You'll be dead. You'll no longer feel separation. You'll be whole."

"My revolution must survive until the Tribes are free."

"There are no Tribes, Tommy. There are no citizens of the Empire. There is no separation. We are of the same mind, but our pasts build an imaginary chasm between us. Abandon the physical experiences that separate us, Tommy. Step out of time. We are one mind divided by false truths. You and I are one. We are one with Timothy. We are one with Peter. We are one with the priests. We are one with the Empire's citizens. Even now, we are one with Mandolin. Give up your precious you, Tommy. Be free."

"You would lead a man away from this world."

"You would lead men to their slaughter."

"At least they die for truth."

"Nobody dies from truth, Tommy."

Nobody dies from truth. Tommy stands up and begins walking again. Douglas catches up with him.

"The end is near, Dougy," says Tommy.

Douglas answers with a whisper, "I know that. I didn't want to die so soon."

"I tried to warn you. I tried to save you. I tried to guide you in the right direction. You can't upset the priests the way you..."

"Fuck the priests."

"You see now...that's great. That's just great. That's what's gonna get you killed." He walks away from him.

"C'mon Tommy, you want to die for a cause, don't you?" he says, chasing after him.

"Not this cause. I just don't get it. The priests do what they do because they wish to survive. I do what I do so the Tribes will survive."

"And that is why I do what I do."

"You're not going to survive," says Tommy. "They're after you, Dougy. You won't be too hard to find if you keep showing up at their Temple. Maybe it's time to move on."

"To where? This is the end of the river. I'm not gonna move. I'm not gonna run. If it's gonna come, let it come."

"Do you think that's wise? Do you want to die? What about the others? Do you think it's fair to them? Don't you think they have the right to know?"

Douglas looks off in the direction of the campsite. They have all gone back to sleep.

"I'll tell them in the morning," says Douglas.

"In the morning. Another morning."

"They said they want to kill me."

"Yes."

"They want to kill me soon."

"Yes."

"I'd like to live just a little while longer," says Douglas. "I didn't want to die so young."

"There's no point in getting old," says Tommy. "Come with me. Me and Bobby are going to go meet Timothy at *Sarah's Inn.* There's room for you yet in the Struggle."

"No," says Douglas. "You go."

"It's too bad you couldn't join us," says Tommy. "At least you would have died for something."

"I knew it would end this way when I started," says Douglas.

"Well, I hope you like rocks."

They both chuckle.

"I didn't mean it, brother." says Tommy. "You're not going to die in vain. Whether you help us or not, we will win this Struggle."

"It is not my struggle."

"Sure it is. You just don't know it yet. The Tribes must survive. The priests are in control of the Tribes and you cannot take it from them. That's how *they* survive."

"That's what they don't get. I don't want to take control. I want people to take control of their own lives."

"Their lives belong to the Temple," Tommy smiles. "The priests play a game where they write the rules. To them, you're just one of the pieces. Maybe you didn't know it, but you grabbed for the power and then you didn't take it. Now the power will be taken from you. If the priests don't rule the Tribes, the Empire will."

"The priests are the Empire."

"That's how you see it?"

"That's how I see it."

"Why can't you see what I see? It can be us gaining the power!"

Douglas's thoughts go beyond the Garden. He thinks of Mandolin, dead now.

"You see only what you want to see," says Tommy. "With you, there is just one answer for everything."

"There is only one truth. There are people in control of man-made order. There are people who allow themselves to be controlled by man-made order. There are those who see the truth, who see how to control order, but do not use it to their own advantage. There is the priest. There is you. There is me."

"You won't listen to anyone but yourself. Maybe that's why people listen to you."

"Maybe."

"The world isn't ready for you yet, brother. I wonder if it ever will be."

Douglas looks to the clearing where the others are sleeping. "At least I will die with friends," he says. "I miss the days of our youth, before this world made its imprint on us."

Tommy looks at his brother and thinks about the time before he left the farm. He nods his head. His smile is more of a grimace. His memories are hard.

They look up at the stars. It is a clear night. One star shines brightly above their heads. The star is more brilliant than any other. It is an alarming light. It is almost too bright. It cannot long remain burning so much brighter than the others without burning itself out.

It Begins

The time has come. Loki is an impatient assassin. Douglas and Tommy may not be going to sleep this night. Maybe they are preparing his speech for Festival. Maybe they are as alone as they are going to be. Loki moves into position, a prowling wolf before the kill. He has brought Tommy's dagger for the job.

The two brothers wait in silence. They have nothing left to say to each other. They are not tired. They do not even know why they stay. They have nothing in common but their DNA. They sit in the Garden not facing one another.

Douglas is sweating. He thinks about how the end came for Mandolin. His twin is right. He wonders how his own end will come.

"I guess I'm gonna leave," says Tommy, standing.

Loki hears him. He will have Douglas alone.

Douglas nods. He gets up. All of his friends are asleep in the Garden. Tommy puts out his hand and Douglas shakes it. "If I don't see you after tomorrow," says Tommy, "maybe I was wrong."

"Happy Festival. Good luck."

"You too."

The two brothers hug. Tommy is more comfortable hugging his twin than when they first reunited.

Tommy is gone. Douglas is alone. He will not sleep this night. He walks away from where the others are sleeping. Loki waits for Tommy to get away. He will go after him in a minute.

Douglas's body is out of his control. It will be stolen by the elders of the Temple. He can run, join Tommy, or wait for the priests to come to collect.

Everyone else is sleeping. Andy, Peter, and Barty are sleeping. Douglas's little brother, Joey, is sleeping. Philip is sleeping. Jimmy A is dreaming. Jimmy A's brother, Matty, is sleeping. James and Johnny Z are sleeping. Bobby is waking up slowly.

Douglas runs his fingers through his hair. He looks at the moon. It is a moon with an alarming light. It is almost too bright. No one who looks at that light sees what he sees. It makes him sad. Soon it will be morning and the sun will outshine its own reflection.

'Sleep,' Douglas thinks as he looks at his friends. 'It is almost dawn. Soon I will sleep forever.'

Douglas is sad. Had he been wrong to think that what he wanted could be won? He thinks about Mandolin and his thoughts go away from her. He looks up at the sky again and it is lighter, but the stars are still bright. It is Festival. Soon it will be dawn.

Douglas thinks about his family. He thinks about Tommy, Jimmy and Joey. He also thinks about his mother and he thinks about the stepfather who used to beat him as a child. He thinks about the real father he never knew.

Tommy goes away from his brother still thinking about him. He isn't far from the Garden when he hears men approaching. Tommy ducks behind a bush next to a tree. He watches the men go by. It is Aron and Zacharus with Temple Guards and Imperial soldiers.

Tommy circles around to head off the approaching group and warn his brothers and *the Ghosts.* He gets to the clearing before the soldiers and they are all asleep. He makes no noise to wake them; he doesn't want to alarm the approaching war party. He goes to where he left Douglas.

As Tommy approaches the clearing, Loki stands up from behind a bush. As Tommy comes closer to warn Douglas about the soldiers, it is already too late. Loki stealthily stalks his prey and brings out Tommy's own dagger.

"Dougy!" Tommy screams, pointing to the spy.

Douglas looks towards his brother's voice and turns around to see his assassin. "Who are you?"

Loki laughs. Everyone asks the same question. He puts his hand on Douglas's left shoulder and hastily plunges the blade into Trigger's gut. He then rips open his stomach in an upward motion. It is not the method he prefers, but he has been discovered. Douglas makes an animal grunting noise. Everything starts to happen in slow motion.

"I am murdered," marvels Douglas. He feels a sharp pain in his stomach. Then he feels nothing at all.

Loki looks at Tommy who is almost upon him. Tommy has murder in his eyes. Loki turns like a wild rabbit and runs into the cover of the bushes and into the darkness of the surrounding wood. The hunter is now the hunted. Tommy starts to go after the spy, but then he looks at his brother who has been stabbed. He puts off revenge and goes to his twin.

Douglas falls into his brother's arms. The knife is well placed. Loki left it in as evidence. He is dying.

"Dougy?"

Douglas looks up at the lightening sky. "All the stars are gone," he says.

"What?"

"It's so light out. The stars are gone."

"What are you talking about?"

"It happens pretty fast," he says. "Life is just a memory. Think of me until I come again."

"What do you mean?" asks the rebel.

"Whenever the Law of man usurps the natural law, a *Voice* will cry out in the wilderness."

Douglas thinks about Mandolin, he'd like to see her, but she is already dead.

"Awake!" Douglas says with his fading breath, "Awake!" He drops his head and closes his tired eyes for the last time. He is not dead yet, but he soon will be.

"Dougy?" Nothing. Tommy shakes him gingerly in his arms. "Dougy boy?" Tommy puts his ear next to his brother's mouth to hear or feel his breath. He's not dead yet. "I never knew you," says Tommy. "If it's any consolation, I wish I did."

The priests and the soldiers enter the clearing where the others are sleeping. The soldiers rouse all the men. Bobby jumps up. "Where's Douglas Trigger?" says Aron.

"What?" says Bobby, now fully awake.

"There," says Zacharus, pointing to Tommy. Peter, Andy and the others are waking up.

"What the...?" says Andy, coming awake. He is greeted with an Imperial spear blocking his path.

"Forget *the Ghosts,*" says Aron. "Who's that there?" He leads the war party to the scene of the crime. Bobby follows them. When they enter the clearing, they see that Douglas is dying in Tommy's arms.

Tommy looks over when he hears them approaching. He kisses his brother on the forehead and lays him softly down on the ground.

"Vengeance is mine," he says.

Bobby comes to the edge of the crime scene and is held back by Temple Guards. He sees Tommy recover the dagger from Douglas's stomach and retreat into what is left of the night. Tommy looks at the knife and sees that it is his. It confirms that Loki is a spy from the Temple of the Tribes of the Holy City.

"It's Tommy," says Aron. He motions for the soldiers to go after him.

"My Lord," says one of the Temple Guards kneeling by Douglas, "the prophet is dead."

"Dead?" says Aron.

"He's dead, my Lord."

"Dead," says Aron, "killed by his own brother. His own brother. Tommy is a fugitive. We must pursue him."

The priests and soldiers leave Douglas where he has fallen. Bobby can't believe that he saw Tommy removing a dagger from his own twin. Peter and some of the others go to him. They do not say anything. They cannot believe what is happening.

Peter kneels down next to his fallen friend. He puts his hand on Douglas's bleeding wound. He puts his hand over his mouth to see if Douglas is breathing. Peter can hear nothing. There is no sign of life. Douglas is dead. Peter's eyes start to tear up. The others gather around.

"Poor man," says Peter. "The only way he could save himself was to save the world."

"Do you think he saved it?" asks Andy.

"It doesn't look like it." Peter looks over to Joey. "Joey, Douglas is dead."

Joey breaks down and his friends surround him.

The harvest will be great, but the laborers are few. Gather the good wheat into the barn and burn the tares.

Festival

On Festival, *the Sons of Light* plan to take over strategic strong points in the center of the Holy City and rally the pilgrims to enlist as warriors. That is the plan. A garrison led by Bobby will capture the Emperor's deserted Imperial army barracks. Though Bobby is no longer with them in spirit, he is loyal and his flesh is with the rebels. Martin Collins will lead another garrison to shut down and loot the company that collects taxes for the Empire. Tommy will lead a garrison to capture the Temple Fortress, the tallest structure in the Holy City, at the northwest end of the Temple, where they will make their headquarters. Timothy will lead a garrison outside the walls to the edge of the Holy City to wait for the Emperor's Imperial Army to return from their desert drill.

Tommy did not catch up with the assassin, but he knows he will catch up with him on this day when he strikes the Temple, for on this day he knows that Loki is a Temple spy. He will also catch up with the priests, which was not a part of the original plan. Tommy waits for Bobby with Timothy and Martin Collins at *Sarah's Inn.*

"Do you think they got him?" asks Timothy.

"I don't know," says Tommy. "I think they were just after my brother."

"What kind of times are we living in when they kill

prophets?" says Timothy.

"I don't think it's different than any other time," says Tommy. "Do you know what one of the priests said to me? 'People of peace usually die in violence.'"

"He is correct," says Timothy. "Peace does not pay."

"People with false power want to keep it," says Tommy. "It's only after he's dead that people listen to what a man said."

"He should have lived. He was your brother and he should have fought with us this day."

"The Emperor was not his enemy," says Tommy.

"So it would appear. Who would have guessed? You know, I did not agree with your brother, but he said the things a prophet says."

"He never called himself a prophet."

"But the crowd did."

"That's why they killed him," says Martin.

"They called him 'the Great Chief,'" says Timothy.

Tommy knows that people besides his brother will die this day. The fighting is about to begin. Timothy looks away from him. They both know that when this campaign is over, the other or both of them may be dead.

Bobby shows up at the inn about a half-hour after Tommy. Since leaving the Garden, his mind has been filled with only one question. He asks it over and over. He asks it to himself as he sits down. "Your brother is dead," he says.

"I know," says Tommy. "I was there when he was murdered."

Timothy doesn't say anything. He watches the two.

"What happened to everybody?" asks Tommy. "Did they take anybody into custody?"

"I know you were there," says Bobby. "I saw you pull your knife from his gut."

The realization of Bobby's accusation fills Tommy's face. "Wo! Wo!" he says. "It *was* my knife. When I was detained by the Council, they took my knife."

Bobby is disbelieving.

"It was Loki," says Timothy. "He's a spy for the Temple."

"Really?"

Tommy is incredulous. "Really. He killed Dougy. I saw him.

He did it with my dagger. And it is with my dagger I will kill him."

"If your brother was murdered by a Temple assassin, why were the priests there to arrest him?" asks Bobby.

"Maybe they did it on purpose to create deniability," says Martin.

"Aron said they were gonna kill him and now he's dead," says Tommy. "You didn't see the Council of the Tribes meet."

"I saw you kill him," says Bobby.

"No. You saw me pull the knife out. They kept my knife when they let me go. They kept my syrinx! I did not kill my brother, but I saw who did."

"Loki, a Temple assassin."

"We did not suspect he was a Temple spy until Mandolin's stoning. Now we know. I saw him murder my brother. I saw him stick it in, my own knife. It seemed like time stopped. I was so close…It was like in a dream when you can't move. I was so close. I could see it happening, but I couldn't stop it. Time stopped, but I couldn't stop it. If I see Loki in battle this day, surely he will die."

Whether Bobby believes Tommy or not they have things to do.

"Gentlemen," says Timothy, "let the battle begin."

"The day all knew would come has come," says Tommy. "Today our freedom will be won."

They stand up and go to the rendezvous. There are hundreds, not thousands, waiting for them. Tommy's dogs are there, where he left them during the night. The rebels wait for more *Sons of Light* to show up. The pilgrims who pass by outnumber the rebels and they are not stopping. They are not at all interested. It is almost time to go. They can't congregate much longer without alerting the Empire and the Great Chief's local authority. Timothy taps Tommy on the elbow and motions to a high spot for Tommy to say something. "Who needs your brother," he says, "you be *the Messiah.*"

Tommy looks at him. Tommy looks at Bobby and Martin. Bobby nods to encourage him. "I don't know what I'll say."

"He never did either in the beginning," says Bobby. "He just started talking."

"Do it for him," says Timothy. "Do it for your dead brother."

Tommy nods his head. He stands on the highest point in the square. Those who know him see him and quite down. *The Sons of Light* all look to him. Some of the pilgrims look at him as they go.

Tommy holds up his hands and it becomes almost silent. "Comrades," he says to his fellow rebels and to the passersby, "Pilgrims! Men of the Holy City!" Some pilgrims are stopping to listen. "Listen to me! Listen to the call of the Tribes! Listen to the call of Festival! Listen to me!" More people are passing than stopping. Some of the rebels are eyeballing the passersby. The dogs are barking. "Awake!" says Tommy.

The Sons of Light cheer.

"Brothers, today we fight! And what man among us has not longed for this day?"

More cheers.

"How long should a people be subjugated before action is taken? I'll answer that question. Not one day more!"

The rebels cheer again.

"We are *God's Favorite,*" says Tommy. "This land is our land. It is *God's Promise.* It belongs to the Tribal Nations. We will run the enemy from Tribal Lands, even if our enemy is our own Great Chief. Let today mark a new Festival. It will be *the Festival of Liberation* from the Empire!"

The rebels cheer and applaud. Some of the pilgrims are joining in.

"This is a call to all pilgrims and passersby," says Tommy to get their attention. "What better way to serve God than to be one of his warriors? We must remove the infidels from *God's Promise.* I call on all pilgrims to unite with *the Sons of Light* to drive the infidels from the Nations of the Tribes. I say it again. Pilgrims unite with *the Sons of Light!* Pilgrims unite with *the Sons of Light!*" It becomes a chant. The rebels start chanting with him. "Pilgrims unite with *the Sons of Light!* Pilgrims unite with *the Sons of Light!* Pilgrims unite with *the Sons of Light!* We must regain *God's Promise!*"

A cheer goes up. A pilgrim speaks: "Why should we fight for your Kingdom when we have already won our own

Kingdom?"

"What do you mean?" says Tommy.

"It is everywhere, but nobody sees it."

The words of his brother. How annoying. Why are his words so powerful? Why do they sound though he is dead?

"Are you a *Ghost?"* asks Tommy.

"I am one who has listened to your brother. I saw you with him. Why do you not speak like him? Where is he today?"

"My brother is dead," says Tommy. His heckler is surprised and shaken. Many in the crowd gasp. They know who he is. "Yes, killed by one of the Emperor's Imperial soldiers. The Great Chief's soldiers were also there. They are the same thing. He is the Emperor's puppet. They are in collusion. My brother died for this revolution. His was the first blood shed in this new age. That is why I fight. My message is his message. His message is my message. If you followed him you should follow me."

"But surely he is alive?" says the man.

"No," says Tommy. "Are you with us?"

The man considers it. He is still shocked to think that Douglas is dead. Was he really killed by one of the Emperor's Imperial soldiers? This world is an illusion. "No," says the man. "I will not go."

"You will not go?" says Tommy. "You will not fight for freedom?"

"I am already free."

Timothy gives Tommy a signal. It is time to go. Tommy can't believe this man. It's like Douglas is raised from the dead.

"Then we will free you," says Tommy, "and when our blood is shed, know that we did it for you. Freedom is not free. It comes at a price. Every man must decide what price he will pay for freedom. All men who would fight for freedom come with me! This will be *the Festival of Liberation!"*

The Sons of Light cheer. Tommy steps down and along with Timothy, Martin and Bobby, they start marching. *The Sons of Light* fall in behind. They are a large and ominous group. Rebels move in to arm the pilgrims. The populace is alarmed. Some of the pilgrims join in according to plan.

Others do not join. Doors close as the rebels march through the streets carrying the emblem of their revolution, the dagger. It is a Holy Day.

All the garrisons of the rebels begin as one large garrison. Their march towards the Temple begins in the lower city. They continue to pick up pilgrims along the way. As Tommy's garrison nears its target, they break off from the larger group to begin the battle. "May nothing remain to give witness that the Empire was ever here," says Timothy. The other rebels continue their march to the upper city.

Tommy's garrison is the first to draw enemy fire. It is not the Emperor's Imperial fire. They are Temple arrows. Jerrod of Cana is the first rebel to die. He dies at the hands of his own people.

Martin's garrison is the next to break off. As they near the street where the tax company is, they charge it. When they are finished there, Collins has a score to settle with Matty. He knows where to find him, but first he will reinforce Timothy's garrison.

Bobby's garrison breaks off as they near their target. Timothy's garrison continues their march beyond the Holy City walls where they will fortify the roads into town.

There is a field and a bakery across from the soldier's barracks in the upper city. Bobby's garrison marches into the field, captures it, moves into the bakery and captures it, before moving in on the barracks. Their intelligence regarding the desert exercise is correct. Most of the Imperial Army is drilling in *No Man's Land.* There is only a skeleton force at the barracks. *The Sons of Light* meet with no resistance along the way and little when they capture the barracks. They experience no casualties, while the Empire looses ten men.

Bobby hears jeering and booing from the street. He goes to the gates of the barracks and sees some of the Tribal crowd on the street heckling his men. Not only aren't they joining in the rising, they are aiding and abetting the enemy.

"You'll get us all killed!" jeers one man.

"Stop what you're doing this instant!" says another.

Bobby is glad that Tommy and Timothy are not there to witness this crowd. It would make them angry and sad.

"Shall we arrest the traitors?" a rebel asks Bobby.

"No," says Bobby. "Let them be."

Suddenly one of the Emperor's Imperial soldiers darts out from hiding. He rushes by Bobby and the other rebel by the gate, pushing them over. He runs into the thickest part of the crowd.

"Get him!" shouts Bobby as he scrambles to his feet. He grabs his bow and an arrow, takes aim at the soldier and pulls back on the bow's string. He cannot fire it. There are too many civilians around his target. Bobby puts the weapon over his shoulder and draws his knife for hand-to-hand combat. "C'mon," he says to the other rebel, "We'll have to go after him."

They both run after him into the crowd.

Timothy's men dig into the hills and the mountains of the terrain outside the Holy City walls. The other garrisons dig in as well in other places. Based on their intelligence, Timothy's garrison stands between the Holy City and "No Man's Land" where the Empire conducts their war games. They do not see battle right away. While they wait for the Emperor's Imperial Army, they also wait for pilgrims from the Holy City to fortify their numbers. Thinks Timothy, *'Surely, if we have victories in the Holy City, they will have to join us.'*

By the time the fighting outside the gates of the Holy City starts, the rebels hold the Holy City. The battle begins when one man from Timothy's garrison fires an arrow before he is given the command. The arrow fells an officer riding on a horse.

"Attack!" yells Timothy after the attack has begun.

The Emperor's Imperial Soldiers are caught off Guard. This is not a drill.

The initial attack of the rebels is so overwhelming that the Imperial Army thinks they are greatly outnumbered. The Empire's casualties in the early stages of the battle are outpacing rebel casualties four to one.

The battle begins midday. It is over by dusk. Few survive.

Meanwhile, Imperial Soldiers have already burned the rebels out of the army barracks in the Holy City and soldiers from the Great Chief's Palace are forming a cordon around the Temple and its fortress. Barricades constructed primarily of household furniture the rebels had set in place the night before the rising began have hindered their enemy's advance, but it is only temporary.

The Imperial Army defeats the rebels in the desert at dusk. They march into the Holy City to take it. A garrison makes its front the Temple of the Tribes of the Holy City. It is the tallest fortress in the Holy City. The garrison from the desert joins the cordon that is being methodically drawn around the Temple and its fortress.

By evening, Imperial Soldiers have set the Temple on fire to flush the rebels out. It is a great, glorious, cleansing fire, and from a great distance, it seems that the whole city is on fire. No rebel is killed in the Temple's fortress. By the time the Emperor's Imperial Army has captured it, the rebels have abandoned it.

This is Festival.

The Card

While the rebels rule the streets, Aron sits with his father-in-law in his office. He can hear a disturbance in the hall. The fighting is coming closer. There is a knock at the door.

"Come," says Zacharus.

A Temple Guard rushes in. "Your Graces," he says, out of breath. "It's the rebels. Tommy Trigger is heading this way and he can't be stopped."

"What do you mean?" says Zacharus. "We have a palace of Guards!"

"If we had an army…" the Guard whispers. "He will not be stopped."

There is a sound at the door and everyone turns. It is Tommy, accompanied by several rebels. He is holding his dagger in one hand and in the other, a sword. There is blood on his hands. He is looking for Loki. He points the knife at the Guard. "Will you join the revolution?" he says.

"I serve God and the Great Chief."

Tommy kills him.

"How many men have you killed?" Aron asks indignantly.

"I'm not done yet."

"Have you come to kill us?" asks Zacharus.

Tommy looks at his men. He looks back at Zacharus. "I have come to secure this fortress."

"Whose blood do you wear on your hands?"

"It began with the blood you shed. This is my brother's blood. We are commandeering your fortress. This Temple belongs to *the Sons of Light.*"

"How dare you," says Aron. "This is the House of God."

"There's a new landlord."

"How dare you," says Aron.

"You kill your own people," shouts Tommy. "You're swine!"

"It is the fate of all infidels and blasphemers," says Zacharus.

"My brother was right about you. You brood of vipers and hypocrites. What you say and what you do are two different things. My brother was right about you."

Zacharus is uneasy. "Tommy," he says, "You cannot begin to fathom what you have gotten yourself into."

"Your revolution is done," says Aron. "The Emperor's Imperial Army will crush your comrades and paint the streets with their blood."

"Listen to yourselves," says Tommy. "You have betrayed your own people."

"You murdered your own brother," says Aron. "I saw you. But you may be forgiven. He was a blasphemer. He was an enemy among us, a wolf in the fold. He divided us when we needed to be whole."

"I did not murder my brother. Is that the story you're selling?"

Loki comes into the garden outside. He had been in the street when the fighting broke out. He approaches his master's office with caution.

"You are the enemy among us," says Tommy. "You are the wolf in sheep's clothes."

"We're your people," says Zacharus. "We support your tribalism."

"Like Hell," says Tommy.

"Your brother was a pawn," says Aron. "He was expendable. He hurt your cause and God's. All men are pawns of God. His death was to be the end of our troubles. This was to be the start of something good. But now this!"

Zacharus shakes his head at his son-in law. He will never

understand when to remain silent.

Loki is at the garden entrance. He hears the men talking. He pauses to listen. He wants to know who is in the room before he enters.

Tommy looks at Aron with disgust. *"You're* expendable," he says.

"No," says Aron, "people like you and your brother are expendable."

Loki peeks around the corner, thinking there is a drape, to see what is happening before he enters, but the drape is gone. It is the drape Peter used to wrap Mandolin in. Tommy sees him when he is revealed and immediately targets the spy with his dagger. The knife finds its place in Loki's heart. He staggers in from the garden mortally wounded. The two Priests are visibly shaken. Loki is shocked. He doesn't move. Then he jerks and raises his sword. He is not dead. He approaches Tommy.

"Agh!" he gasps, "Agh!"

Tommy advances on Loki, easily knocks the sword out of his hand, pushes him against the wall, and chopping his head off, he pulls his knife out of the headless corpse. "I'll need that," he says.

He turns back to the two priests. They are panicked. "Your God is a jealous God and avenging," says Tommy. He slashes the throat of Zacharus with the dagger and stabs Aron in the chest with the sword. He sits down at Zacharus's desk while they are dying. Speaking to his fellow rebels he says, "This is the Temple of the Tribes of the Holy City. It is reclaimed by *the Sons of Light."*

Tommy springs up from Zacharus's desk and rushes out the door with his knife and sword.

Harvest Time

'The Hierophant goes into the world and opens a door. As he passes through, he doesn't notice if anybody is following him. Some people want to go with him, but they look away and lose sight of him and so they are afraid. Some people try to tell other people about the door, but they don't know where the door is themselves. They tell others about the door, but they know they will never pass through it. Some who know about the door have built the wall and aren't about to tear it down or pass through it themselves. Some think they have seen the door and they try to build other doors just like it. To hold up the doors, they build great Temple walls. To guard the walls, the doors are locked. Some accept money not to walk through the door. Others watch the Hierophant pass through the door, but they do not have the courage to go with him. They wait for a time when the Hierophant will come again to tell them why they live.'

The End

James Tripp is a Los Angeles based stand-up comedian. Before entering show business, he was a political aid, a reporter for ***The Martha's Vineyard Times*** and was the news director for WMVY-FM radio in Vineyard Haven, Massachusetts.

Coming Soon:

The Kingdom

www.ingramcontent.com/pod-product-compliance
Lightning Source LLC
Chambersburg PA
CBHW072057020726
47501CB00003B/617